C.K. Brown has had a varied career including music and finance. During this time, he has written songs, poetry, short stories, and newspaper articles. This is his first novel and was mainly written in lockdown. Recently retired, Chris then completed this novel. It is a spy thriller with romance underpinning the story, set in 1971, but with some modern themes. Chris lives in South Staffordshire with his wife, Carole.

C.K. Brown

The Z Affair

AUSTIN MACAULEY PUBLISHERS

LONDON * CAMBRIDGE * NEW YORK * SHARJAH

A CIP catalogue record for this title is available from the British Library.

ISBN 9781035855957 (Paperback)
ISBN 9781035855964 (Hardback)
ISBN 9781035855971 (ePub e-book)

www.austinmacauley.com

First Published 2024
Austin Macauley Publishers Ltd®
1 Canada Square
Canary Wharf
London
E14 5AA

Thanks to Jane Jordan photography and Andy Perks for their assistance.

Chapter One
Berlin, Late October 1971

Bombed-out desolate buildings, weeds and mud; not changed since the last time he was in Berlin a couple of years ago. A cold, dark night.

The rain swept in from the nearby river Spree. Philip Trent took a last drag on his cigarette and threw the stub into the wet wasteland. He pulled his collar up pushed his trilby down and turned and faced the Berlin Wall.

He was in a ruined area of the city near the wall and Bernauer Strasse was just around the corner. This was in the north of the city and several kilometres from Checkpoint Charlie and all that circus surrounding it.

73, Bernauer Strasse had been famous for underground escapes via tunnels. These had been found and blocked up by the East Germans, alongside the sewer system, also used for escape.

There was one hidden sewage pipe however not found, and was still used by the British Intelligence Services when necessary. It surfaced on the floor of a disused bakery on the Western side.

Trent turned to the man next to him, lit up by the nearby dim yellow lamps which bathed the deserted area.

'What time do you think our man will be out?' He said as he lit another No 6 cigarette.

'In the next twenty minutes,' the man tersely replied. He was in his late forties and had a very upper-class accent.

David Thomas was in fact Welsh, but elocution lessons and an Oxbridge education had obliterated his accent. He was slightly overweight, testimony to good living. He wore his faded old school tie and a Savile Row suit which had seen better days.

Thomas was number one in Berlin for the British Secret Intelligence Service or MI6. He spoke excellent German and was an expert in getting people out of East Berlin when needed.

Trent did not work for MI6, but his department—'The Outfit'—had borrowed Thomas for this escape mission.

If Thomas' upper civil servant manner bothered Trent, he did not let it show. He had to work with this man to get a tricky job done.

They both lapsed into silence, the tension building as the clock ticked. Sweat even in that cold and wet evening showed on Thomas' face in the yellow gloom. Trent remained cool.

*

Several hours earlier, Philip Trent had landed at Berlin Tegel Airport. His passport showed he was Stephen Brown, a commercial traveller, and he carried only a small suitcase.

The West Berlin Customs officer was a thin, blond, bespectacled young man, with a naturally suspicious disposition. He spoke English with only a slight accent, and after studying the passport:

'Mr Brown?'

'Yes?'

'Can you please sign this form.'

'Of course.'

'Is your stay business or pleasure?'

'Strictly business; home tomorrow.'

'Your only case?'

'Yes, change of clothes.'

'Ja, Herr Brown, please proceed.'

'Vielen Dank.'

The man stamped the passport and pasted the Customs stamp on the side of the case. Trent pushed on through the crowded terminal and out to the taxis. He breathed in the cold autumn air and hailed a taxi. He asked to be dropped by Zoologischer Garten, Tiergarten (the Berlin zoological garden). His rendezvous with Thomas was to be there.

He was early so he ordered something to eat and drink from a small café in the gardens, overlooking the zoo. He glanced at a newspaper left on the table, a copy of BILD with a picture of Willy Brandt Chancellor on the front; Trent's German was not good enough to read further.

Despite the cold late-October weather and the late darkening afternoon, Trent sat outside the café and ate his meal. He'd not eaten anything since yesterday lunch time as he'd been tied up with his superiors. He had sauerkraut and a small selection of German sausages (when in Berlin…), washed down with a small glass of Spaten Oktoberfest and a schnapps.

He took in his surroundings, families well wrapped up, entering the zoo. The smell of Karo cigarettes in the air, the imposing Brandenburg Gate in the distance. Surrounded by ruins from the war, the gate stood alone in an exclusion zone in an arc of the Berlin Wall. No one was allowed to visit. Trent had first seen it on leave from the army some ten years previously. He still wondered how the gate remained untouched by all the devastation around it.

A sudden breeze blew across the park bringing with it dead autumn leaves and assorted rubbish. Trent shivered, stretched, and lit another inevitable cigarette.

A man approached him, and spoke.

'Bist du Englander? Sprechen Sie Englisch?'

'Konnten Sie langsamer sprechen. I am English.'

The other man finished. 'Can you tell me the way to the British Embassy?'

'Ich verstehe nicht,' Trent replied.

This exchange was the simple password dreamt up by MI6. This was his contact David Thomas, who handed him a package, to be opened when cleared of the park.

This was his gun and ammunition, brought in via the diplomatic bag to the British Embassy. A Smith and Wesson .38 police special revolver with a sawn-off barrel, together with a shoulder holster. Not a good idea to carry through Customs!

Nothing else was said. Thomas beckoned him and Trent followed him out of the zoo gardens to a nearby car park and climbed in the car. They then went off to Bernauer Strasse.

David Thomas had been seconded from MI6 for this job. He ostensibly held a minor diplomatic role at the embassy, but in fact, held a wide-ranging intelligence brief and had worked in Berlin for fifteen years.

Originally from Tenby in Pembrokeshire, he'd long left his roots behind him. His career spanned the army in Korea, Oxford and a degree in English literature.

Then various intelligence departments, before landing in West Germany and then Berlin. His aptitude for picking up languages standing him in good stead.

Whilst he'd changed his persona from Welsh to a "posh" civil service type, he still looked a typical stocky Welshman. He was in his late forties, balding and his remaining hair grey. His blue eyes should have been bright but were slightly bloodshot (part of his hangover from the previous night Trent surmised). Although they'd never met, Trent had been well briefed about him.

Their mission was to ensure the safety of an agent, Ernie Johnson, coming through Thomas' sewer escape route. Trent was then to get him back to London.

There had been a flap back in London. 'We must get Johnson out!'

The escape plan and Thomas had been arranged and Trent dispatched.

He did not know the reasons behind the panic, only the urgency. Ernie Johnson he vaguely knew as a man his "Outfit" and "6" used in Berlin and he'd dealt with a couple of times previously. He was known as the ferret for his ability to sniff out intelligence. He also spoke excellent German and actually looked very much like a ferret. Unprepossessing, he had the skill to fade into the background and keep his eyes and ears open. Whatever information he now had, Trent's superiors were anxious to obtain.

Trent pondered on this as Thomas steered his 1965 Mercedes-Benz 230SL through the busy traffic. They moved away from the Tiergarten, onto the Alt-Moabit and north towards their destination. There had been few words on first meeting. Berlin now flashed by and Thomas was now talking about the 4 Power agreement, also known as the Quadripartite agreement, which had recently been signed by the UK, Soviet Union, France, and the USA. Trent only half-listened but picked up that it was once again hoped that tensions would ease between East and West.

He reflected on the divided city, themselves driving through the Federal Republic of Germany and the other side of the divide the Communist German Democratic Republic. Then all of the city of Berlin, an island within the communist GDR. Ten years since the Berlin Wall was raised.

Trent shook the thoughts from his mind to focus on the job ahead.

Eventually, they arrived at the designated safe house near Bernauer Strasse. Parking at the rear of a dilapidated café, they went up a rusted fire escape to the flat above.

A one-bed flat; the Wall and an observation tower were in sight. Camouflage nets, tank obstacles, barbed wire all covering the wasteland across the road from the café. All laid out before the grubby windows.

Peeling paint, a threadbare carpet, the smell of cabbage, sweat and badly processed sewage. As well as, there was a small bathroom, living room and kitchen.

Trent looked through the grimy, condensed windows towards drab Berlin. The distant rumble of trams, trains and far-off traffic.

'In fact, the windows are completely bulletproof,' Thomas said, handing him a cup of espresso coffee with a tot of rum.

'Our man should be safe here.'

Trent grunted and lit a cigarette.

'We've been using this now for several years and our system is foolproof.'

He again made no comment, and Thomas, like other Welsh people Trent had met, talked enough for both of them.

'When the border troops of the GDR closed the Bernauer escape route, they overlooked one sewer pipe leading to the bakery, and it's that we use. It's about a kilometre from here, and we also have a special route back. You'll see.'

Thomas had a small coughing fit on the rum-laced coffee. He then continued.

'On the face of it, our friends over there are trying to improve things a bit, we'll see how this new agreement works out. There is easier access to travel visas at present. But I still think they're lying two-faced commie bastards.'

He clicked a switch on an old transistor. "Brown Sugar" crackled out.

'That'll help cover any long-range sound surveillance.' He finished his coffee. 'Come on, let's go.' He left the radio blasting…

Trent checked his gun in the holster, beneath his raincoat, and then they left the flat out into the autumn rain now falling heavily. They then walked through the ruined shambles in the shadow of the wall.

So now they were on Bernauer Strasse and they approached the old bakery with caution. The rain was steadily cascading on the surrounding ruins and seemingly suiting the location and occasion.

Then everything moved quickly; David Thomas was surprisingly fast. Trent followed keeping alert, hand on his gun.

They entered the old bakery via a green, moss-covered metal door and then went down to the cellar.

Thomas removed an old cupboard in the corner and lifted up a hatch in the floor. Immediately, the smell of ancient and modern sewage filled the room.

'The sewage from the East always smells worse to me,' Thomas's flippant comment echoed in the small space. 'Here he comes.'

There were muffled noises and curses, and then Ernie Johnson appeared via the open hatch. Covered in the delights of the tunnel he'd crawled through, he looked worse than he normally did. He muttered something about needing extra money for all this and then both he and Trent followed Thomas up to the ground floor.

Ernie Johnson was so ferret-like. He had blond hair and a fair complexion, almost albino-like. His hair stuck up in a tuft like Tintin and the indeterminate colour of his eyes was hidden behind tinted (now slightly tainted) glasses. He thought the glasses made him look hip or cool or whatever the jargon was.

Thin, shifty, medium height, not even his friends (if he had any) would call him handsome. Trent and his organisation had used him a couple of times for information and he knew that he'd been involved in the black market in Berlin. MI6 had then blackmailed him into working for them, rather than face criminal charges. Their paths had crossed a couple of times, but Trent couldn't really say he knew him.

Johnson turned to Trent. 'Nice to see you again, Mr Trent.' It was a high-pitched whine. 'Look, before we go, take this. It's for London.'

He handed him a small booklet, a tourist guide to East Berlin. (who knew?) Thankfully, it was in a plastic container as Ernie did not smell or look too good.

Upstairs, Thomas said: 'I'll tidy up in the cellar later, let's get Johnson out of here. Trent, take a recce outside.' Thomas was still very much in charge of the operation.

Philip Trent slowly looked out the darkened doorway and surveyed the area through the driving rain.

Far off over the rubble and bombed-out buildings, he could make out three shadowy figures approaching with intent, the yellow lights catching them. One man stood head and shoulders over the other two, and obviously they were making for the bakery. Trent took his gun from the holster. 'Foolproof system, my arse!' He muttered.

Normally, Trent would have faced up to these potential assailants and taken them on. However, his job was to get Johnson home.

'Trouble up there,' he pointed. 'Need to get out quick.' His finger twitched on the trigger.

'No problem,' replied Thomas. 'Follow me.' They followed him through thick weeds and broken glass; an eerie yellow world of desolation.

They reached a nearby building and went up to a ladder round the back.

'Up we go, we'll be back at the flat in no time. These Johnnies won't find us!'

On the rooftops, they walked through an array of chimney pots, on both sides panoramic views of Berlin, even in the downpour. It was precarious in places; don't look down! But Trent had to admit a very effective escape route.

The view on the Western side was brightly lit and the light around Tiergarten down to Potsdamer Platz, which looked like a building site, could be clearly seen.

To the east, everything seemed darker, although Alexanderplatz and the Television tower could be seen through the gloom.

Eventually, the three descended on another ladder and found themselves adjacent to the "safe house". Back in the flat, the three wet and dishevelled agents threw off their raincoats.

Thomas then pulled out his rum bottle and shared round the drink, "to keep out the chill". He said to Johnson: 'You can shower in a minute, and there's a change of clothes.' Thomas then turned the radio up. *Chirpy Chirpy Cheep Cheep* filled the room with its dreadful noise. Berlin radio sometimes picked up the worst sounds of the British hit parade.

'First, I think Trent would like a verbal debrief.' He looked through the murky window. 'But watch this, chaps.'

The road below was now full of West German police "investigating" a supposed stolen car. 'Maybe we are blown,' mused Thomas. 'Maybe they know this flat. However, the police outside are our insurance. You'll be surprised what arrangement we have with the commissioner.' He laughed. 'And at what cost? Still, we may have to change places, safe house; mmm, most unsafe I think now…'

He took another slug of rum. 'Perhaps you two would like a quick chat; I'll go and wash.'

The music now switched to Rod Stewart and played on to cover their conversation from any surveillance. As Maggie May belted out, Trent watched the police below and then turned to look at the unkempt Johnson, who seemed nervous and was sweating despite the coolness of the room.

He turned to Trent. 'The Guide Book has the stuff for London. They told me to give a verbal overview as well.' He stood by the window and wiped his forehead with a dirty handkerchief. He started:

'The Z. file…backed by the Stasi…'

Stasi…Stasi…Stasi…A shattering of bulletproof glass, like a knife through butter. No response from the police outside. No noise of a gun. Obviously, they had heard nothing.

Trent took in the hole in the plate glass and dived away from the window. Johnson lay dead on the floor, with what looked like a harpoon in his chest. Blood splattered over the floor.

'What the…!' Thomas came from the bathroom, towel in hand, muttering a string of expletives!

Trent tentatively looked through the hole in the glass, gun in hand. In the distance, he saw three figures he'd seen earlier, the giant in the middle. They were standing in the bombed-out ruins high above the police. There was some sort of weapon in the giant's hand. Could only just make it out.

The giant raised his hand in a mock salute, then they were gone into the night…

Chapter Two
27 October, London

Article in the *Daily Express*, London, 27 October 1971

The "Zombie" Killings

Yesterday in Hampstead, north London, there was a violent robbery at Lloyds Bank.

The police reported that three men in plastic masks raided the bank with shotguns.

With no regard for life, they shot and killed two innocent bystanders. The bank guard and one of the customers were killed instantly.

One of the witnesses said that there was no provocation and that the lethal shootings were deliberate.

The robbers escaped with an undisclosed sum of cash, shooting at the ceiling as they went.

One of the assailants was described as "a giant of a man". He was the leader and it was he who carried out the killings. He was wearing a "Zombie"-like monster mask.

The names of the victims have not yet been released.

Chief Inspector Alcock, the officer incharge of the case, declined to comment when asked if this incident was connected with a spate of similar violent robberies across the city. Robberies that some commentators referred to as the "Zombie" crimes.

See editorial comment re rising crime across the country, on page 18.

Philip Trent paused reading. The mention of a giant took him back to Berlin. No, it couldn't be, could it? A coincidence? He had a few papers spread across the table. There were similar articles in other papers.

The Mirror focussed on recent bombings across the country—thirteen killed and no one yet claiming responsibility. It also discussed the theory of a linked connection between the armed robberies and a plot to destabilise the country.

The Mail also pitched in with the wave of strikes sweeping across the UK, and agreed with the possible links with rising crime and terrorism.

Trent pushed the papers aside; he lit a cigarette and the smoke rose to join the yellow-stained ceiling. He sat deep in thought.

Before he left for Berlin, a communist plot re-mass sabotage had been mentioned. Could all this be part and parcel? Was his mission to Berlin related to this alleged plot?

Well, anyway, he'd find out more in the morning when he'd meet Colonel Stewart, his boss.

A creature of habit, every Wednesday he could be found at Il Portico, a small family-run restaurant on Kensington High Street. It was long and narrow with tables against the walls each side. There were only a few people in and at the back, in a small area cordoned off for their regular customers, sat Philip Trent. The management provided for his every need including a selection of newspapers for him to catch up on the news. He was always a good spender! Always a good tipper!

On a Wednesday, it was reasonably quiet and he could be left to his own thoughts and solitude at the back of the restaurant. This suited him, he was generally happy with his own company, not of a gregarious nature (Bloody miserable, anti-social, were the comments of a certain lady of his acquaintance).

Anyway, he liked the Italian ambience of the place and the food. He could already smell the aroma of cooking filling the air. Since being based in London, his eating habits had changed—Faggots, Pease pudding, chips and beer replaced by more expensive dining.

Luigi, the head waiter, approached. Although dressed in the standard white uniform, his flamboyant, colourful nature normally shone out. He had a warm and friendly personality, always with a smile, always helpful, but something was different tonight. He seemed distracted.

'Signor Trent, wadda you wanna tonight?'

'Evening, Luigi. I'll have a Peroni to start please, with some scallops. Main, veal Milanese I think, with spaghetti. And a bottle of Valpolicella Superiore. Thanks.'

Trent, a man normally of few words, but often he'd talk with Luigi before and after the meal. Both had similar interests: rock and roll and football. Trent would talk in his soft Birmingham accent and Luigi in his extravagant Italian.

Although Trent was sure that he was actually a born and bred east Londoner.

Trent for his sins supported West Bromwich Albion, and Luigi, West Ham. They would normally have a good-natured banter about each other's teams, but tonight, a subdued Luigi took his order and departed for the kitchen.

Trent wondered about this. He finished his meal with two cappuccinos and a brandy, and lit a cigarette. When Luigi returned to clear away, he asked if something was bothering him.

Luigi, his accent now gone, when he spoke, it was pure east London.

'Y-you've been reading and seen the news, Mr Trent? All these...'

He looked around nervously. 'All these robberies, explosions, violence. So-called Zombie robberies. So terrible, the world now; so, so terrible.'

His voice now a whisper, he shook his head, hand trembling, and face white. He continued: 'In Canning Town today—where my wife works—there was another of these robberies. Someone at the bank killed, again this giant, this giant bloke in a monster mask. My wife, she was a few doors down, but she heard, and all the panic, the chaos.'

'Was she alright?' Trent asked.

'Yes, yes, she's fine; insisted I came to work tonight. But...but...' His words trailed off.

Trent went to the small bar near the kitchen, poured a brandy, and gave it to the nervous Italian.

'Any clues who was behind it?' Trent finished his drink and cigarette. Again the "giant bloke" stirred in his mind.

'Who knows; the IRA, anarchists, baader-meinhof nutters, who knows.' A shrug of the shoulders.

Trent paid, gave a sizeable tip to the distressed waiter, and walked out into the cold night. He decided to walk the eight miles back to his flat near Osterley Park. That would clear his head and ready himself for the meeting with his boss in the morning. He tightened his leather coat around him and set off.

He had returned from Berlin and reported to his superiors three days before. He had expected a bollocking, particularly from his immediate boss, Colonel Alec Stewart. He had not returned with Ernie Johnson intact, but they only seemed concerned with his gift—the East Berlin guide book and the microdot held within it.

They asked him to return on Thursday (tomorrow) for a "full chat" as the colonel put it. Never mind, he had a more interesting afternoon planned after the meeting.

Walking down the High Street, kicking the fallen autumn leaves into the air, he noticed in the cold the parked cars were beginning to frost over. His thoughts took him back many years...thoughts normally blocked out, not wanting to revisit.

It was the cold taking him back and it returned him to the small room in his grandparents' house. Freezing in the winter, you had to put your shirt in front of the coal fire before you could wear it. This reflective mood continued...

His parents dead, his grandparents had brought him up in their council house in Smethwick.

Bill and Bessie. Bill was salt of the earth, typically working class—working in a factory—Tangyes. His nan did part-time at Smethwick Laundry. Whilst proudly working class, Bill was also an old-fashioned patriot. He had loved the king and then Elizabeth II. Churchill was his hero. Trent had that patriotism instilled in him.

Suddenly, the past tumbled out...

The distinctive smell of M & B mild, Park Drive, his grandad back from the pub. Down the allotment with Bill; out fishing at the canal.

At the Hawthorns—the Albion—his grandad, a steward.

Memories cascaded...

Bomb shelter, now a shed—outside toilet. Toast on the coal-lit fire, the wireless playing *Music While You Work*. Standing for the national anthem, camp coffee, cups of tea, budgie singing in the cage, fish and chips, Sunday roast, Bisto.

- Playing football down the Rec
- Nicking sweets from Granny Glees
- Flicks—first fumble with Lynn on the back row
- Fists first—fighting, always fighting...

He'd been ill when he was six with measles-related encephalitis and he'd missed a year of school. It had left him edgy, full of electricity, and nervous energy. Did this lead him to always be in fights? Maybe; maybe, but they said his father had always been in fights as well.

His main memory of illness was convalescence, in bed whilst kids played in the street, and he could hear the distant ice cream chime on a warm summer evening.

His grandparents provided a warm, safe home. So sad he was when they both died close together.

Grandad Bill finally succumbed to First World War gas and then shortly after, his grandmother to cancer; but truly a broken heart.

Violence had always been a part of him, although often he fought for the right reasons.

There was the time when he rescued his mate, Steve, in Smethwick. The action in Africa, rescuing his comrades, earning the bloody VC; a cross to bear. He hated it! Again, his childhood friend, Steve, among the rescued.

Then the fight in Hereford. A typical scenario, story of his life…

He'd gone for a quiet drink in a Hereford pub and gone to the aid of a local lass. First, she was insulted by her boyfriend and then he'd hit her. A local lad tanked up on scrumpy cider. Trent, "the Saint", intervened on her behalf.

The local's mates then joined in (five of them!) and a fight developed…like a scene from a John Wayne movie. The upshot—the locals unconscious on the floor and a wrecked pub; further upshot—Trent arrested by MPs and facing court-martial…until his old commanding officer, Colonel Stewart, had rescued him with a job in his newly formed security unit, the Outfit.

Then many other acts of violence under the orders of Colonel Stewart.

All seemed alien to his day-to-day existence. When not on a job, he lived in a sparse, small flat in Isleworth near Osterley Park. His next-door neighbour, Mrs McDougal, a widow in her seventies, he paid her to do the housekeeping. She had a dog—a black and tan border collie called Tess. She had semi-adopted Trent and he regularly took her for walks and to the pub, the Hare & Hounds, near the park.

Mrs McDougal was short and stout with an over-balancing large bosom. She had iron grey hair with iron grey eyes to match. Stern was the word; her whole demeanour said stern, from her lined, unsmiling features to her dress—country tweed with a hint of tartan. However, this front hid a heart of gold and her occasional rare smile lit up her face and eyes, revealing a dour and dry humour.

She had moved south to England from Aberdeen with her husband many years ago. He had been a civil servant in the tax office and he'd left her with a solid but not spectacular pension. Her only son had emigrated to Australia and she had sort of, as far as anyone could, adopted Trent. His money for housekeeping being very gratefully accepted.

So there she lived in the tiny flat with Tess, the dog, a cat called Sid, and Bunty, the budgie. The flat was very old-fashioned, not changed since the war, but very warm and cosy. There was always a cup of tea, homemade Dundee cake or shortbread biscuits, and on special occasions, a tot of Scotch whisky.

Trent actually, and surprisingly, liked to pop in from time to time for a chat. Although her accent was often impenetrable. He compared his flat to hers. His was bare; minimalistic he called it, although others would say cold and empty.

Her's was cluttered, old-fashioned and homely.

The rest of his time was for exercise—the baths, the gym, boxing, running, etc. All using up that nervous energy inside him.

Sometimes going to the football matches in London, or home to see West Brom. Out drinking with his occasional friend, Kev Bloomer; then there was Thursday afternoons.

Violence and football! In March 1969, he'd been to see the Albion at Stamford Bridge, Chelsea. It was an F.A. Cup quarter-final and Albion won 2-1. After the game, Trent decided to walk back to his flat, nine miles away. The evening still chilly, he pulled his Baggies scarf tight around his neck.

Moving away from the crowds, he went down a side street he knew. There in the badly lit street, he saw four skinheads in Chelsea regalia. Straight from central casting for hooligans; straight from Chelsea Shed End.

They were picking on two Albion fans who'd turned down the wrong street. An elderly gentleman and his young grandson.

'Pick on someone your own size!' He gestured to the two West Brom fans to move away. They did so, as the four "heroes" turned on the newcomer.

'Turn right at the top of the street; it'll lead you to the main road.' The two went quickly, glancing back nervously.

'Well, what have we here? Fucking Baggies scum.' The leader of the pack produced a knife.

'You're gonna die tonight.'

'Look, lads, just walk away. I don't want anyone hurt.' The four convulsed in laughter.

'Your funeral,' Trent said and faced up to them.

A knife flashed, missed. Trent kicked the leader in the balls. There was a whirlwind of violence as his fists and feet worked in tandem, smashing out at the nearest two. They collapsed, bleeding and unconscious.

'Do you want some more, Chelsea scum?' The two looked at their fallen comrades and fled.

Violence, he justified that melée as "defending the weak". Although he had to admit he'd enjoyed it.

So walking back to Osterley on the cold autumn night, he thought about himself. A patriot: for God, Queen and country. A thug, an occasional assassin.

As his boss recently had said: 'In the right job'.

Then he thought about the strange meeting with Colonel Stewart before the Berlin mission and the links between his conversation with Luigi, and what was touched upon in that meeting—sabotage!

Chapter Three
October, London, Shortly Before Berlin

Shortly before the trip to Berlin, Colonel Stewart had ordered him to a meeting in Whitehall. 'It's a review of all intelligence personnel—MI5, 6, Special Branch, us—the lot. Carried out by an independent board. Waste of time.' The colonel never one to mince his words. 'But there seem to be rumours of something amiss; an upsurge in Eastern Bloc activity and talk of planned sabotage here. So the powers that be have ordered this review, to analyse our strengths, and you've got to go!'

So on a cold late-October day, Trent took a tube to Westminster station. He was not looking forward to this meeting, not his cup of tea at all. He marched through the mid-morning crowds, past a completely bald saxophone busker, discordant tune echoing on the tunnel walls. He threw a couple of coins into a waiting hat. Not too bad—at least he recognised the tune, *Strangers in the Night*.

Then he went up the escalator, past cinema adverts, forthcoming concerts and scantily clad models in scanty underwear. His nan wouldn't have approved of them, no not at all.

He came up into the chilly Westminster air. A news vendor shouting about some armed hold-up in Brixton. A rush of wind scattering leaves, blowing someone's bowler towards the river. The traffic on Bridge Street was snarled up and Trent was glad he didn't have a permanent car and the temptation to drive into the city.

He walked along the Thames embankment, gulls crying, swooping over the water. His destination was a nondescript shabby civil service building away from the Houses of Parliament and major offices of state. Almost as if they were ashamed of this drab edifice.

A sign outside the doors announced coyly "Department of Health and Social Security". A small rusted, scuffed sign that he could barely read.

He was met in reception by a sullen security guard and taken upstairs. They went through a vast hall where numerous workers were busy writing out cheques (dole money?). These, including many long-haired, seemingly students, were working part-time. There was an echo of voices and cigarette smoke rising to the flickering office lights above.

They went down various other corridors, no words spoken by the security man, until they came to a door at the end of a long hallway. He knocked, there was a muffled "Come in", the door opened, and Mr Security left without a nod or a word.

It was a bare office, with a long table and various chairs, nothing else. The walls of peeling paint, a mix of dark green and an indescribable grey. It overlooked the Thames, which flowed past the dirt-smeared windows, a murky autumn brown.

Surprisingly, his boss, Colonel Stewart, was there sitting in a corner. Affecting nonchalance, drinking coffee and smoking a large cigar. He nodded, said nothing, smug, self-satisfied as ever.

Trent stood in front of three civil servant types behind the battered table. Three wise monkeys or whatever was best to describe them. They were hard to depict—faceless men—men of government. All in grey suits and although a little early, all wearing poppies. Trent blinked, the light from the window behind the three inquisitors shining in his eyes.

In the middle, the obvious senior monkey seemed to be another ex-military type in his fifties. He'd probably gravitated to the civil secret service after the army. Possibly, a crony of Sir Richard Abbott, the colonel's boss. The old school tie, old pals network, in action once again. He gestured to Trent to sit down.

'Good afternoon,' said the senior one. 'Thanks for coming…eh, Mr Trent.' No coffee or cigarettes were offered. He wore his superiority well.

'Just a few questions. Colonel Stewart I understand has explained the rationale behind all this…'

No names, no introductions. He didn't wait for an answer. 'Yes, good. Now this won't hurt.' Just like his dentist. His mirthless smile revealed a badly fitting set of dentures, speaking of dentistry. He then pulled a sheet of paper from a file and placed it in front of them.

He then started to go down the sheet of paper, which was a summary of Trent's career. Trent had long ago learnt to read things upside down and he took in his "potted history".

The senior chap read out extracts and Trent only half-listened as words like "excellent service record", "prone to violence", "working-class background" floated past him.

Philip Trent
Extract from Personnel File
Top Secret; Private and Confidential

- Born 1.4.1940
- Smethwick, Staffordshire
- Father killed at Dunkirk
- Mother and her parents killed 1942—bomb raid
- Brought up by paternal grandparents
- Age six, seriously ill in hospital—missed school
- Despite illness passed 11-plus
- Attended Holly Lodge Grammar School
- Expelled before 'O' Levels
- Had several manual jobs
- Became a Teddy Boy, 1957
- Nearly went to prison following a fight
- But let off when conscripted into army
- Joined North Staffordshire Regiment
- Which became Staffs Regiment 1959
- Grandparents died 1960 and 1961
- Army tours of duty included Germany and Africa
- When National Service finished, stayed on
- Awarded V.C. in Africa for bravery
- Promoted to corporal
- Recommended for SAS 1963 (a special operations section). Briefly married in Hereford—not divorced, separated.
- Served in various locations including Borneo and Aden
- Promoted to Sergeant
- Late 1967, another fight in Hereford, leading to court-martial
- This quashed when Colonel Stewart recruited him early 1968 for his new operation.

Health

- Height: 5ft 10ins
- Weight: 12 stone
- Supremely fit
- Despite a liking for cigarettes and alcohol

Skills

- Expert in firearms
- All types of combat/self-defence
- Mountaineering
- Swimming
- Surveillance techniques

Hobbies

- Keeping fit
- Food/drink
- Football
- Music
- Women

Summary

- Extremely patriotic and able officer. Prone to occasional bouts of ill-discipline and violence. In fact, has a talent for both. Despite promotion to N.C.O in the army, essentially a lone wolf operative.

See medical and psychiatric reports.

N.B. Trent is more suited to working in the field than intelligence/office work.

What Trent did note upside down was some green ink scrawled over the page. Sarcastic green ink from Colonel Stewart's fountain pen.

"Pleb" next to Smethwick

"Thug" next to "fights"

"Ha!" next to "VC"

"Boozer" next to Health

"Prostitutes" next to Hobbies

"Psycho" next to Summary

The colonel's sense of humour! Infantile?

He glanced briefly at his boss but kept his thoughts on the report to himself. These musings were interrupted. 'Right, you start with the old interrogation, Jenkins.'

The main man gestured at his colleague on the right, Mr Nondescript. He said this with a smile that never touched his cold eyes.

'So…er, yes, Trent,' Jenkins stuttered. 'What politics do you have? Who do you vote for?'

Trent suppressed the urge to tell him to go f- himself. He continued with the pantomime…

'I don't do politics; I don't vote.' The man in the middle raised his eyebrows, but said nothing. Jenkins continued.

'So you don't vote Labour then?'

'No, nobody.'

'Why's that?'

Trent again was careful in his answer. 'Always just followed orders—a soldier—don't pay attention to those at the top.'

'Was your grandfather a communist?'

This from the other non-entity on the chief's left, and out of the blue. The colonel, Trent could see, stifled a laugh.

'No, he always voted Tory, a great fan of Churchill.'

'But he was in a union.' Jenkins picked up the questioning.

Trent smiled. 'You had to be where he worked, but you could say, he was an old-fashioned working man, but believed in King and country. A patriot, stood up for the national anthem, respect. Yes, respect. And he always preferred the Tories to Labour.'

'What paper do you read?' This suddenly came from the man in the middle, the chief. Trent stared through the grim window at tugs and other boats on the Thames. He suppressed his rising anger. 'I don't order a paper, I sometimes buy the Standard, read my neighbour's Sunday papers. Get the news off the wireless, or the TV.'

'So not *the Mirror* or *Morning Star* then?'

Trent looked at the senior man with ill-disguised contempt. 'I sometimes read *the Mirror*; don't buy it. Let's get this straight. I'm a loyal, patriotic soldier, well ex-soldier, who serves my country. I follow orders.'

Jenkins again. 'OK, so what do you think of the communist threat generally, and our information that the threat is being ramped up.'

God, he could murder a pint, a cigarette, a walk by the Thames. 'I'll do what I'm ordered to do…If I'm told to go up against the Reds, then I will.'

So on and on and on…more questions about his past, army record, the VC, etc., etc. He was getting very bored and restless. His patience was very brittle.

In the end, Colonel Stewart called a halt to proceedings. 'Thank you, gentlemen; I think that's enough.' He nodded at the three men. 'My summary of his report sums this officer up. I stand by that.' He turned to a bemused Trent. 'Come on, you could do with a drink.'

They left the drab government building and the colonel, without a word, steered Trent to St Stephen's Tavern on Bridge Street. He ordered a brandy for himself and a pint of best bitter for Trent, then lit an expensive cigar. They then had a debrief of the annoying meeting, which only managed to annoy Trent even further.

He was feeling angry, dazed and confused by it all, despite the colonel saying don't worry. 'Load of red tape, bureaucratic bullshit. Don't worry; we're on your side. Despite all that hoo-ha, you're the right man for the job.' His accent was well-bred, upper class.

'Well, Sir, I never doubted it.' He was in the right job—vocation—he was sure of that, but it was strange for the colonel to emphasise the fact.

Still, feeling better after the pint, they parted on reasonable terms, the whole thing seemingly unreal.

In fact, Trent was irritated to the extent that he made some of his own discreet enquiries. He discovered no one else at the "Outfit" had had to go to a similar meeting.

He cast his net wider and was even more concerned to find that seemingly no one else in the intelligence world had been vetted, that he could find.

Did they in fact suspect him of being a potential traitor—or worse, a double agent—or was it his supposed working-class background?

Chapter Four
London, 28 October

The next day after his night out at the Italian, Trent breakfasted on a bacon sandwich, brown sauce, with orange juice and a coffee. His flat was minimalistic by any standards: a small kitchen, living/dining room, two small bedrooms, all sparsely furnished. He listened to the radio and had his first cigarette of the day.

Then looked out over frost-covered rooftops as a plane, Concorde, flew overhead, descending to nearby Heathrow.

It was 6.30am and he had to be in the office by 9am. No time for an early morning run or dog walk.

More bad news came: further violent robberies happened across the country, including a security van attack in nearby Hammersmith. The BBC radio announcer was now referring to them as the Zombie raids due to the monster masks worn by the robbers. In addition, strikes had now hit the capital and public transport had completely come to a standstill. Also, he caught a vague fragment, something about the Congo becoming Zaire—a changing world!

He apologised to Mrs McDougal that he could not take Tess for a walk.

Mrs McDougal, with her broad Aberdeen accent, said she understood.

Trent did not own a car; if he ever needed one, he would hire. With no public transport, he'd have to go into town by taxi. He would also have to put on a suit; colonel's orders, a rare event.

Trent sank into the back of the black taxi cab. Dirty old London passed by slowly, the morning traffic worse than ever. A mixed jumble of Cortina's, triumphs, escorts BSA's and also even an electrical milk float floated by. The frosty morning melting into wet slush, the passers-by, a blur through streaked condensed glass. His thoughts were on Berlin and the meeting in front of him. Then an afternoon of relaxation.

The driver, pleased to get a fare all the way to the centre, tried to engage in conversation. Typically, he covered all subjects going—the weather, politics, Tottenham beating Forest soundly—then moving on to the strikes and growing violence. Typically, he blamed "the foreigners".

Trent, not in the mood to converse, answered with grunts, "Yes" or "True". They passed Fullers Brewery, a red post office van was involved in an accident. The stop-start-stop-start of London traffic lights. A group of hippies passed holding balloons, on their way home from some all-night party. Kew Bridge, Hammersmith, Earls Court. The way he'd walked last night from the restaurant. Then on through Knightsbridge and into back streets known only by the cabbies and their famous "knowledge".

The "Outfit", his employers, were based in Southampton Street between Old Covent Garden market and the Strand. The front of the old building was an accountancy firm dealing with wealthy clients. A genuine business owned by Samuel Goldcrest, personal friend of Sir Richard Abbot, the head of Trent's organisation.

Trent nodded at the pretty secretary in the accountants' reception, went up the narrow stairs through a side door up to the third floor, and into his bosses' inner sanctum.

He only came to these offices above the accountants a few times a month, but was always amazed that in the rabbit warren of a building there was so much activity.

He had no real idea what anyone did but in the various small offices, there were at least thirty working. He knew the colonel also had a network of spies and informers across the country and Europe, all reporting into this building. The buzz of computers, ringing of telephones, radio operators taking messages—the background hubbub of a busy headquarters.

The "Outfit" as it was called had no real title. It had been set up by Harold Wilson, then prime minister, in early 1968 following an alleged coup against his government by right-wing establishment figures. "Alleged" to the outside world, the attempted coup in fact had been "in fact".

1968 had been a year of unrest across the UK, Europe, and the world. Students had nearly overthrown De Gaulle's government in France and he had briefly fled the country. Students had demonstrated in Grosvenor Square against the US Government and across the Atlantic America saw continued riots against their involvement in Vietnam.

Underpinning the student and surface unrest, more sinister forces had been at work. The rise of Irish republicanism, terrorist groups such as the Angry Brigade, and many others, seemed to signpost a time of full-scale revolt.

In a way, the right-wing coup was an answer to all this predominantly left-wing agitation.

Wilson had no truck with right-wing or left-wing revolutions. Forever a pragmatist, he set up a secret organisation reporting directly to him, and gave it no name. In due course, it unofficially became known as "The Outfit", the new prime minister, Ted Heath, allowed it to continue.

The organisation was to stand aside from MI5, MI6, the Special Branch, etc. Its brief was wide but in effect was there to root out any potential insurrection against the country and deal with it, by fair means or otherwise (the PM not wanting to know the means).

This took it up against terrorists, organised crime, left- or right-wing agitators, communist agents, etc. Unfettered by normal police procedures, it was considered that the ends justified the means.

This certainly was the view of Sir Richard Abbott. In his early sixties, Sir Richard in many ways epitomised the establishment and the status quo he was there to defend.

An Eton man and career civil servant, he had worked in many facets of policing and intelligence, charming and smarming his way to a high position.

His knowledge of the secret world and contacts throughout all aspects of the intelligence and wheels of government made him the ideal candidate to set up the "Outfit".

A private income and several city directorships allowed him a standard of living above even a top-class civil servant. He had a mansion and estate near Marlborough, called the Manor House, an apartment in Mayfair, other properties, and a fleet of cars and servants. He was separated from his wife and grown-up children and could be seen with fine wine and food in the best clubs in London.

His overweight look reminiscent of Orson Welles in the Third Man era before he'd grown a beard, all covered by a well-tailored Savile Row suit. He had balding grey locks, a pink face, and utilised a pince-nez. In his top pocket, a silk handkerchief poked out. Overall, he exuded wealth, privilege, and self-satisfaction all in keeping with him as a Baronet with inherited land and title.

Where Sir Richard was a strategic thinker, his number two, Colonel Stewart, was a man of action, and he ensured that the whole operation operated efficiently. He had a wide military service and had been in Philip Trent's Staffordshire Regiment. In 1963, he had recommended Trent for the SAS (Where he had ended up in a top-secret section carrying out clandestine missions abroad). Then Stewart had followed his commanding officer, General XXXXXX, into the Intelligence Corps.

He worked in various intelligence divisions for the next few years, including MI5 and MI6. He became known as a "rainmaker", a man who "got things done". Old-fashioned in his views, he eschewed the gadgetry sometimes prevalent in intelligence work. Eventually, he helped set up the "Outfit" in early 1968 and then rescued Trent from the military police and court-martial, and Trent became part of the team.

Colonel Alec Stewart, in his early fifties, also liked the good life. However, he retained the look of a very fit man. Short grey hair, clean shaven with piercing blue eyes, his whole body language screamed "military". At 6ft 1in, he was taller than Trent, a scar on his right cheek, and he wore suede shoes with a two-piece suit and regimental tie. The only hint of vanity in a large, gold signet ring on his right hand.

Nothing was known of his private life other than he was also seen in the best clubs and restaurants often with a beautiful lady on his arm.

Trent, phlegmatic as usual, sat outside Sir Richard's office, silently cursing the No Smoking sign. Babs, the strict personal secretary to Sir Richard, glaring at him—grey bun, glasses, angular, with eyes only for her two bosses.

She was in her fifties, and had worked her way up through the civil service and had been with Sir Richard for nearly ten years. She was unmarried and, typical of career women of her generation, was in effect married to the job and fiercely loyal to her boss. Prim, pristine, grey government uniform. She wore no lipstick, no make-up, and hid behind a pair of thick, horn-rimmed spectacles. Severe outlook—her mouth turned down, reflecting her general dissatisfaction with everything and everybody. She was a slave to her typewriter, to her filing cabinet, and lost in a world of red tape.

Her whole universe was this drab office, the small reception room outside Sir Richard's and the colonel's offices. A sentinel for the two main men in the "Outfit". Cerberus on guard.

Eventually, she beckoned to him to go forward and Trent entered Sir Richard's office. He was comfortably seated behind a mahogany desk, the whole room subtly proclaiming his wealth and power, portraits of Queen Victoria and Bismarck on the wall (but not one of the current Queen?).

There was also a water colour of his stately home in Marlborough, and some prints of fox hunting. Otherwise, the office was as minimalistic as Trent's flat. There was no paperwork on the desk, no filing cabinets, no "Top Secret" stamp. He had a phone and a globe on the desk and a map of the world on the wall. The only other furniture was an expensive-looking drinks cabinet in the corner.

This all contrasted with the colonel's office next door, which gave the impression of frantic activity. He also had Queen Victoria on the wall, along with Wellington, and paintings depicting Rorke's Drift and the Zulu assault on the British Army.

There were bulging filing cabinets, papers strewn on the desk, an ashtray overflowing with cigar stubs. A bookcase with books on military history and the British Empire, and the inevitable drinks cabinet.

Trent usually met the colonel in his office and he supposed it was now a dubious "privilege" to be in Sir Richard's sanctum.

The colonel sat on a hard chair adjacent to Sir Richard and he curtly asked him to also sit. Both puffed on insanely expensive cigars. He was not invited to smoke.

It was boiling hot in the office, the radiators in the building were either too hot or too cold and needed a good kick to work anyway. Sir Richard, like a reptile, or cobra, seemed to thrive on this atmosphere.

Trent felt sweat prickling on his back and armpits. This wasn't only the heat, he was always slightly nervous in front of these two. He'd rather face overwhelming odds in battle or be in a gun fight.

'Well, what did you think about the fiasco in Berlin?' Colonel Stewart spat out, whilst Sir Richard appraised him through the pincenez and cigar smoke. The colonel twiddled his green ink fountain pen. Trent, like back on the parade ground, sat up straighter, trying to stand to attention in his chair. He looked beyond his two chiefs at the world map on the wall. Why was it still showing all the red of the British Empire? India was independent surely.

'I think, Sir—and, Sir—that the whole thing was blown; a mole of some kind informed on us blew the whole plan…'

'You think there was a mole, hey?' The colonel's sarcasm dripped. A pause, a glare, then he relaxed. 'Well, Trent. We think you're right, absolutely, absolutely. Probably MI6, their end. Can't trust these other people. Well, we're setting up an enquiry for the leak. Two good men looking at it now. Anything else? Anything further to report?'

'Yes, Sir, there's more. The whole setup…' He paused; how to articulate the thoughts racing round his head—

'Seemed, well, unreal. In fact, just that, a setup. They knew Johnson was coming to see me with the stuff. They could have killed him anytime. So why after he handed it over?'

The colonel and Sir Richard exchanged glances, privileged thoughts way above Trent's head.

'Yes, indeed,' Sir Richard interjected looking at Trent like the pleb he believed him to be. Like something unpleasant on his shoe. He was glad that he normally only saw the colonel. At least for all his sarcasm, he treated him like a soldier and could be reasonably civil. He really could do with a fag right now!

'Our focus,' Sir Richard continued, 'must now be on the data brought out by Johnson via the microdot. Some very interesting gen that correspond to our thoughts. Way above your pay grade of course.' He looked over at the colonel, who nodded. 'Let's go and see the professor…'

After his patronising words out of his mouth, he muttered, 'Tally Ho,' rose, and wobbled out of his office.

Stewart gestured to Trent to follow him. They went after their chief through the maze of corridors until they came to a fairly modern room at the back of the building—the conference room.

Trent had only been here a few times before. It was a fairly large meeting room, with seats for about ten. There was a small stage, a podium, a screen, and a projector.

The three men sat at the front, before the stage. Sir Richard was sweating slightly. Babs brought pots of coffee, even for Trent, and they waited. The two senior men lit up cigars and also let Trent light up his more plebeian No 6 tipped.

A blanket of smoke filled the room, the door was flung open and in walked the "Outfit" employee known as "the Prof".

Chapter Five
London, 28 October

The Prof was not a professor of science. Nicknamed because a) he looked like a mad scientist and b) because of his diligent and academic approach to this work.

He had worked with Sir Richard Abbott for many years. His real name was Jim Clarke and he was a collator of intelligence, an analyst, and a strategist all in one. A major cog in their intelligence wheel. It was said he had set up and ran the colonel's spy network and oversaw the computer system that backed everything up.

He was somewhere in his forties, although this difficult to pin down. Unbeknown to most of his colleagues, he did in fact hold a professorship of philosophy from Cambridge University. This was at a time when MI5 were recruiting top graduates from that university. However, it was his love of research, statistics, computers, and data that had cemented his career.

He had a high forehead, slightly balding head at the front, giving him the "egghead" intellectual look; what remained of his hair was white and unruly. Age: indeterminate. Height: medium. Spectacles perched on his nose. His whole demeanour was dishevelled and untidy. Shirt usually hanging out, fly often undone. Shoes never brushed. This all covering a brilliant and analytical mind.

'The affair in Berlin, the Johnson balls-up…this confirmed many things to us with regard to some of the communist bloc's intentions towards this country.' Sir Richard gave a small preamble, his chins wobbling. 'When I was at Buck House, Prince Philip expressed concerns about all this trouble brewing, although he knows nothing of what we're going to discuss now.' He paused for effect; typical name-dropping.

'Now over to you, Prof, for your views on all of this, please.'

Prof stood in front of the screen behind a podium, positioning himself so that the three men were all facing him. Trent extinguished his cigarette and sipped on the coffee. It was good.

The Prof shuffled uneasily. He looked nervous in front of his superiors. Although the very nature of his job meant he must have to do regular presentations. But this was not his natural metier. Graphs, charts, intelligence, data, analysis were where he was happiest. He held sheets of paper in his hand, which shook slightly. He brought himself under control, looked at his notes and shakily started.

'Well, gentlemen,' the prof's voice was nasal and surprisingly vaguely posh Scouse. He stared over the three, never looking at them direct.

'As you are aware, over recent months there has been a rise in violent crime, with many murders. This has baffled our police.' He took a sip of water from a carafe in front of him.

'In addition, we have seen more bomb attacks across all the country, with no one claiming responsibility. Furthermore, there has been an increase in industrial action in all sectors.' He scratched his shaggy white hair and continued. 'Our intelligence sources across Europe have pinpointed a co-ordinated plot to destabilise this country and we also expect this to rise significantly over the next few weeks, with some particularly nefarious action against a major target. We have also ascertained that…' A pause, another sip. '…somewhere behind all this, various terrorist and anti-British groups have combined to make this work. Here's some of the data we collated.'

The projector flashed and figures, graphs, etc. hit the screen; the prof stood aside, pointing out details.

Philip Trent stifled a yawn and mentally switched off from this array of data, until the professor finalised…

'In summary, the microdot brought in by Ernie Johnson from east Berlin clarifies a lot of our suspicions.' He cleared his throat. 'They call this conspiracy the Z File. For reasons I think will be made c…clear as we go along.'

'He had a source deep in the East German security police—the Stasi if you like—and it would appear that Moscow is behind this coordinated plot, although very coy about it. They are staying well in the background So staying in the shadows, they have made it appear that any plot is by the hand of a rogue element in the Stasi; ahem anyway, that's where funding is coming from.'

The Prof was now warming to his subject and spoke without stopping:

'Somehow they've recruited a faction in the IRA, the Angry Brigade, PLO, UK communists, et al, and a new militant Islamic group, who believe they speak for the new Madhi. The overall aim is to create chaos, anarchy and economic ruin on these shores. Use anyone with a crackpot idea to overthrow the government.

'As I say, they've already started with these murderous violent crimes, bombings and strikes, and this will escalate.' He finally finished for a breather and another drink.

Sir Richard intervened. 'Ahem; as you see eh…yes, Trent, things are critical and newspapers and TV are sure to get hold of more things soon and make things worse.' He waved his cigar. 'However, the PM and cabinet are sceptical and scared of over-reacting. We need further evidence and, if feasible, to get to these people and destroy them. If we can get this evidence, I have the ear of the PM and I can get things moving. Get a fully resourced operation against this threat.

'There is also a further problem in that; right-wing elements are also clamouring for more government action in the wake of all this. Over to you, Colonel Stewart.'

The colonel poured himself another coffee, savouring the aroma. 'Yes… you have read of Sir Adrian Joyce, more right-wing than Enoch Powell, an honourable member for Churchdale in Oxfordshire. He recently crossed the floor of the House from the Tories. Supposedly an independent, he is now part of a splinter group of the National Socialist movement here. Also in the process of setting up a new party—the GB National Party.

'Neo-Nazis, some call them, and his supporters have been demonstrating in areas where ethnic minorities live. Echoes of Moseley and his blackshirts. Anyway, they're the antithesis of this new communist group. Floggers, hangers, anti-Europe, anti-decimal, racism, etc., etc. Ahem…Anti-queers. He's causing a stir in parliament and in the press. So…ahem…this all leads to a very unsatisfactory and volatile situation. Any queries so far, Trent?' Those piercing blue eyes focussed on him like gun barrels.

Trent lit another cigarette to give himself time to think. Finally, he said, 'Well, I can see from the papers, telly, that things are getting worse.' He scratched his head. 'Few questions; why am I here and what do you want me to do?' Blunt as normal.

He looked directly at his two superiors.

'Also, still not sure why Johnson was killed and do we know who that giant was? Seemed to be the leader?' He finished. 'Any connection with this giant who is killing over here, this Zombie character?'

'To the point as usual.' The colonel half-smiled, whilst Sir Richard nodded.

'Prof, tell him about the giant,' Stewart ordered and the professor, startled, became nervous again; he blinked in the direction of his superiors.

'Yes, well, er, er, we believe him to be Wolfgang Mueller. A mercenary. An ex-Nazi, ex-C...communist who has worked for everyone, in-including Castro. N-Now here and c-causing trouble. He's somewhere in his late forties and was born on the East German side, in the Leipzig area. First heard of in Buchenwald concentration camp where, although young, he had a reputation for cruelty. This led to a dubious eh, promotion to Auschwitz where again his talent for torture and death was very useful to the Nazis.

'After the war he vanished, but he seems to have somehow found favour in the KGB and Smersh. N-next known to be part of the ruthless put-down on the Hungarian uprising of '56.

'Since then, he seems to have been an...an independent operator, a mercenary of sorts working for the highest bidder. Including, as I say, Castro. That is until recently when he re-surfaced in the S-Stasi as the man with the job of co-ordinating death and destruction here.'

'We had heard rumours about him before, but the info you brought from Berlin is specific. He is the Stasi's man over here fermenting trouble.'

The Prof's initial nervousness now vanished, so he continued: 'Also, he seems to be taking part in some robberies and killing without mercy. P- probably f- for fun.'

Trent was now so transfixed with the story unfolding, he didn't even light a further cigarette. The coffee in front of him went cold; he sat forward with alert interest.

'He is the man who we are certain killed Johnson with some sort of rocket-powered harpoon, to slice through the bulletproof glass. He is the man we need to track down, although it is unlikely that he is the brain behind things. Interestingly in the latter stages of the war, he was caught up in a bombing raid which, with the scarring on his face caused by that, and his height, he became known as "the Zombie". But more often than not as Z.'

Chapter Six
Still London

"The Zombie", the giant of a man whom Trent had "met" in Berlin. The giant with an evil past, who was killing without mercy and with a purpose. Known as Z to some.

Wearing a monster-type mask in the robberies, the press had latched on to the Zombie soubriquet. Also quoting the approaching Halloween (although at present more celebrated in the US than Britain).

The Prof continued. 'Interestingly, the evidence gathered by the police of the robberies shows that the same fingerprints have turned up at various scenes of crime. No matches, so those involved are not career criminals. Also, we have no prints on file for Mueller. Ballistics also reveal that they are using the same weapons time and again.

'On a couple of occasions, Mueller has removed his mask, almost as if he wants it to be known he is involved, and he is taunting us. Here's a police artist's impression of him from a surviving witness.'

He passed a sketch to Trent, who commented: 'Not a pretty picture, would look better with the monster mask on.' He received a glare for this vague levity from the colonel, all serious stuff today...

So that was what Mueller looked like. He would like to meet up again with this "thing" and deliver rough justice. He repeated his earlier question: 'So what would you like me to do?'

The colonel picked up the mantle. 'This info from Johnson also indicated that a "gentleman" called Ajmal Khan is involved here; monies from a secret source in the Stasi are paid to him.'

Another puff of the cigar, a clearing of the throat. 'The Zombie theme—Khan owns a business in Birmingham that imports and sells monster toys, including these masks. The name Zombie Plastics Ltd was used to manufacture at a unit in Wales, but now imports and sells as a wholesaler. Interestingly, only just changed its name to Zombie; could be an inside joke by these people.'

The colonel paused, stared hard at Trent to emphasise a point. 'Chief of security there is this Wolfgang chap. Although under the name of Roland West, ha! The Berlin info reveals all this and Khan would seem to be a puppet for Mueller—West whatever.'

He continued: 'As it happens, Khan is of interest to the local police. They believe he is up to his neck in drugs, extortion, prostitution, and the rest. We also think he is the front for this extreme Islamic group and getting funds from the communists to stir things up. With us so far? Not boring you, are we?'

Trent still said nothing under the colonel's close scrutiny. The colonel appraising him with gimlet cold blue eyes then went on.

'The Birmingham flatfoots have no proof however. Now you have a friend there from the army, who is with the CID.'

Trent raised his eyebrows quizzically. 'Well, yes, Steve Ray, a DI. We were also at school together.'

'Yes, I know,' the colonel smirked. 'You were called up at the same time. I remember you both in the Staffordshire.

'Anyway, we've arranged with his superiors for you to have a nose around Khan's warehouse, meet the gentleman, as his sergeant. Once you have the layout of the place, you could break in, see what you can find.'

Trent still quizzical. 'OK, oh, and what do I say to the locals?'

'You are part of Special Branch looking at Khan as a potential threat to our country. Prof here will supply credentials and Babs has arranged all travel, hotel, etc. in Birmingham for tomorrow. Any further comment? No, ok. You will report daily to the prof, of course.'

Trent shook his head; it was a lot to take in. He looked at his watch and the colonel noticed.

'Well, off you go. I know you have a meeting later.' Another smirk; Sir Richard nodded. There was no farewell from Sir Richard, only a grunt.

It was just after 1pm when he left the office, his large leather coat wrapped round him tightly. The late-October weather was ice-cold, and the sky was gunmetal grey. He walked up to Henrietta Street and to Leicester Square. He had two hours before his "meeting" in a hotel near Portman Square.

Trent made a decision—he'd go to Soho and the Coach and Horses—see if he could catch Kev Bloomer there, his journalist friend. See if he had any background on the current disturbing events. The press viewpoint!

Crossing Leicester Square, it was lunchtime and office workers, with no worries about any of the Zombie nonsense, milled about. Their faces red, in the chill afternoon, their breath visible in the air.

They sought somewhere for their lunch break—a meal at the Golden Egg or a Wimpy or some such place. A drink at the pub with reheated cottage pie—no thanks. He'd have a snack and a pint at the Coach and Horses.

He passed the Odeon, *Bedknobs and Broomsticks* the feature. A sign promoting the premiere of *Diamonds Are Forever*, coming December. Made a change from all the sex movies appearing all around London. Another advert—*"No sex please we're British"*. Michael Crawford at the Strand theatre.

A newspaper vendor was shouting his incomprehensible sales pitch for the *Evening Standard*. The news poster declared: *"Another series of robberies... Zombie killer strikes"*.

Trent purchased a newspaper, left the square, and headed up Wardour Street towards Soho. He passed crowds of people—men all long hair and sideburns, even middle-aged men, with their greying moustaches. Women often in maxis. Whatever happened to the mini? A crowd of bobbies hung around a Doctor Who police box surreptitiously smoking and drinking tea, their breath creating clouds in the cold. *Something about policemen on the street...*this random thought ran through his mind. A Beatles favourite of his mate, Steve, who he was shortly to see again.

He felt slightly at odds, his hairstyle still military-short, and his clothes conservative; not that being trendy normally bothered him. Trent was impervious to dictates of fashion and fancy. However, even he could feel slightly out of place amongst all these long hairs and peacocks of London. He breathed in the refreshing cool air, glad to be out of the office hothouse. God, now for that pint, then an afternoon of promise.

Chapter Seven
28 October, Soho and Beyond

The Coach and Horses in Greek Street was a magnet for journalists, bohemians, alcoholic hard-drinking artists, poets, film stars, and so on. Run by Norman, London's rudest landlord, it was a lunchtime haven until closing time. Then afternoon drinking often continued at one of the nearby exclusive private clubs, such as the Colony Room.

The pub still had a 1930s feel with the bar and wall panelling from that era. There were still Art Deco Lino floor tiles and a spittoon trough, and a well used battered piano in the corner.

Trent ordered a pint of Fullers Bitter and a packet of cheese and onion crisps, that would do for lunch! Paid in the new decimal coinage (he was with Adrian Joyce on this—bring back pounds, shillings and pence), then luckily he found a seat. He wondered if Sir Richard and the colonel were off to one of their clubs, leaving the prof alone with his packed lunch. He tasted the beer, good but not as good as Banks' or Pardoe's back in the Midlands.

He looked round the smoky, crowded bar and there was Kev Bloomer holding court. He caught his eye and beckoned him over.

'Have you time for a quick chat? What do you press boys think of all this Zombie stuff…? Robberies, strikes, y'know; do you think it's all a coordinated plot?'

'Frightfully busy, dear boy, tete a tete with that TV star.' A nod in the direction of a handsome young man nursing a cocktail.

'Could be a good story; also have a feeling might get lucky. Catch you later. Could give you the lowdown tonight, old boy; catch up on footie as well.'

'Got to go to Birmingham tomorrow for a couple of days, will meet up when back.' Kev nodded, he didn't really want to know about Trent's business, although he'd heard rumours—hush-hush and all that.

Kev rejoined the young man and his entourage at the bar…he seemed vaguely familiar to Trent. Some TV show he'd seen?

Kev always reminded him of George Melly, large, flamboyant, running to fat, with those extra-large lips. The epitome of perhaps how Shakespeare imagined Falstaff. Handkerchief in his top pocket, expensive suit, but always in a scruffy state. A sort of posh prof, Trent surmised. A vodka and tonic always in hand; cigarette ash covering his front (alongside other stains). A character!

He claimed to be bisexual but no one had ever seen him in female company. A brave and open homosexual even before it became legal in 1967. Also a brave and tenacious journalist, with a brief that covered all topics.

He'd been born in Dudley and had pulled himself up to his current position by his flashy sock garters and braces. Only a few years older than Trent, his journey had been via grammar school, a course in journalism at night school and a job at the Birmingham Daily Mail (now the Birmingham Evening Mail).

He left for London with an excellent reputation, which he solidified with a series of scoops working for the Daily Blank! His latest had been initial exclusive coverage of the Baker Street robbery in the previous month. Criminals had tunnelled into the Lloyds branch in Baker Street and broken into safety deposit boxes. Through Kev's police and government contacts, he released the story first and gained all the kudos going.

They'd met, surprisingly, after the West Brom-Everton F.A. Cup final in 1968, at a celebration party. Kev was from the Midlands, a football fan, but somehow along the way had lost his Midlands accent. Now posh, so very posh.

He'd tried it on with Trent until discovering he was very much heterosexual. They remained good friends, going to the football or pub-crawls every so often. Also, he provided some interesting titbits of gossip from time to time.

Trent picked up the paper, lit a cigarette, and had another pint. Why was he getting a bad feeling about all this? The news continued about further "Zombie" atrocities and were now linking them with a further explosion at a pub in Coventry, seven killed. Sir Adrian Joyce was asking questions in the House. There followed an article on Joyce:

Is Sir Adrian Joyce the new Winston Churchill? Well, he certainly seems to think so. He dresses conservatively—three-piece suit, bow tie, handkerchief in top pocket, and a gold pocket watch. With an added bowler and cigar, very Churchillian!

Not from the aristocracy, however, a self-made man in his early fifties. Born in Nottingham and from a modest background, he built a fortune from the textile industry lace manufacture. Then joined the Conservative Party, and was always the darling of the right side of the party. This probably precluded a rise to the top and he always remained an MP. This surely led to his decision to leave the Tories and set up a new party, The GB National Party.

Winston Churchill? He was always concerned with the rise of Nazi Germany in the thirties. Joyce is also concerned with an outside threat—communism. But equally, he is concerned with the internal threat of rising crime, violence, and terrorism. In fact, he says that the internal and external problems are intrinsically linked.

The new party have links with the quasi-fascist group, the National Socialists, and many critics say that he is the opposite of Churchill. In fact, a Nazi.

Michael Foot, the left-wing Labour MP, in fact describes him as a total anti-democratic fascist.

Sir Adrian denies this accusation. The new party, he states, espouses traditional values. Those of patriotism, loyalty, strong law and order, and strong armed forces. A Britain not polluted by the idea of Europe and other malign foreign influences. In particular, a stand against communism and support for the Vietnam War.

"The G.B. National Party is building a broad church of support with its stronger approach to the problems facing the country," says Sir Adrian. "My thoughts are for the families of the victims of the recent bombings. An example of terrorism faced by Britain and what we will wipe out. Terrorism that we believe is supported by the communist regime."

Whether you believe in what Sir Adrian is saying, and he is certainly a controversial character, many are flocking to his cause.

The terrible recent events seemed to have galvanised public support for him and it will be interesting to see how the new party fares in the next election.

Whilst this paper offers no support to this new force in politics, we do grudgingly recognise that he voices many things popular with the general public. We shall see how things play out…

He ordered another pint and read the paper cover to cover.

When he finished, he slung it aside in disgust and pushed his way through the teeming bar and waved farewell to Kev.

'Oh, cheerio old thing!' Kev's voice boomed above the hubbub. 'Off for your Thursday dalliance with prostitutes, ha ha ha. Have a good time!'

Trent glowered at him and made his way out into the cold and on towards Oxford Street, trying to shake off the feelings of doom.

Chapter Eight
Portman Square Hotel

Prostitute, Camille was certainly that. A high-class one with very rich clients and expensive fees. Courtesan would be a better description. Colonel Stewart had introduced them some years before and it had almost been love at first sight, if not that then lust at first sight!

Normally, she would work at the expensive hotels perhaps twice a week—The Ritz, The Savoy. Thursday afternoons were reserved for her and Trent, at a modest hotel near Portman Square, on Gloucester Place. Afterwards, they'd go for a meal, a show or the cinema. Sometimes even a club.

The hotel was old-fashioned, a faded townhouse in need of some loving care. As Trent entered, he saw in the dining room all the live-in guests seated around the room, separately. A mix of retired majors, rich widows, etc.; Terence Rattigan's *Separate Tables* came to life. Waiting for afternoon tea, each lost in their lonely world. Trent moved past these relics of their own past, their sad faces staring into their own abyss. He nodded at a couple of them, but was largely ignored. Surely not him in thirty years? Dead, he hoped!

He went up to the first floor, politely knocked and entered *their* room for the afternoon. It was of a very old style—high ceiling, mirrors on the wall, ornate lighting, Adam fireplace. The room was large, large enough for the very sizeable double bed. There was a bureau, hard chairs, and uncomfortable sofa, all springs.

On the bureau were scattered a few leaflets, for London sight-seeing.

Next to the bed on a side table was champagne on ice, two glasses ready. In the bed was Camille. She had fine blonde silken hair down to her shoulders. A lock escaped, falling over her right eye. She had high Slavic cheekbones, pale skin and delicate, laughing brown eyes. She had long lashes, all her own, and a smile always played on her full lips.

45

She was 5ft 7ins-ish and had agile, feminine movement. There was a hint of muscle and strength from regular trips to the gym and she had firm attractive breasts. She always reminded Trent of a sort of blonde Emma Peel-Diana Rigg in *The Avengers* TV show, with a mix of a sophisticated Grace Kelly. Those were admirable attributes although as Trent admitted, in fact she was just gorgeous.

Camille was a true feminist, without losing her femininity. Totally in control of her life, always relaxed, content with the state of the world and the state of the nation. She also liked the good things in life, best clothes, without being showy, good food and wine. She was also well-read and cultured.

In fact, she was the complete opposite of Trent, although he'd picked up and appreciated some of her traits. He now liked decent food and wine, and even read books! She did say he was still verging on being a misanthrope though. Another victory, she'd improved his vocabulary.

Camille Morris was originally of an old aristocratic Russian family, the Muravievs. As Camille told it, her mother had fled the Russian Revolution for Paris in the 1920s and then moved to London, living in genteel poverty. She changed her name to Morris to not attract attention, to not stand out. Camille had turned to her "vocation" so that she could live in a style that had escaped her refugee mother. Her high cheekbones the only clue to her Slavic origin. Camille was slightly older than Philip Trent and her father had been a mystery, never revealed by her mother. Although, she believed him to be French, hence her name, Camille.

She took another sip of champagne; Trent offered her a kiss. Outside, the dark autumn afternoon glimpsed through the blinds.

'You stink of beer, fags and onions, you animal...' She gave a throaty chuckle and pushed him away.

'Sorry, called at—'

'Yes, the Coach & Horses,' she interrupted. 'With that fat drunk friend.'

'It was business, and you know his name is Kev.'

Chuckle again. 'Yes, I know who he is. He's still let us say an imbiber of mammoth proportions, a tittle-tattle reporter, and a bad influence on you.'

'I thought that was you?'

'Me, nothing but saintly good, look how I've improved your life.'

'My love life?'

'Yes, mmm...suppose so, but also your life, good food, wine, books, culture, better than all that chips, beer and football.'

'Well, not entirely.'

'No, you still stink, go get a shower and a mouthwash.'

In the shower, he sniffed suspiciously at the feminine soap and gel, shrugged and started to lather. Arms went round him; a soft kiss on the neck…

No sex please, we're…

Censored by the Lord Chamberlain's Office 1971.

After their exertions, Trent lay looking at the ceiling, smoking; such a cliché. Camille, healthy, didn't. She was still wet, covered by the thin sheet, the damp outline of her breasts showing through, the dark shadow of mystery below. Blonde hair wet, a hint of perspiration on her forehead. She then started the conversation, knowing Trent was never that loquacious at the best of times.

'We're getting like an old married couple.' She was well-spoken but not too upper-class.

'Never, well, I hope never,' replied Trent. Their bickering was always gentle and with some humour. Camille perhaps saw something in Trent beyond his dubious profession, worthy of love without judgment.

'Do you remember when we first met?' She asked, looking directly, searchingly into his eyes. Something that made him feel vaguely uncomfortable, although Camille had no such inhibitions.

'How could I forget.' He'd never seen anything so sensual, sexual. Yet so, so nice. Anybody so intelligent and sophisticated, yet good fun. He'd been hooked, even when Colonel Stewart had delighted in telling him what she did for a living.

They'd met at Rules Restaurant at the colonel's instigation. He thought they would "get along" and he was right. Although nothing the colonel did was without reason. At the back of Trent's mind, he always considered that she'd been instructed to keep an eye on him for the colonel. To spy on the spy. He also knew she did the odd bit of work for the colonel.

The colonel didn't stay after the introduction.

'That bloody colonel really enjoyed telling me about you. After it was obvious I was taken with you; sadist!' He stared out into the dark street outside, afraid of his feelings.

'Taken with me, were you?' She smiled and threw a pillow at him. 'And were you OK with what I do?'

'Can't say I'm over-chuffed. However, I've known from day one, and how do you say it, I've compartmentalised it. Same as with my job really.' He paused.

'Just happy to be with you.'

He thought, *She's not judging me and my job,* so he could hardly point a finger.

So they'd fallen for each other in Rules; she, a courtesan, to be polite, and he, a sometime assassin to be less polite. After the meal, they'd gone to one of the trendy clubs Camille knew, and then to this hotel for the first time.

This all was getting too near an emotional knuckle for Trent and he changed the subject.

'How's your week been?' He asked, putting his cigarette down and taking a drink of champagne.

'Busy-busy; went to the Tate Gallery, mmm…the gym, the theatre and, oh, afternoon tea at Claridge's.' No mention of any of her clients. 'How about you?'

'Nothing much; been to Berlin, work.' Non-committal, he picked his cigarette up and took a deep drag.

'What shall we do later? I thought the Ivy, and then a club. What do you think?' She said, changing the subject.

Trent pulled a face. 'Oh, but you know me and dancing.'

'The place will be packed. You'll be drunk and who cares…' He knew he'd go just for Camille.

'Can't be late; off to Brum tomorrow, on business.' He also knew he would be late!

They always went out after. The colonel had first introduced Trent to good restaurants, decent wine, and Camille had continued this education. She had also introduced him to culture—theatre, ballet, opera, decent cinema—to no avail. She'd taken him to see The Band at the Royal Albert Hall (well, you like rock & roll)—the smell of cannabis filling the old hall—old Albert would turn in his grave! He'd rather see Chuck Berry coming to London next year (that's rock & roll!)

Philistine! She'd said. Although he knew she'd gone because she fancied Robbie Robertson.

At first, Camille wanted to pay for everything; now they took it in turns (although admittedly, a strain on his pay packet). The hotel was free due to some mysterious past favour to the owner.

Most of the time she didn't talk about his work. She knew from the colonel that he worked for the government, and his work could be dangerous, but no specifics. This time was different.

'Your drinking and smoking, over-exercising, is it your job? Something you're trying to black out? All that danger, for Queen and country? Please talk to me, Philip.'

Trent did not reply. She continued: 'I do worry about you, you know.' She looked lovely, concerned, blonde hair tousled, falling over her face. He was lucky, even on a part-time basis.

But he couldn't reply. He didn't want to break that self-built barrier, that reserve that he held as a protection against his inner feelings. Feelings best kept hidden, particularly with his line of work. Hidden even from Camille, and even from himself.

He mumbled something. "Basically, I'm still a soldier, obeying orders, not to reason why and all that…"

'I'm sorry, Philip, I know you don't want to talk about this. That I'm another safety valve. I do, do really care in my own way. Me and that queer drunk are your only friends! Oh, and that bloody dog.

'Look, Philip, as I'm opening up about things, let's go further. Let's say that I really do care for you, but…' She gave a long, dramatic pause. 'But I also seem to have fallen in love with you.'

This was the first time she'd said this.

Trent couldn't just yet say the expected words. Instead, he grunted and said: 'Y'know, why is everyone this week trying to analyse me? You're as bad as the colonel and his cronies.' (He thought of that meeting, the assessment of him as a security risk.)

At the mention of the colonel, the mood changed. Trent started to pace the room, naked as he was. His muscled scarred body on view. Camille knew he didn't like this attempt to peel back the hidden layers of emotion. She pulled back from this line of conversation.

'Philip, I'm sorry. Come back to bed.'

Now all coquettish, sexy—the courtesan.

He couldn't resist; he climbed back into bed and they fell into an embrace.

Chapter Nine
To Birmingham, 29 October

With a slight hangover, he'd got back home at 3.30am. After the Ivy, a nightclub, then another bout of strenuous lovemaking, he really couldn't stand the pace. The alarm clock awoke him at 7.30, a few brief exercises, a cup of coffee, and a walk round the park with Tess, the dog.

His head clearing, he explained to Mrs McDougal he was away for a couple of days and gave her the housekeeping money. She replied in a strong accent, difficult to understand. He was sure she did it on purpose and as he left, a smile twitched on her stern lips. He then caught the tube into Euston, carrying a small overnight bag and attaché case. He wore his long, leather coat against the gathering cold and took his only headgear, a battered old trilby.

Whilst the "Outfit" did not spend much on weaponry and gadgets, the expenses were generous. So Trent travelled First Class British Rail to Birmingham. From experience, he knew that BR did an excellent breakfast and once on the train, he was served by a smartly uniformed BR steward and he tucked into bacon, eggs and coffee. His hangover quickly disappeared and he sat back and looked out at the passing landscape.

- Past a large power station billowing steam to the sky.
- Endless pylons, a stain on England's green fields, carrying the electricity to towns and cities.
- Closed stations, broken glass, platforms of weeds—courtesy of Dr Beeching.

Trent cursed this progress and picked up the newspaper he'd purchased at Euston.

More strikes, violent robberies and bombings. A new phenomenon being a spate of hoax bomb calls across the country, causing further panic. Protesters—right and left—on the march. Adrian Joyce to the fore in the news and parliament, with his ever popular right-wing rhetoric.

Camille had not been totally correct about his friends. There was also DI Steve Ray, his childhood friend, although he'd not seen him for a few years. Always too busy!

They were to meet at Steelhouse Lane Police Station at 1pm, then go for the interview with this Ajmal Khan. Police Sergeant Trent, it said on his warrant card (arranged by the prof and Babs, along with his additional Special Branch ID).

Trent arrived at New Street station and stepped out into the city chill, a fog forming. He noted the recent reconstruction, together with the new Pallasades shopping centre above the station. Grumpily old-fashioned, he detested the changes. He remembered the steam trains coming into the station as a kid, he remembered the old Snow Hill station now gone (Dr Beeching Again!)

Progress! He looked at the modern "futuristic" buildings incongruously alongside the older buildings.

He preferred the old, grubby, dirty look, with character. The Rotunda, a carbuncle on the city skyline. It already looked dated. He did admit that not everything was rose-tinted, however. The slums of Winson Green and Aston were being pulled down, and they were no great loss. The city had seen the second-highest tonnage of bombs in the war, something he knew personally with the loss of his mother. So with bomb damage, slums and a massive housing shortage, an extensive redevelopment was taking place. Would the new high-rise towers and buildings be any better? Only time will tell.

He had been booked into the Midland Hotel in Stephenson Street, opposite the station. He had his attaché case put into the hotel safe there, full of his "tools of trade". He'd brought his smaller Beretta, which he kept in the holster beneath his coat. He disagreed with Fleming's armourer, he liked the gun. Then he hired a car through reception to be delivered later.

He left for his appointment and there was an old obvious drunk on the corner of New Street. 'Gotta shilling for a cup of tea, guv!' Someone else clinging to the old currency! Trent gave him a few coins and smiled as the old chap walked up Corporation Street to Yates's Wine Lodge, where he could get a "dock" of cheap wine from a barrel on the counter. Passing over New Street, he

51

remembered trips to Lyons Café with his nan, a rare treat when she came shopping to Birmingham.

He followed the old rascal up Corporation Street, past the famous Nathan's Jewellers clock and C & A's. And then into Bull Street, past Lewis's and a turn into Steelhouse Lane and the police station The station had been built in 1933 in neo-Georgian style, and obviously had seen better days. A dirty grey building in a dirty grey street.

He showed his "Special Branch" ID to the desk sergeant and was shown up to CID. Steve Ray met him in the hall outside the main CID offices.

He never really changed, a couple of inches shorter than Trent, but still just about regulation height. Hair slightly ginger (much ribbing in school!), bright blue eyes, freckles and as always a boyish, engaging smile. The hair was longer than would have been allowed a few years ago and he had the almost modern obligatory sideburns. The long hair did not hide a scar on his forehead however, a football injury from years ago. He was in plain clothes as befitting someone in CID. Very seventies plain clothes—brown suit, flare trousers, and a floral kipper tie.

An optimist, outgoing; the opposite of Trent. He also definitely didn't look like any sort of policeman.

They shook hands warmly. Then there was that typical awkward moment when after a long time of not seeing each other, the old friends were lost for words.

After a minute or two, or so, Steve spoke first, smiling, 'So you're in Special Branch today?' Trent typically grunted, Steve continued, 'Thought you were in some James Bond department MI…whatever.'

This avenue of conversation ground to a halt, Trent changed the subject.

'Hear you're married now, Steve, how's that going?'

Steve smiled. 'Yes, to Jackie, a nurse. You can meet her later. Come over for supper. She's dying to meet you. Any chance you getting hitched?'

'Not much.'

'Any…?' He looked straight at his friend. 'Any, what I mean, going steady?'

'I have a er…lady friend,' he replied cautiously, and left it at that.

'Same old Phil, give nothing away.'

'Same old Steve—heart on the sleeve.'

The two pals smiled shyly at each other.

'How's your mom and dad?' Subject changed again.

'Fine—Still go to the Hawthorns with dad when I have time.'

'Policing in the second city; busy?'

'Crime on the increase, not helped by this stuff on the news. Seems to encourage copycats, well here in Brum anyway. Don't forget tonight…mmmm yes…let's go and see the boss.'

He could hardly refuse the invite to supper, although he did have some nocturnal adventures later, which Steve, the policeman, would not want to know about, officially at least.

Steve introduced him to his boss, Superintendent Ken Roberts. There was a shaking of hands again, although Roberts did not look that enthusiastic to meet Trent. He toyed with the Special Branch card but did not look at it. He was obviously an old-school policeman who looked as if he'd be more than happy to beat up suspects, and maybe plant evidence if required. Maybe Trent, however, did him a disservice. Steve seemed to look up to him. A man overfond of the whisky bottle and like Trent an habitual smoker. The ceiling of the office was nicotine-yellow; a half full whisky bottle on his desk.

Roberts's nicotine-yellow hair matched the ceiling and he constantly cleared his throat. He was in short sleeves, sweat marks showing at his armpits. The small office was red hot, the radiator blasting, a strong smell of whisky battling with an aroma of fish and chip takeaways and sweat.

He sat behind an old wooden desk pitted by a thousand cups of tea/coffee/whiskey. There was no concession to computers with files flung around and no concession to cleaners either. Everywhere was dust and the summer's cobwebs were still dangling from the ceiling. What looked like mouse droppings were in the corner!

There was a dirty condensation-covered window overlooking a backyard and the back of the nearby court buildings. This was the nerve centre of the battle against serious crime in Birmingham. A large map of Birmingham and its environs adorned the wall, Roberts' patch.

Roberts' grey face and lines showed a man living with the stress of crime in the second city. Trent thought a heart attack on legs. Roberts dropped a cigarette butt into a cold cup of tea and turned to Trent-

'Special Branch, hmmm? Our Mr Khan is a danger to national security?' He was sceptical. 'Up to his neck in all sorts, but a terrorist?' Scepticism was always his first instinct.

'I don't know, you spooks from London (Ignoring Trent's local background) Whatever next, waste of time…hmmphm.'

He stared at Trent through bloodshot suspicious eyes appraising him, Then with a sigh, he relented.

'I understand you know our Steve from old, well…' He trailed off, put his feet on the battered desk, offered Trent a cigarette, and the meeting slightly thawed.

The superintendent became almost cooperative, professional, he nodded at Steve, and took up Khan's story.

'Well, this Khan character appeared from nowhere in the early 60s. All his paperwork in order, but a bit of a mystery.' He took his feet off the desk and blew a smoke ring towards the yellow ceiling.

'Set up various businesses, all seemingly legit, but we believe a front for his dubious activities.' Roberts waved his arms and cigarette, ash and sparks flew through the air.

'We suspect him of…hmmppphhh…running protection rackets, involved in drugs, prostitution, rack rents. Nothing proven and his own community protects him, closing ranks out of fear. I'd love to nail the bastard and if your lot can help, then all the better.'

Now firmly on the same side, he continued.

'Lives a life of luxury the c…Smart detached house in Edgbaston. Attractive young English wife. Although it's also said he has a wife and children back in Pakistan.' He tutted, his frustration visible.

'So, he lives an expensive lifestyle. Properties all over, including France. One of his businesses is Zombie Plastics Ltd, specialty fancy dress, including monster masks. Originally manufactured at his own factory in Wales but now imports from the Far East. The business been about for a few years, but he only recently changed its name to Zombie. His local wholesale place is in Hospital Street in Hockley, and as requested, we've made an appointment with Khan this afternoon and…hmmmmpaa…I think that's it.'

A few cigarettes later, but no tea or coffee offered, and they decided on an approach for the interview with Mr Khan. Trent and Steve then set off for Zombie Plastics Ltd in a squad car.

Not much was said in the car, they'd catch up later. They parked in the street opposite the unit, and skillfully navigated the abundant dog mess littering the pavement. They'd arrived slightly early so Trent could survey the place. Steve guessed his intention was to break in later, but tactfully this was not alluded to.

The building was of red brick, darkened by Birmingham pollution. Built in the fifties, approx 8,500 sq feet, it was mainly for storage with two large roller shutter doors at the front. In the sizeable parking space were several vans and a top-of-the-range Jag; Khan's, one assumed. A solitary tree, sorry for itself, at the side of the yard, the few remaining leaves autumn brown.

Trent ran his eyes over. At the front was a palisade fence, standard. Behind it, another barbed-wire fence with "Danger: Electric" signs. Security cameras evident. A couple of tough-looking security guards loitered. No sign of Wolfgang/West/Zombie. All a bit over the top for a plastic goods place. A security guard opened the gates and they drove into the yard. Trent eyed the expensive security alarms on the outside of the building and the floodlights strategically placed, like searchlights.

They entered the building, the sizeable storage space nearly empty except for a few cartons stamped with the names of Far East cities and two fork-lift trucks. A couple of warehousemen wandered around. There was a mezzanine floor on the left-hand side and the security guard gestured to go up. There were a couple of offices there and a small kitchen. They went up the metal staircase. Trent was suddenly aware of the gun and holster banging beneath his coat. They could see two figures through the window in the largest office and Steve knocked.

Chapter Ten
Hockley Warehouse

'Enter.'

The man behind the desk who greeted them was nothing like Trent envisaged. A gangster? A terrorist? The man in front of him was a tall, good-looking man, with grey hair, perhaps in his late forties, a trimmed neat moustache, and a hint of sideburns. He was about 6ft, had matinée idol looks, an Asian Charles Boyer perhaps. His well-manicured hands were festooned with gold rings, a gold chain round his neck. He was dressed casually but expensively—sports jacket, silk trousers, silk shirt. He exuded charm and was the epitome of wealth and taste. A waft of costly aftershave hit the two "policemen". The successful businessman around town.

He rose and greeted Trent and Steve like long-lost friends. Next to him was a thin, bespectacled nervous man, who he introduced as his assistant, Ayub, who hopped about on two feet.

'Inspector...ah...Ray, an unexpected pleasure, and your colleague...?' He paused, his black eyes momentarily glinting at Trent.

'This is Sergeant Trent, new to our division.' They both showed their warrant cards, which Khan waved away. He continued in a very cultured, melodious voice.

'Now, gentlemen...Tsh, what have I done now? I don't need my solicitor present, do I? I have him standing by at Challinor & Roberts, only ten minutes away.'

'No, no, nothing like that. It's a more general enquiry, not related to your good self.' Steve gave him his best winning smile.

'Good, good. Coffee, gentlemen. Ayub, can you organise? I'm afraid you can't smoke. I forbid it in here.' They both nodded and whilst Ayub went to the small nearby kitchen, Trent quickly scanned the office.

It was very sparse. A map of the world on the wall. Two desks, telephones. A large computer in the corner. A filing cabinet—and most interesting—a very secure-looking Chubb safe in the wall. On Khan's desk, there was a photo of an attractive blonde, much younger than Khan. Obviously, his English wife.

Ayub returned, he placed down a pot of coffee, milk, etc. Rubbing his hands like an obsequious Asian Uriah Heep, he asked how they liked it and served accordingly.

Khan sipped at his coffee. 'So how may I be of assistance? Always happy to help our local police.' The snigger on the tip of his tongue never materialised.

Steve continued the interview. 'Well, it relates to an employee of yours.' He glanced at the notebook in his hand. 'A man I think you know as Roland West, but perhaps better known as Wolfgang Mueller on the continent.'

Khan raised his eyebrows. 'West, yes, he was in charge of security here but has been missing the last few days. Wolfgang, Mueller means nothing to me. Are you sure that's who he is?'

'We, yes, are.' Steve nodded. 'When did you last see him?' He produced a pencil to take notes.

'Let's see now…Ayub, when was West last here? You know everything here, don't you, Ayub?'

Ayub scratched his chin, gave a nervous grin. 'Last Saturday.'

Steve leant forward, staring at Khan. 'How did you take him on?'

'Let's be fair. You're asking these questions. What has he done?'

'He's wanted by Interpol and other agencies for criminal activities in Europe.'

'I see…'

'So how come he ended up here?' Steve asked again. Khan signalled to Ayub, who fetched a folder from one of the cabinets. He opened and spread various papers across the desk.

'You see,' Khan continued. 'He came from a reputable London agency that specialises in security people. Also good references. He was here about four months.'

The two "policemen" looked through the papers that seemed genuine.

Steve looked up. 'Did you never query the name West, when he's obviously German?'

'His accent was non-existent, at least I didn't notice one. I didn't feel the need to question him, his credentials seemed genuine.'

'You've no idea where he went?'

'No. Ayub, you saw him more. When did you see him last?'

'As I said a few days ago… Saturday I think; then he just didn't turn up for work. We never heard anything from him.'

Trent spoke for the first time.

'Why do you need all this security? State of the art security cameras, very rare in this country? All for—how do you say—a novelty business?' Khan seemed surprised. He'd forgotten the "sergeant".

'Well, Sergeant.' A pause, he looked at Trent carefully. 'Yes, Trent, whilst the warehouse is empty now, at times it is very full. In fact, we've just sent out a big delivery. The stuff is very popular. The 31st is approaching and whilst Halloween hasn't caught on here yet, as in the States, we have high hopes of this improving. Confident for the future.

'So a big demand, lots of goods stored here, and this city is full of criminals, particularly with all that's happening in this country.' He bit his lip, barely suppressing a smile.

Steve replied politely. 'Thank you, Mr Khan. If you can think of anything else, please let us know.'

'Well, gents, if that is all. I'm a very busy man. I'm sorry we can't help any further. Ayub will show you out.' With that dismissal, the meeting came to an end.

They left the warehouse site and drove back towards the city centre.

'What do you think, Phil?' Steve asked as he swung right down a side street.

'Smarmy bastard, wouldn't trust him an inch.'

'Look, Phil, I know you can't say much but it seems an obvious coincidence. Zombie Plastics and all this Zombie hoo-ha in the papers. Even more trouble today, I note.'

Trent was non-committal. 'All I can say is that the powers that be are trying to sort out all this mayhem.' What he couldn't actually believe was that this Khan was involved in terrorism. Crime, yes. Terrorism, no.

Steve changed the subject. 'Jackie's looking forward to meeting you tonight; you know the address. Do you want a lift?'

'No, thanks, I hired a car earlier. A few things to do first and I've got a task after your place.'

'OK then, is 8.00 OK? Won't pry into your task, may get me into trouble.

'8.00 is perfect.'

'Oh, and try to be a bit more discreet with that gun of yours. Don't want to frighten Jackie.'

So he'd noticed his gun then!

Steve dropped Trent off in New Street; the autumnal fog now thickening across the city centre.

He headed to a red telephone box near the station. He'd been told to report in daily to "The Prof". There wasn't too much to say, the main gist being that Wolfgang Mueller alias West had vanished, and he'd take a good look at the warehouse later.

Back at the Midland Hotel, he retrieved his attaché case from the hotel safe. Up in the room, he removed a wallet containing burglar tools, a pencil torch, and a spare clip of bullets. Ready for the evening. He put them in hidden pockets in his long leather jacket.

It was 5.30pm; an hour's kip, a shower, then off to Steve and Jackie's in nearby Halesowen. He'd pick up a bottle of wine on the way from an offy.

Chapter Eleven
Halesowen

The hired car was a Cortina. Trent bought a bottle of Liebfraumilch wine from the off-licence. A little sweet for him, but not much choice.

Halesowen was seven miles from Birmingham on the edge of the Industrial Black Country, looking out onto the client hills. Trent knew it as a place many from his hometown aspired to move to. If they really did well, they'd aim further at nearby Hagley (Go West young man!). Halesowen existed before Birmingham and was even mentioned in the Domesday book. Following Birmingham, most of the old town had been redeveloped and replaced with a horrible shopping centre and everywhere pedestrianised. Trent hated it!

On the outskirts of Halesowen was the large Mucklow estate, built in the fifties. On the periphery were several newer, medium detached houses overlooking the Clent Hills. Mr and Mrs Steve Ray lived in one of these. It was set a little way from the others. Trent parked his car, the Clent Hills invisible behind the night and fog. A few fireworks exploded, telling him Bonfire Night was not far away. He knocked on the door and Steve answered. He handed over the wine and hung his leather coat up in the hall. Its secret contents well secreted, so as not to offend Jackie's sensibilities. He was dressed typically in jeans with a black polo jumper.

Steve took Trent through to the living room to meet his spouse.

The living room was dimly lit by shaded lamps, the décor a swirl of orange and brown, a TV in a cabinet, a hi-fi and a picture of a Spanish lady on the wall. The outside world closed off via Westfalia curtains. Fog, ice, and fireworks all locked out.

Some strange music was playing low; the room was pleasantly warm. Steve took him to the kitchen where appetising smells drifted out. He introduced him to Jackie. A faint smell of pot? (Naughty policeman!) A copy of the music mag, *Sounds,* lay open on a pouffe, something about Deep Purple…

'How do you do?' He shook hands politely. Jackie, a bit more forward, gave him a smacker of a kiss. She looked him up and down. 'So you're Steve's long-lost friend.' Black Country-blunt. 'How come we haven't seen you lately and, well, er…me not at all?'

They'd been two years married, he'd been invited, but had been on a mission in North Africa at the time.

'Sorry, I missed your wedding,' he insisted. 'Sorry, always seem busy.' Always the lame excuse.

He stalled, never one to start a conversation. Last time he'd seen Steve was at the Cup final in '68, same time he'd met Kev Bloomer. Even when he occasionally came back for the football, they hadn't met up.

He summed up a lively, petite brunette with a strong local accent. Pretty. Brown eyes, late twenties, in a fashionable Laura Ashley dress. Jackie, the nurse, Steve, the cop—an ideal couple.

'Anyway, you're here now.' She smiled at him. 'Thanks for the wine; meal in ten minutes. Steve, get him a drink for goodness sake.'

Although mock-stern, Trent could tell that there was a real warmth between them.

Steve gave his boyish smile and produced a large can of beer: Watney's Party Seven. Trent smiled. 'You always had a shit taste in beer.'

Ice broken they fell into laughter. Trent bought up football. 'What do you think of Don Howe as a manager then? You've probably seen more of him, can't get up here much.'

'Well, we just lost to Leicester and we were crap.'

'Southampton tomorrow, nail biting.'

'Yeah, not much hope.' Steve took a sip of beer. 'But you know Jeff Astle— Still king, so you never know. Need a new manager.'

It was going back all those years: Football, beer, boyish banter, catching up. Trent offered him a ciggy like the good old days behind the school bomb shelter.

Suddenly, a switch and Steve became serious. He knew Philip had something to do with the Zombie crisis but didn't push the matter openly, he kept it general.

'The bloody news, all bad news. Strikes, riots, crime rampant. That nazi bastard Joyce ranting about immigrants and these Zombie mask holdups. The lads at the station believe the commies are stirring things up. Rumours hey. What's your thoughts?'

Before Trent could evade the answer, Jackie announced mockingly, 'Dinner is served.' They went through to a small dining room next to the kitchen. All warm and comfortable, not like Trent's minimalistic cold basic flat.

The meal was—starter: prawn cocktail; main: chicken kiev, sweet: black forest gateau. Followed by cheese and biscuits. Steve opened the Liebfraumilch and poured.

It was a very pleasant evening. Trent relaxed in their company, sticking to the beer, even if it was "shit". They all lit up cigarettes; no pot appeared.

Jackie described how she worked at nearby Hayley Green Hospital for infectious diseases. Trent knew it from when he was ill as a kid. Steve pointed this out but before he expanded, Trent changed the subject abruptly.

'This music—what, excuse me, Jackie—what the hell is it?'

She nodded. 'Yes, it's rubbish, isn't it? I like Tamla Motown myself.'

'It's Jethro Tull, new progressive stuff.' He looked laughingly at Trent. 'Not your cup of tea?'

'Last time I saw you, you were into the Beatles, weren't you?'

'Well, I've moved on—like the modern stuff—Led Zeppelin, The Cream, Caravan, East of Eden, Pink Floyd. I like all this modern underground stuff.'

Trent looked at his friend again—ginger hair slightly long, sideburns, a flower-power shirt, flared jeans. Not like an off-duty cop; the opposite in fact to conservative Trent.

Steve winked at his wife. 'Phil never moved on. The permissive society passed him by. Still into all that old rock & roll.'

Trent nodded thinking of Chuck Berry, Little Richard, Buddy Holly and even Elvis in his early days.

'Who's your favourite then?' His friend teased him.

'My favourite is still Carl Perkins, and his version of Blue Suede Shoes is better than Elvis's.'

'Good old stick in the mud.' To Jackie, he said: 'He never changes y'know.'

'Anyway, what happened to the Beatles?'

'Oh I still like them, but I've opened my mind to other things.'

They talked about the Beatles and other sixties pop groups. Trent could never really get into many of them, but they both had a shared memory.

'Do you remember back in '61 in Hamburg on leave?' Steve turned to Jackie. 'I told you we saw the Beatles, there in a club on the Reeperbahn before they were famous.'

'Yes, they played rock & roll then, real loud and stomping. Lennon as Chuck Berry, McCartney, Little Richard, and Harrison—fantastic—Carl Perkins. They went all soft when famous.' Trent was stuck in his music mud. He sipped at his beer—wasn't drinking much—had a busy night ahead. Steve was way ahead and now on the whisky.

'Want a drop to keep the chill away?'

Trent said yes: he had a cold night ahead. The evening wore on, the whisky doing its job, giving him a warm feeling to the pit. He hadn't felt this relaxed in years. What a lovely, friendly couple. Why had he allowed things to drift for so long?

Jackie talked about her nursing, with humorous tales of patients and their exploits. The men talked more football and Jackie mock yawned.

Trent noticed and asked her about herself and her background. Jackie had always lived in Halesowen and had been brought up in a small terrace down by Halesowen Town Football Club. She'd somehow passed her 11-plus and went to the local grammar school. More interested in boys, dancing and music, she'd left with one O-Level in English. Enough to get her into nursing.

'How did you two meet?' He asked.

'At a dance at the Tower Ballroom, y'know Edgbaston, near the reservoir.'

Trent visualised the big bands there, him a Teddy boy eyeing up the girls without great success. The band condescending to play some ersatz rock 'n' roll in the middle of their normal swing set.

'We went out for a couple of years,' she continued. 'Got engaged, married; you know how it is.'

Trent obviously didn't but nodded. He couldn't help but notice the look of love and devotion that she gave Steve, and his returning warm, humorous smile.

They revisited their youth—nostalgia reigned—more artificial yawning from Jackie.

Their escapades: truancy, scrumping, fishing for sticklebacks and tadpoles, climbing trees, football in the mud, sledging in Warley Woods, that first pint...

'D'you remember that first pint?' Steve said.

'It was half, wasn't it? Half of mild,' replied Trent.

'Yes, down the Two Brewers. Your grandad spotted us from the bar, banged our heads together. Happy days.'

'What about the stink bomb?' Steve continued the memories. 'Threw it in the Pheasant pub.'

'Right stink when I got home as well.' Trent smiled at the memory. Then rock & roll, Elvis. The pictures, Saturday morning, The Girl Can't Help It.

'D'you know Jack, our hero was always in trouble, fights—the Teddy boy.' Steve was slightly drunk now.

'However, he was normally fighting to protect someone, including me. Came to my rescue at school. Got him into trouble, luckily got called up and escaped justice. Then in Hereford, he rescued a lass in distress and half-wrecked a pub.'

Trent interrupted. 'Everyone this week seems to be analysing me and my past.' He raised his eyes to the ceiling.

It became a bit more serious now. Steve was still talking to Jackie. 'He also saved my life; I told you before. In Africa, in the army. He rescued a whole pile of us wounded. Took out an enemy outpost singlehanded. Gave him the VC for that.'

Trent remembered the flashing lights of anger as he attacked. Shook his head; he did not wish this to continue. He never wanted to remember Africa, which only returned to him in his nightmares. The VC, a constant embarrassment. He looked at his watch, nearly 11.30pm.

'Well, folks, I've had a great evening. Truly. Haven't talked so much in years! Nice to meet you, Jackie, at last, and thanks for the meal.'

He finished his whisky, fetched his coat, and shook them both by the hand. Jackie, quite emotional, kissed him on the cheek. 'Come and see us again soon.'

He shook Steve's hand. 'Nice to catch up, Steve. I'll see you tomorrow for a debrief.'

With that, he stepped out again into that cold autumn night.

Chapter Twelve
Back to Hockley

Trent drove back into Birmingham along the Hagley Road. Then went through the back streets of the Jewellery Quarter, an area of small workshops and alleyways. He parked in Hospital Street, two hundred yards from Zombie Co Ltd. He walked up the street, a scant few street lights, dim in the swirling mist. Dark shapes of factories and warehouses surrounded him.

He'd transferred the gun and wallet to his main pocket for easy access, and he now tentatively approached the warehouse. From his early survey, he saw it as a piece of cake to get in, with or without security guards, alarms, etc.

He stopped, surprised. Ajmal Khan's empire was in total darkness. He touched the gate and it swung open. He picked up a chunk of wood lying nearby and threw it at the barbed-wire electric fence; nothing!

He entered the yard; the security lights were turned off but he could still see that the vans had gone and no security was in sight. A ghostly quiet enveloped the whole area.

A quick sweep of the building informed him that the security alarms weren't on, nor the fancy cameras. No need for his burglary kit but he kept his gun handy just in case.

The main door was wide open. Curiouser and curiouser? A tingle ran down his spine...Danger? A portent? But to what?

He flashed his torch around the empty warehouse. The boxes had gone, as had the fork-lifts. All that remained of the men were a couple of cups on a trestle table and one cold cup of tea knocked over. A half-eaten samosa was on a plate. The men had left in a hurry just like a Marie Celeste.

Still with gun in hand, torch in his left, he went up the steps to the mezzanine floor. The first office and kitchen were completely empty, so was the main office. He put his gun away. Khan's office seemed more interesting; his flashlight showed the Chubb safe in the wall open but empty. The two cabinets empty bar stationery.

There was a faint smell of burning in the air; odd. He shone the torch on a large waste bin in the corner. There were the charred remains of burnt papers. Why burn them? Why not remove them like everything else? A slight niggle niggled at the back of his mind.

He bent over the bin, there was one piece of paper not fully burnt. A clue?

It seemed to be some sort of proforma order for goods from abroad. He could make out "plastic goods" and what seemed to be a word: "Penglog". The rest was indecipherable. He took a plastic wallet that he'd seen in the filing cabinet and placed the charred paper gently into it. Was the word Eastern European? Russian? He'd get the prof to look at it tomorrow.

Trent stood thoughtful for a couple of minutes. Why flee? There didn't seem to be any reason. Why burn the papers? Panic? He decided he'd go wake Steve up and find out Khan's address in Edgbaston to see if he'd fled from there as well. It was now 1.15am.

He left the building, drove back into the centre, and parked the Cortina at a car park near the station. The hotel was closed up but the night porter let him in. He used the public phone in the foyer to phone Steve. It rang out and Trent surmised that they were both dead drunk and out for the count.

He asked the porter for a brandy. It had been really cold outside, and went with it up to his room, to try and warm up. Sitting on the bed, he drank the brandy down and decided to walk up to Steel House Lane police station and obtain Khan's home address. Firstly to see if he was still there and then perhaps carry out a rougher interrogation than that they'd carried out earlier.

He put his nefarious tools and ammo clip into his attaché case. He'd keep the gun, just in case! He went downstairs to arrange with the porter for the case to go back into the safe.

As they were talking, the phone went to reception. The porter answered.

'It's for you, Mr Trent. It's the police.' He handed the receiver to Trent.

'Hello, Steve…'

There was a sinister chuckle. 'Sorry to disappoint you, Mr Trent.' A slight German accent. 'I'm not Steve, or the police. You may know me as Z.' Another chuckle. 'Now listen, you stop harassing Mr Khan; this is a final warning. You'll see what we'll do to you; ask your friends, Mr and Mrs Ray.' With an evil snigger, he cut off.

Trent stepped back, momentarily numb. Wolfgang Mueller! How? Why? His thoughts raced. God, Steve and Jackie! He grabbed the attaché case, pushed past a bemused porter and ran into the street, barely noticing anything outside, including the fog now lifting.

He got back into the Cortina, flung the case into the back, and put the Beretta on the sidecar seat. Not normally fast, heart racing, he put his foot down and raced down the Hagley Road towards Halesowen. He focussed on the road, and the drive; he must remain calm and detached whatever he may shortly find.

He drove down Mucklows Hill overlooking Halesowen lit up below. The fires/ furnaces of Coombswood and Round Oak burning red. The steel works and factories of the Black Country beckoning into hell!

Chapter Thirteen
Tragedy in Halesowen

Trent now drove slowly onto the Mucklow estate and then up to the small group of detached houses where he'd been earlier. He parked someway from Steve and Jackie's house and approached carefully, gun in hand.

The fog was evaporating and the Clent Hills were now visible, black shapes against the dark sky. The fog was going but now replaced by a ghostly mist drifting in from the nearby fields. The faint street lights shone, catching frost now forming on the ground.

The nearby houses were all in darkness, the mist surrounding Steve and Jackie's house giving it a wraith-like feel. It was the only house where a glimmer of light from the hallway could be seen from behind the thick curtains. The only sounds were of water dripping from nearby branches and a distant hum, which as he got closer he realised that it was the radio playing.

He went down the drive past the neatly kept garden. All his senses were at a fever pitch, internal alarm bells screaming care and danger! There was something terribly wrong as he approached the house; the front door was slightly ajar and he could hear the music loudly now. Kid Jensen on Radio Luxembourg thumping out late-night rock music.

Trent decided to go round the back, down a side passageway to their small back garden. There, in their ordinariness, was a tool shed, an apple tree, a clothesline, and a pair of wellingtons lying in the wet grass.

The back door to the kitchen had been smashed open. Holding the gun at the ready, Trent pushed it open with his foot. His senses still heightened, the tension sharply hitting, his heartbeat was loud, booming in his ears. The kitchen was in darkness; there was a vague smell of chicken kiev, smoke and beer. He turned the light on.

The house, warm earlier, was now as cold as the chill outside, as cold as a grave. A teapot, cups, and various pots and pans were scattered on the floor.

He called Steve's name, although he knew it to be futile. He moved slowly towards the living room; another smell above that of the evening meal. A familiar, sharp metallic smell. The hall light was on, the radio was still playing. He reached out and turned the living room lights on…

Chaos! Mayhem! The nice neat suburban world of Jackie had been turned upside down. Furniture knocked over, glass everywhere, the Spanish lady knocked off the wall. The TV, hi-fi smashed, the dining table and chairs up-ended.

There was destruction everywhere and it was obvious Steve must have put up a hell of a fight. There was blood on the carpet and walls—that metallic smell—all the noise must have been covered by the radio, and there was also some distance to the other houses.

And there in the corner of this suburban nightmare, covered in blood, were the bodies of Steve and Jackie, trussed up like chickens.

He'd seen many deaths but this was different; this was personal. He couldn't look at the scene. This was his fault; he'd brought death to this house and the innocent couple. The innocent, friendly, normal couple.

No, it was Wolfgang Mueller, the man on the phone, who'd done this.

Suddenly, he felt faint. He dropped the gun and staggered to the kitchen and was violently sick. He saw the empty bottle of Liebfraumilch on the sink and thought of the happy evening earlier. A lump came to his throat and he felt something unfamiliar, tears pricked his eyes.

He went back to the living room where he saw a grotesque Zombie mask pinned to a lampshade, a macabre joke staring down at the tableau of death. Tears then streamed down his cheeks and he cried for the first time since he was a very young boy.

Chapter Fourteen
London, 30 October

Trent walked through Osterley Park. A cold but sunny midday. He was walking with Tess, the border collie. Sodden leaves were strewn about, the swans, geese and ducks still on the pond which was not frozen yet. Kids played on the swings and slide, and in the distance majestically stood Osterley House, designed by Robert Adam and with enough elegance to attract Cary Grant to film there some ten years before. They walked past the Chinese lake pagoda and for a moment, he forgot everything in the tranquillity of that pleasant autumn day.

Hard to believe in all this peace, the horrors of the night before. The wireless earlier also proclaiming more riots, robberies and bombings, trouble the background in his life.

He'd finally arrived home at 9am. Time for a couple of hours' sleep, a shave, a shower, a walk, and then off to a meeting at the Outfit's office. What a hell of a night! His friends brutally murdered and then the police after...

The phone in Steve and Jackie's house had been ripped from the wall. Trent went to a phone box at the corner of their road. He first phoned the emergency line to the office, to the prof at his home. He briefly and without emotion told him of the events of the night and asked for protection for Camille, Kev Bloomer, and Mrs McDougal.

Any friends of his could be a target. He knew the prof would sort it. He arranged to meet the colonel the next afternoon.

The second call was to the police and he asked them to get Superintendent Roberts, if he was asleep, to wake him.

The police then descended on that quiet suburban road with all that entailed.

Superintendent Ken Roberts seemed to put all the blame on Trent back in the Steel House Lane interview room. His first words: 'Look, Trent, I've spoken to friends at the Yard. They've never heard of you, neither have Special Branch. So who are you? Hmmmmmphh…Also that Beretta and your burglar tools in the car—interesting. We'll see if you have a licence for the gun…hmm.'

He blew a smoke ring in the air, no cigarettes or refreshment for Trent. 'So first tell me what happened.'

Trent went over and over the horrific events of the night. Even his attempted illegal break-in at the warehouse. Trent could tell that Roberts was forcing himself not to thump him. Well, good luck with that.

'Look, Roberts, you know I had no part in this. Christ, they were my friends. You'd do better trying to track this Khan and Mueller, or West whatever, down.'

Roberts relented slightly. 'Khan's house is also empty, first thing we checked. His wife also gone.'

So it went on; they even breathalysed him. Good job he'd not drunk too much and it was an age away. Shame he hadn't hidden his gun and case.

In the end, Trent insisted on a phone call and they finally relented. Another call to the prof, now his first point of contact, strings were pulled and Robert's chief constable intervened.

He retrieved his weapon and attaché case and left the police station as dawn was breaking, out onto the street with the milk van, heavy frost on the ground. Back at the hotel, he collected his belongings, arranged for his car to be rebooked for another seven days and then headed out of Birmingham, past the half-built spaghetti junction towards Rugby, the M1 and the south. Revenge was still uppermost on his mind, and that persistent question: why didn't they just kill him if he was seen as such a threat to their plans?

Back from the park, Trent, although not very hungry, had a lunch of toast and marmalade, Robertsons with its infamous picture on the label. The toast burnt black as he liked it.

He gave a few bits to Tess, the shared dog, and stroked her. She was always a comfort in times of stress.

He rarely had phone calls and then there were two in the space of twenty minutes.

The phone rang. 'Hello, Trent here,' he said brusquely.

It was Roberts; Trent had left him his number for an update, the aggression and suspicion of the night before now gone. A subdued, deflated superintendent now, and he spoke almost gently. They'd had an early post-mortem on Steve and Jackie. Their throats had been cut and they believed it was in an Islamic ritual halal way.

He let that sink in and continued: 'I'm afraid that Jackie was also badly raped.'

Trent did not hear much of the rest of the report, the cold rage was surfacing.

'Difficult to pinpoint a sequence of events, but we are working on that.' The next bit was probably hard for Roberts.

'Look, Trent, I'm, er…sorry about last night; got carried away in the heat of emotion. I know they were your friends. We'll get the bastards. I'll let you know when the funeral is. Ok?' The call trailed off and ended.

Staring out the flat window, a noisy plane swept past towards Heathrow. It was Concorde, but he hardly noticed as he pondered his next move. How to track down Mueller, Khan, and all those involved in this stinking conspiracy? One thing he did know, he wouldn't be attending his friends funeral. Guilt, embarrassment? How could he face their parents and family? Cowardice, yes, but better to concentrate on revenge.

The phone jangled again. It was Kev Bloomer, again a rare call to the flat.

'Phil…Phil…er, er…look, I'm sorry about your friends in Birmingham.'

'What? How do you know?' Trent was incredulous.

Kev continued: 'Look, old thing, it's going to be in the early evening editions of the papers and the TV news. Then in the dailies tomorrow. I've seen the proofs. The murders, the plots, Khan and his gang. With you and your VC award bang at the centre. You seem to be the designated tragic hero in all this.'

Trent could hardly believe it. Who? How? Why?

Kev concluded: 'Let's meet up later and talk about this, over a drink. I'm sorry again, old boy.'

After a moment's thought, Trent said: 'Sorry, Kev, thanks and all that but I'm going to be busy for the next few days.' (He didn't say searching for the killers of his friends-vengeance at the top of his agenda.)

The call finished and he took Tess back to Mrs McDougal. He spoke to her about some bad news hitting the telly later and telling her not to worry. Also said he may be away for a few days. Trent also phoned Camille (again a rarity) and briefly told her of the events. He also said he'd be away for a bit and would see her when back. He was brief to the point of being curt. He did not want to hear any more sympathy. Emotions suppressed, all focus was on the job ahead.

Making sure his armoury and his attaché case were hidden in the secret panel at the back of his wardrobe, he took the Cortina off towards the city and his meeting at Southampton Street.

Normally, he loathed the London traffic but in the mood he was in, he didn't fancy the crowds on the tube. At least the traffic should now be starting to leave the city, the opposite direction. He took the London Road and passing a newsagents' in Isleworth, he saw the sign outside with what he'd been dreading: "VC hero in Mystery Murder!".

Chapter Fifteen
London Office

Bang! Trent slammed the newspaper down on the desk. The prof, used to the normally quiet, laidback Trent in the office, was astonished and leapt to his feet. His normal nervous manner increased and he stuttered: 'Trent, y-y-you're back.'

Trent had bought the newspaper and parked the car in a side road, he had read the lurid contents, angrily chain-smoking. It was all there as Kev Bloomer had predicted. His "potted" history, the VC, exploits in Africa and the rebels. Now working for "Scotland Yard", etc., etc.

The rest was basically the truth—the links with the "Zombie" murders, the tracking down of Khan, the death of the policeman and his wife—his friends. The ritual killings! The mask! Christ! Where had they got all that from? There must be a leak the size of the Grand Canyon at the Outfit.

His anger intensified as he sped off along the Great West Road towards the city, down the so-called "Golden Mile" past Thirties Art Deco factories, including Beechams and Gillette. He needed urgently to see his chiefs at "The Outfit" to discuss. He arrived at Southampton Street early evening, now dark but slightly warmer, and rain was falling over the rushing crowds in the Strand.

Babs had met him as he entered the offices on the top floor. There were half a dozen empty desks, silent phones, a giant tape recorder, the reels not turning. She informed him that Sir Richard and the colonel were out and that the prof would see him shortly in his room. This hardly improved his mood. He noticed something different about her; what was it, this strange expression like a constipated gargoyle?

With a start, he realised that this was Babs showing sympathy. The only other two people in the office were huddled up in the corner in deep conversation. One he knew, Smith, and he nodded at him. The other character he didn't know well; it was Jones he believed.

Whilst waiting, he looked through the grimy windows, lights winking and twinkling in the falling rain. Across the rooftops, he could just about make out Leicester Square, Nelson's Column and closer, the rooftop of the Savoy. And then further out, Soho—the seedy strip clubs, sex shops, and prostitution all hidden now in the dark autumn night.

Babs then took him to the prof's lair and returned with a pot of coffee and two of Sir Richard's best china cups. This was unheard of, then Trent realised this was more of the sympathetic Babs. He courteously said, 'Thank you.' He then stood by the window listening to the outside rain.

The prof then stumbled in deep in thought and he didn't seem to notice Trent; scruffy as ever, he sat down, and Trent then slammed the desk with the newspaper.

The desk and the room were a complete shamble. Piles and piles of files on the desk and floor, in no obvious order. In a small space on the desk, next to Trent's coffee, was a teapot, pasteurised milk, and sugar. On top of a filing cabinet were books on botany and flora and a book on Conan Doyle.

Sherlock Holmes? Perhaps this tied in with microscope and magnifying glass also on the desk. Together with, even stranger, the violin in the corner.

There was a small window at the back, overlooking the back of dark, soot-covered buildings. The windowsill covered in plant pots with peculiar floral growths dangling down the civil service grey walls.

Finally, in the middle of this jungle/jumble, there was a deckchair!

'I'm very sorry, Trent, about your f-f-friends and all that.' The prof scratched his white unruly hair.

'OK, oh, and where exactly is the colonel?' Trent still terse. 'Surely he could have been here to discuss matters?'

'Sir Richard and the colonel had to go to a security council meeting at No 10. To discuss the w-w-orsening position across the country.' The prof still eyed the untamed animal opposite with some trepidation.

Trent sighed, took a deep breath, and at last sort of relaxed; it wasn't Prof's fault. He lit a cigarette and took a sip of Babs' excellent coffee.

'All this stuff in the paper, where the hell is it coming from? Is this the same source that leaked everything on the Johnson affair?'

'As you know, we're looking into that. The colonel has g-got Smith & Jones on it. Although, he still thinks it's MI5/6 or Scotland Yard. Not us.'

Trent knew Smith, although hadn't had any actual dealings with Jones. Smith was a sarcastic arrogant thug and he didn't like him much, but if the colonel had chosen him, then who was he to quibble? He pointed again at the paper.

'They knew everything. What's going on?'

Prof looked at him sympathetically. 'Look, Trent, as far as I can see, it's your Victoria Cross. It gets you publicity and that's what Khan and these others want, to stir up things in the country, and the publicity is grist to the mill. It could even be them you know telling the press. Don't worry, we'll get to the bottom of it.'

'That medal, always a bloody problem, hardly helpful for a secret agent!' Trent took another deep breath and changed the subject. 'Oh, and er…thanks for putting security on Mrs McDougall and the others.'

'Ye…yes, that's fine…although the colonel did moan about resources.' No sympathy from that quarter then! The prof then got down to brass tacks. 'Look, we have a mission on this Khan fella. Colonel Stewart wants you to follow up a lead in Paris. Feels it's best you're out of the c-country with all this hoo-ha about you going on.'

Trent, with a sudden thought, interrupted. 'Oh, before I forget, have a look at this, found it in Khan's warehouse in Brum.' He handed him the plastic envelope with the half-burnt paper with only the word PENGLOG legible. He half-smiled. 'Never know it could be a clue. Some sort of order form it seems.'

The prof examined it thoughtfully. 'Excuse me a sec.' He left the room, leaving Trent to light a cigarette, swig some more coffee and stare again without seeing out the window at the autumn wet.

The prof returned. 'We'll know a bit more in a minute.'

Trent asked, 'What about Paris?'

Again a scratch of his head, again when he got going, his nervousness abated. He continued: 'Look, Trent, we'll cover Paris in a minute. First, let me give you a resumé of the current situation. This evening on *Nationwide,* the BBC ran a feature on the murders in Birmingham. They focussed on how they seemed to tie in with everything happening, with you investigating this plot and the conspirators murdering your friends. Then, for the first time, they talked of a coordinated plot against this country.'

He let that sink in. 'Even worse, this to be followed by a full *Panorama* exposé next Monday. This will include everything on you and your investigation.'

The professor's stutter/nervousness was now miraculously gone. 'That publicity will add fuel to an already incendiary situation, hence our master's regular trips to Downing Street. Let me give you an update on the state of play in the country.' He broke off as he collected his thoughts.

'There are strikes everywhere, not just London. Much worse than Tom Jackson's national post-strike and the Kill the Bill demonstrations earlier in the year. They're whipped up by left-wing unions and agitators. But most certainly manipulated by outside forces. Here, have a look at some of the ringleaders.'

The prof scattered a collection of photos across his already shambles of a desk. Trent gave them a cursory glance, lit a cigarette, and nodded to him to continue.

'Also these robberies with extreme violence are getting worse. Overseen by this Mueller—Z or Zombie, if you like. Police have found no trace of him or Khan and his wife, they've vanished into nothing. Bombings, actual explosions and persistent hoax calls about bombs, are on the up whilst you were in Birmingham. Seemingly, this by this coalition of terrorists, including the IRA, the Angry Brigade, and Muslim extremists. Our intelligence people and MI5 have also come-come-up with these photos of those that we think are the key men for the terrorists.'

Again, Trent gave them a brief look. The prof poured himself a cup of tea, which must now have been cold.

Trent helped himself to coffee, leant back, and had a drink. He could hear the persistent rain beating on the filth-engrained windows. The professor returned to his subject.

'All this backed by the communist bloc. This is confirmed by all intelligence sources and the microdot you brought out. We've tried to keep some of the worst of it from the press, but to no avail.

'Thrown into the mix is Adrian Joyce and his new GB National Party causing agitation. He's causing the biggest stink, him and his fascist supporters. Blaming communists for everything, and it looks actually, as if he's right there, but also blaming all foreigners. Shouting about the er…ahem…ritual murder of your friends and pointing the finger at all Asians. Hindus, Sikhs included, although the ritual killing was supposedly Islamic. He's getting a lot of support in the gutter press as well as from the general public. Xenophobia, I think, it's now being called. Anyway, blaming all foreigners for your woes.'

The prof drank his cold tea and pulled a face. 'Urghh...where was I? Oh yes, we've tried to damp things down, to stop alarm spreading. But we're failing and number 10 seems reluctant to put a block on the news coverage. The country seems to be almost on the verge of civil war and chaos. The pound has taken a battering and the stock market is plummeting. This is why Sir Richard and the colonel are pushing the PM and cabinet for a state of emergency to be called. For Sir Richard to then takes control of things with extra police and military powers. The government is cautious, but you can see, Trent, that things are very dire.'

Trent normally ignored politics but even he could see matters were getting out of hand. However, his main aim was the destruction of the Zombie, Khan, and their masters. Mainly for revenge, but this as it happened would also bring a halt to the conspiracy. Two birds and all that. He said as much to the prof, who nodded his agreement.

Before he could continue, the phone on the shambolic desk rang. He took it. 'Hmm...yes, OK; yes, thank you.'

He turned to Trent. 'Well, it would seem that Penglog is actually Welsh.'

Trent started. Khan's other warehouse was in Wales. 'What does it mean?'

The prof also lit a cigarette. 'Penglog translates to skull, and it could be that it relates to an island in Wales—Yns Penglog—Skull Island.'

Chapter Sixteen
London

'Skull Island? Wasn't that something to do with King Kong?' Trent asked incredulously. The prof didn't know; he knew very little about the cinema, arts or culture; only work interested him it would seem (And maybe Sherlock Holmes and plants…).

Trent was all for going off to Wales to have a look at Khan's warehouse and the island. The prof pulled him back and reminded him: 'The colonel, and also Sir Richard, want you…er, out of the country away from the news and the BB-B-BBC. You're to follow this Paris lead-up, and anyway, it ties in with Khan. We'll look into this Penglog place whilst you're away. When you're back, de-decide a plan of action.'

'Oh, what's this Paris thing then?' What the prof said made sense to Trent; he would try to suppress his inner feelings for the time being.

The prof carried on: 'Alphonse Jourdain, who works for the Sureté and is attached to Interpol, also does some work f-f-for the colonel. I think you know him.'

Trent concurred. 'Yes, vaguely, I met him in '68.'

'Anyway, he has news about Khan's smuggling operations in France. The colonel wants you to meet him in Paris, to get verbally what he's got, and he'll show you Khan's operations. It also gets you out of the way. It's…er…all arranged to meet him tomorrow. A win-win situation, proverbially, so to speak. By the way, keep updating things daily to me, day or night. Colonel's orders.'

Trent was told Babs had tickets for the late-night flight to Paris, together with francs. He was also advised that Alphonse would contact him in the morning at the hotel. There was no time to organise a gun via the embassy. If one was needed, then he was told Alphonse would provide for him.

The prof's final words were: 'You've had a difficult couple of days, Trent. Go to Paris. Keep your head down, relax. Have a sort of holiday, a break. With the colonel's blessing.'

Holiday be damned, he'd get this trip out of the way then pursue Khan et al.

As he went through the main office, he came upon Smith and his confederate, Jones, sitting behind one of the old battered desks (which reminded Trent of school). Smith and Jones were the colonel's chosen ones to winkle out the source of the leaks.

Smith was pugnacious, sarcastic, rude, and forthright. An ex-squaddie who made Trent look like a pacifist and a diplomat. He did unnamed dirty jobs for the colonel, dirtier even than those given to Trent.

He was a little older and taller than Trent. Muscles burst through his suit, and he had the look of a nightclub bouncer. His blond, greying hair was in a crewcut style to cover his approaching baldness. He had bags under his eyes, was unshaven, and looked as if he hadn't slept for days.

Gary Smith had been cashiered from the regular army and had drifted to the French Foreign Legion in 1960 where his "skills" were put to use in the French/Algerian conflict. Algeria finally won and Smith turned to crime on his discharge and spent some time in prison.

Colonel Stewart came to know him through his contacts and recruited him to his previous team in intelligence. Smith did surveillance and strong arm stuff in this role, and then followed the colonel to his new position in the Outfit. He continued to work closely with the colonel.

Smith spat sarcasm and bile through broken bad teeth, with breath that could strip paint. Trent had never taken to him, but luckily, rarely saw him, thank goodness.

The other man was a different kettle of fish. He knew this to be Jones, although rarely saw him. He was quiet, watchful, and studious. His dark hair fashionably long and he wore specs, the sort seen on Michael Caine. Trent knew he often worked with Prof on weird and wonderful projects.

He was short, dapper and appraised Trent coolly through his specs. An academic and certainly not on the rough and tumble side of the business. Alan Jones had studied classics at Oxford coming out with a first, he had an affluent background and his father had been involved in local politics. He often quoted in Latin or Greek.

After leaving university, he'd worked for the Conservative Party and even considered standing for parliament. This until MI5 came calling and he ended working for Sir Richard Abbott in analysis and strategy. He then followed his boss to the Outfit and continued working closely with Sir Richard, although his alleged immediate boss was the prof.

Divorced with two kids he never saw, he was another wedded to his job. 'Well, if it ain't our TV star.' Smith's sarcasm dripped. 'The VC hero who's gonna save the world.' His accent was sarf London. 'Can't even save his friends. Hey, Jones.'

Trent had that flash through his head, knew inevitably this could end in violence. He fought hard to discipline himself to ignore the idiot.

Jones was more placatory. 'Come on, Smith, leave him alone, he's having a rough time.' His accent was well-bred and grating. 'Dona Nobis Pacem,' he quoted. How the hell he worked with Smith Trent never knew! Chalk and cheese.

'Let's essence amicus,' Jones continued to show off his Latin. 'Let's be friends, boys.'

Smith, however, looked as if he was up for a fight and he clenched his fists. 'Whatever you said, fuck that.'

Who knows what would have happened next? Luckily, Babs entered the office. Trent gave an inward shrug—Smith was not worth it—and without a word, he left.

Outside, the rain was turning to sleet and the streets pitch dark; few people were about.

He drove out of the city, the rush hour having subsided. A few rockets exploded in the sky heralding the approach to 5 November.

He turned the radio on; Slade stomped out *Cos I luv you*. He should have appreciated them. Noddy Holder's voice reminding him of Lennon in Hamburg, and Slade were "cousins" from the Black Country. However, they were not real rock & roll.

It was OK, but a violin?

He slid a cassette into the car's player. Carl Perkins' greatest hits. He'd recently purchased it from HMV in Oxford Street to go with a new cassette player he'd bought. So he could compare with his record player and collection of singles and LP's.

Gone, gone, gone blasted out, stinging rockabilly guitar. "Gone"; Trent lost himself and all his concerns in the music for a while.

He collected enough clothes and toiletries for a week from the flat and then headed out to nearby Heathrow. As he left, he noted the Outfit men outside the block of flats on guard for Mrs McDougal as promised by Prof.

His passport again showed him to be Stephen Brown and he donned his trilby and dark glasses against any marauding nosey press.

He'd leave the hired Cortina at the airport and then catch the night plane to Paris and to a booked hotel he hoped stayed open all night.

Chapter Seventeen
Paris, 31 October

The plane had landed at Charles de Gaulle airport in the middle of the night. Too late for the Roissybus, Trent took a taxi into Paris (more extravagance!). The drab suburbs were hidden by the dark and rain, and Trent was thankful for that as they were a little depressing. Soon he'd see the bright lights of Paris centre; gay Paree!

The hotel was a small, discreet, old-fashioned establishment in the rue Saint-Honoré, a lengthy road, spreading from the Arc de Triomphe to Place de la Concorde. Luckily, it was open all night and he blessed the efficiency of Babs.

All Parisian hotels, except possibly the Ritz and the Hotel George V, are small and cramped. Was Bijou the word? And this was no exception. He booked in and arranged an early-morning call. The old, rickety cage of a lift took Trent up to his small (petite!) chambre, where he soon collapsed on the bed and fell into a blissful sleep, the nightmare of the past days banished…for a while at least.

The early-morning call woke him at 7am Paris time (he'd altered his watch the night before). He showered and shaved, and feeling refreshed, he glanced out of the small window at the wet rooftops outside. It always rained in Paris. He remembered 1968, sent to monitor the student riots, it had rained then.

He slipped into memories. May 1968 was one of the earliest assignments for the colonel; this nostalgia was getting out of control!

There were demonstrations, civil unrest, general strikes and occupation of universities. It started with protests against capitalism and American imperialism, and then descended into anarchy. Culminating in riots in central Paris with over six thousand students battling with fifteen hundred gendarmes.

Trent kept a low profile, watching from the sidelines. Then reporting back to the colonel regarding government concerns that the troubles may spread to

London. However, he treated it as a semi-vacation and a way of getting to know Paris.

Expenses weren't so good then and he stayed in a run-down hotel. This was near the famous flea market in Porte de Clignancourt, and fleas were the operative word in that hotel.

He wasn't sure how but he'd met an English girl called Poppy. A French student at Trent Polytechnic and an archetypal hippy. She had hitched over to Paris in solidarity with her French "comrades". He remembered his first journey on the Métro, the smell of garlic and Gauloises, the French cigarette. An assault on his senses, then the light, the noise, the rain, the traffic as he ascended into the Place de L'Etoile and the Arc de Triomphe.

And there, he'd somehow met Poppy, a skinny English hippy girl with large blue eyes, brown hair, and no make-up. They started a brief affair; no, not even that, a brief three-day fling. She had looked half-starved and he made it his goal to feed her up. This was obviously before he met Camille.

So he took her on a round of meals, under the archways in Place de Vosges, a baguette at a street kiosk in the rain, expensive lobster in Montmartre. All washed down enthusiastically with wine/beer; anything.

Then Poppy had taken him to strange dark nightclubs—weird music, light shows, the smell of pot heavy in the air. Pot that he always declined when offered. He watched the freak dancing and the stoned hippies fighting (love and peace?). Not really his scene.

Poppy had been sleeping rough with other students and down and outs on the Métro. Moved on by the gendarmes in the middle of the night, they ended up on the platform at the Gare du Nord. She didn't need much convincing to share his digs and also the fleas. Like chalk and cheese, she had jokingly called him the Barbarian. He wondered what the colonel would have said about their strange relationship. "Fraternising with the enemy" he would probably say.

More fleeting memories—walking by the Seine; Ile-St-Louis, a golden glow as the city awakes at dawn. Notre Dame, romantic, holding hands, can't help the Parisian cliché. Boulevard St Germain, Les Deux Magots, Poppy enthusing: famous for its art and literature custom: Picasso, Hemingway and Sartre. Trent commented: 'Famous for its very, very expensive cup of coffee and carafe of vin rouge!'

The Louvre, Eiffel Tower, Opéra de Palais Garnier—tourist rat traps. Trent much preferred the back streets of Marais, which suited his character somehow—dour and dark, where Poppy was all gaiety and light. Anyway, they were far from the riots. Far from his job, playing truant.

Eventually, they inevitably drifted apart, lost in the madness of that Parisian Spring.

In a small cosy dining room next to the reception, petite dejeuner was being served—bread rolls, marvellous creamy butter, cheese, ham, fresh orange juice. This set him up for the day and strengthened his resolve for anything that lay ahead. He waited for Alphonse to contact him.

Smoking a cigarette, sipping coffee, he picked up a daily newspaper on a nearby table, *Le Figaro*, and his relaxed feeling immediately changed.

On the front of the paper were photos of Ajmal Khan and his wife (he assumed). Next to it, a much smaller photo of President Pompidou, and although Trent's French was limited, he could make out most of the story.

- atrocities in the UK
- drugs! Terrorism! Murder, etc.
- the Zombie attacks
- Communist conspiracy
- where is missing VC hero? Philip Trent…

(Thank God, there was no photo of him!)

Perhaps a certain smugness in the editorial tone that it was all happening to the old enemy, not in France.

Before Trent had time to take in the news, the waiter beckoned.

'Monsieur Brown, s'il vous plait, le téléphone pour vous.'

He nodded. 'Merci,' and went to the reception to answer the phone.

It was Alphonse Jourdain wishing him good morning in a cheery voice and giving him instructions to meet. Ten minutes later, he turned into Avenue Matignon and crossed the busy Champs Elysées at Rond Point. The rain had eased, the sun was weakly shining and a slight chill was returning. He could see the Arc de Triomphe in the distance; the cafés all busy up the straight avenue, despite the weather.

Walking down the Avenue Montaigne, he could make out the Eiffel Tower, the top lost in a low-lying cloud, and then there was his destination, Le Bar des Théatres.

The bar was opposite the Comédies des Champs Elysées. Many theatrical types used it alongside the doyens of the fashion houses in that street. In contrast, the bar was now full of hard-drinking, smoking French locals who sat at the cramped bar at all hours.

Trent entered the old-style bar with predominance of red, including the awning along the entrance. The chairs and tables were jammed together and there was a smell of well-polished wood fighting with the scent of cigarettes and alcohol.

And there away from the crowded bar was Alphonse Jourdain. Debonair as ever in a tailored suit from Pierre Cardin, and a flamboyant carnation in his buttonhole. He was somewhere in his mid-forties, his hair peppered with grey and he had a devil-may-care twinkle. A handsome man, a ladies' man, with his dark brown eyes and fashionable Sergeant Pepper moustache and sideburns.

Trent knew he took good living seriously, but despite a slight paunch, he still looked reasonably fit and exuded Gallic charm.

'Mon ami, mon ami, Monsieur Trent, Philippe, bonjour.' He was almost a Gallic cliché, how you'd imagine Agatha Christie's Hercule Poirot to be (except he was Belgian). Trent recoiled from the typical kiss on the cheeks.

'Bonjour, Alphonse, and how are you?' Trent responded.

'Well, well, Philippe, please have something to eat.'

In front of Alphonse were the remains of croissants, pastries, coffee, and a glass of cognac.

'No, thanks, merci, Alphonse, I've eaten.' He shook his head.

Alphonse continued. 'Oh, la, how about a nice cognac to get the day in perspective?'

'A little early for me; just coffee please.'

Alphonse waved to the waiter and ordered more coffee. He offered Trent one of his cigarettes. Trent declined; he could smell the foul-smelling French cigarette, it smelt of dried manure! He lit one of his own as Alphonse sipped his brandy and again continued.

'You know to a Frenchman, the breakfast, le petit déjeuner, is the least important meal of the day; the lunch, the dinner or supper, these are important— but I forget myself. With these trivialities—' His voice dropped. 'I am so very, very sorry about the death of your friends and all this trouble you have. Sacré bleu!' His eyes flashed around the bar and noted the tables now filling up. His voice dropped again to a whisper and he continued.

'We will talk of these things in a more secluded place I know. I have much to tell of this Khan and co. But the colonel has asked me to entertain you, to take your mind off things before you return to the fray. A vacation in gay Paree, mon ami.'

Trent had also noted the place getting busier. 'I understand, we'll catch up later.'

Alphonse waved his hands in the air. 'Philippe,' he said excitedly. 'Every week, I have a special day and this is it. You are privileged to join me. Le petit déjeuner, it is the start of an epicurean day. Then lunch at a gourmet restaurant, have pastries and cakes in the afternoon and perhaps supper in the evening at some nightclub.'

Trent smiled. 'I guess there's some drink involved as well.'

'Obviously, mon ami. Of course, and the best for Alphonse.'

Trent thought back to 1968 and remembered Alphonse, the playboy. How had he survived in Interpol and working on the side for Colonel Stewart? He was pretty sure that the colonel's network of spies provided Alphonse with some good leads to criminality, which pleased his superiors. Alphonse, of course, got the kudos.

Quid pro quo, Alphonse delivered regular information on the French and continental affairs. All for cash, of course.

Alphonse finished his drink and they left the café, out into a now cooler morning. Alphonse's car was a battered old Citroen CV3 and was parked awkwardly in a very illegal position. His reputation with the Paris police protected him from traffic law, and to evidence this, he waved at a nearby police officer, who waved back.

They drove north back towards the Champs Elysées. The manic Paris traffic confirmed to Trent that there was some sense in driving a half-wrecked car. There was a cacophony of car horns and swearing, and Alphonse swerved his way through the melée. They headed through the back streets towards the Pigalle district. Alphonse didn't say much as he concentrated on driving.

He suddenly stopped in the middle of Pigalle outside a dour grey office block.

'There, mon ami, is Khan's import and export office. It is empty now, I think, but we'll go and have a closer look a little later. But first priority, an excellent lunch awaits!'

87

Chapter Eighteen
Meal in Paris

Quartier Pigalle has been famed since the last century for its red-light district and the cabaret bars of Moulin Rouge and others. Overlooked by Montmartre and the Sacré Coeur, their destination was about half a kilometre from Khan's office. Alphonse parked in a narrow back street.

'Voila! The next stage of our culinary adventure.' He pointed at a very nondescript, in fact seedy, run-down looking establishment, with no name on the front.

They were greeted by an equally nondescript, seedy maitre d' who obviously knew Alphonse well. After plenty of backslapping and cheek kissing, they were shown to a discreet corner at the back of the restaurant away from other diners. The establishment was slowly filling up, it now being lunchtime. Here, Alphonse said, they could speak freely without being overheard.

Trent asked him the name of the place. Alphonse said something indecipherable that Trent didn't catch and he didn't bother to pursue it. Instead, he took stock of the restaurant—small, dark, cramped tables, lights turned low to hide a general lack of cleanliness. Alphonse promised a gourmet meal "par excellence", with wine. Trent hoped food poisoning didn't follow.

Alphonse noticed his reservations. 'Do not worry, mon ami, the food is superb, I have never suffered afterwards! We will dine here, go and look properly at Khan's place. Then an expensive martini at Harry's Bar, afternoon tea at a little place I know with the best cakes in Paris. Then the nightlife—supper, girls, who knows…'

With further reservations about cakes (no sweet tooth) and girls (?), Trent responded: 'Is this all just a French pub crawl?'

'We will order now, then talk business.' Alphonse ignored his comment and handed him a small scrawled handwritten list (la carte, the menu).

Alphonse ordered moules mariniere, followed by sole meuniere with a bottle of Sancerre. Trent ordered coquilles Saint Jacques, blanquette de veau, and a red Bordeaux (He could just about decipher the menu). 'I see you're a sophisticate now. Back in '68, I remember pie or fish and chips were your favourites. Meals out with the colonel has certainly expanded your horizon.'

Yes, and with Camille, Trent thought to himself.

'Enjoy it all; just don't go to the toilette here unless you have to. It would offend your Anglo-Saxon sensibilities, the hole in the floor. You know.'

May prove difficult with all this drink, Trent mused.

Alphonse seemed to want to talk about anything but the actual matter in hand. He actually seemed a little nervous.

Trent reflected on the genial man in front of him. He thought of 1968 again, when Poppy had vanished into the rainy mists of Paris. Alphonse was the colonel's man in France and Trent's liaison there. He had taken it upon himself to show Trent the city and educate him in the culture and the good life. To show this Anglo-Saxon peasant some sophistication.

Alphonse had been in the military and had fought in the Indo-China war in the late forties, early fifties. A war that had segued into the American involved Vietnam War.

Following that, he fought in the Algerian War. Leaving with the Légion d'Honneur, the French equivalent of Trent's VC.

He had then worked his way up through the police to a senior detective at the Sureté. This led to Interpol, where he had also become an agent of the colonel.

His path had been littered with divorces, mistresses and illegitimate children. This together with his luxury apartment in the 1st arrondissement and a penchant for the high life, meant he needed the extra cash and this was provided by the colonel.

After a few minutes, Alphonse said: 'How have you been keeping this past few years? Er…I mean other than your er…present difficulty.'

'Well, you know, the colonel…'

'Oui, oui, the colonel.' Alphonse tried the Sancerre in an iced bucket by the table and smacked his lips. 'Do you know that the soldiers used to call this area Pig Alley, their favourite red-light area.' Trent again tried to get him to return to the Khan situation without success. Alphonse talked about everything and anything. Politics, economics, gossip, he touched on Jim Morrison's death in

July (*Who?* thought Trent). He went on and on until finally, he relented at Trent's insistence.

'OK, Philippe, always impatient. I look at all of this happening in England, in the UK, or whatever, with a horror. We expect riots, revolts in France, it's our national way. Ever since the revolution in 1789, in fact. But in your country? I remember as a child the German occupation here in Paris, dreadful. And then the liberation, the fights, the battles in the street. Terrible carnage; wouldn't wish that on your nation.

'I know politicians here look at the situation with disbelief, not in England? All that ridiculous Zombie rubbish as well. Could it happen here? Could it spread here? They're even fretting about Britain joining the EC. Now I understand a bomb went off this morning at your post office tower in London, no casualties…'

'About Khan, what have you got?' Trent interjected, again trying to bring him to the point of this meeting. There was a delay in conversation as the starters were served and there was more savouring of the wine. Between mouthfuls, Alphonse continued:

'I've shown you Khan's import/export office. We'll go and look at it again later, as I said. I'm sure it's empty and we should be able to break in easily. Now Interpol and the Sureté have been keeping close tabs on this Khan for some time, we are certain he has been smuggling raw opium in from Pakistan in his lorries. Then distributing across Europe from his warehouse in Marseilles. He is also recently started moving opium into the UK and converting to heroin himself. Using his novelty business as cover.

'We are also sure that of late he has been smuggling vast shipments of arms into Britain. It is also known that he left Marseilles yesterday with a final shipment. He has closed up his operations here as far as we can see.'

Trent finished his starter. 'How do you know all this?'

'We have had a spy in his camp for some time and we even know where he is heading now.'

'Where's that?' Although Trent had a feeling he knew the answer.

'To his storage facilities somewhere in Wales. Where he also processes the heroin.'

Wales! Yns Penglog no doubt. The ridiculously named Skull Island. Well! Well! The target moves closer.

The main courses now arrived with their delicious aroma. Trent sipped his glass of Bordeaux—delicious—and listened as Alphonse continued.

'At a guess, they're building up a massive armoury for some sort of terrorist strike in your country.

'Now, I'm sure you want to get over to Wales, to wreak vengeance, or whatever. But I'm under instructions to keep you here. So tonight, we'll enjoy ourselves and then tomorrow, we'll go and look at this warehouse in Marseilles. Oh, and also Khan's chateau in Avignon. Probably a waste of time, but there you are. In the morning, I'll show you some photos of the Marseilles place.

'Now, you haven't a gun, have you? I, of course, never carry one, but tomorrow, I'll sort it out for you. Now please, let's forget all this. How are you finding the meal?'

Trent agreed it was excellent, as he polished off his wine and then the rest of the meal.

'We'll have coffee, then go to these offices.' He lit up one of his evil cigarettes. 'Oh, by the way, recently Mr Khan also was having regular meetings with some very dubious characters—characters of East German origin. In fact, communist agents.'

Chapter Nineteen
Death in Paris

Alphonse parked the Citroen in the narrow street. There was just room. Khan's office was in an old, probably 19th century building. It was three storeys high and Khan was on the second floor. All the buildings ran into each other and they had all seen better days. Alphonse pointed at a small passage at the side of the building.

'Down there is a fire escape around the back which will take us to the back of Khan's offices. As I say now deserted but there may be something there of interest.'

Whilst they'd been in the restaurant, the sun had crept out; now the afternoon was drawing in, a reluctant sun taking its bow and casting long shadows over some of the buildings. They started to cross the street.

Suddenly, out of nowhere, four large ugly Frenchmen appeared, full of menace. What they used to call in Paris "Apaches". The front two had weapons in their hands and they all wore heavy steel-capped boots. One had a lead pipe and the other swung a chain with what looked like razors on the end. The two in the rear produced large, vicious-looking knives. All evil-looking bastards. Trent could smell the sweat. Obviously, they were expected and this was no random attack. There was a look of complete astonishment on Alphonse's face. 'Mon Dieu, putain!'

Trent knew enough French to understand the last word and he echoed it. 'Fuck!' If only he had a gun!

'Geronimo, Vive la France!' Alphonse shouted and dropped into some sort of martial arts defence pose.

Trent, no stranger to street fighting, had a brief flashback to Chelsea and the yobs. A familiar flash of light, precursor to violence, and he stared at the assailant in front of him straight into his eyes.

He knew martial arts but remembered his old trainer in the SAS: 'When the chips are down, forget finesse. Surprise is the key. Hit them everywhere and as fast as you can, nowt subtle. Balls, head, throat, chest, knees. No Queensberry rules, as quick as you like!'

Trent, the street fighter, with that added skill. He dodged the swinging chain, rolled to the floor and kicked out at the assailant's legs very hard. The "Apache" stumbled back and Trent leapt up bringing his forehead straight into the thug's face, the "Glasgow kiss". A squelch of blood and Trent followed up with a hard karate chop to the neck. His quarry completely floored; he grabbed the lethal chain. The man, although tough, was no match for the professional.

He heard panting to his left and swung around. Alphonse was struggling with his opponent on the floor. The other two, he noted, were warily holding back, knives ready. Waiting he supposed for their victims to weaken.

Trent swung the chain catching the man on top of Alphonse on the back of the head. He collapsed dead in a bloody heap, some of it covering Alphonse's nice expensive suit. He helped Alphonse up, who was tutting and cursing in French about the mess. No "merci mon ami". They turned to face the other two who circled warily. Alphonse had picked up the lead pipe; Trent had the chain, they were now armed. Things evened!

They were ready for a continued fracas, when there were three soft noises— Phut! Phut! Phut! Three shots. What? Where? Alphonse looked puzzled, put his hands to the back of his head, and looked at more blood now on his hands. 'Mon Dieu, my suit ruined...' With that, he fell over joining the two they'd been fighting, also shot, together with Trent's "victim".

There was another silenced shot. Trent somersaulted and landed behind the Citroen. It wasn't for him, however; it had hit the first wounded attacker, and now in front of him were the four hooligans and Alphonse, all dead. No shot directed at him? Then a half-hearted shot pinged on the car roof and silence.

There were probably two snipers on the roof of Khan's place, with silenced telescopic rifles. Was one of them the German, this Zombie character? He took a quick look. Yes, two killers up there, getting ready to leave. Seemingly in no hurry. One of them could clearly be seen despite dusk approaching, the lights of Paris now coming on and reflecting on the roof.

No, it wasn't Mueller, Z or the Zombie. Trent knew that man now lit up by the street lights, he'd seen him only yesterday. It was Smith, from the office, the

Outfit. The man the colonel had entrusted with finding out who the traitor was. Well, he didn't have to look too far, did he?

The colonel's chosen man. Well, for once, Colonel Stewart had been wrong in his judgement and the choice of an employee. Was the other man with him Jones? No wonder Smith knew where he would be and that he would be unarmed. The Apache thugs, a distraction before the snipers attacked and obviously working for Smith.

He glanced at Alphonse, the man was obviously dead—once so full of life— "Joie de vivre". There was no time for regret. People, curious, had now appeared in the street and police sirens could be heard getting closer. The two killers had vanished across the rooftops.

Trent dropped the chain, picked up the lead pipe, and ran across the street and into the small side alley. He was going to get that bastard Smith!

Around the back of the building, he found the fire escape and ran up the metal steps to the rooftop. Passing the glass doors to Khan's office, he could plainly see that it was empty as Alphonse predicted. Anyway, no time for that now!

He reached the top and he could see a good distance over higgledy piggledy rooftops and there was no sign of his quarry. They had gone! There were plenty of rooftop doors and hatches in sight and they could have gone down any one of them. He could see the crowd below had grown and several police vehicles had appeared.

There was clanging on the fire escape and shouting, the police were coming up. Smith (and Jones?) had well gone, time for him to go as well. Didn't really want to get snarled up with French police and their bureaucracy.

He broke into a trot avoiding chimney pots, TV aerials and sometimes even washing. Trent cursed the lunch and drink, not conducive to running across the rooftops of Paris. The police were in pursuit behind him; he flung the lead pipe aside and continued on the precarious journey.

It was getting darker and more lights were coming on; the Sacré Coeur and Montmartre now brilliantly lit up. The Eiffel Tower and other sights also now showing brightly against the dusk. He had a flashback to Berlin and going across those rooftops. If he had time, he could have appreciated the panoramic view.

Now breaking into a sweat, the police behind were keeping up. He stopped to leap over a small gap between buildings and then climbing up where the roof was at a different level. He needed to get down and away from the pursuers. In all the confusion his old hat has been lost- no time for sentimentality.

Stopping behind a tall chimney pot to catch his breath (also cursing too many fags!), he noted a deep channel running down the roof to catch an overflow of rain. He could hear the police getting nearer and could see now their flashing torches. Making up his mind, he dropped into the channel and crawled to the edge, praying that he couldn't be seen.

At the end of the channel, there was a drainpipe going into the dark below. Quickly testing it for strength, he then shinned down, hoping it would hold, and also hoping they wouldn't hear him as he descended.

Chapter Twenty
Escape from Paris

Trent watched the police clatter over the rooftops, shouting, lights flashing. Luckily, they hadn't seen him. He seemed to be in a small weed-ridden backyard, junk and rubbish lying about.

When he was sure it was all clear, he moved to the bottom of the yard. There was a wooden fence, which he climbed over, and he found himself in another back alley in "Pig Alley". There was no one about and he followed the illuminated Montmartre area on the hill, knowing this would take him to the Metro.

He came up on the Boulevard du Clichy. He could see the Basilique du Sacré Coeur on the hill, next to Montmartre itself and the Place du Tertre. Famously home to street artists and tourist 'rip-off' restaurants. Also, he passed the Moulin Rouge and its famous bright red windmill. Once an area of reasonably modest dance halls and cabarets, now an area of sleazy sex shows and prostitution. Toulouse-Lautrec would have turned in his grave (or would he?).

The Boulevard was packed with cars, buses and bikes fighting for space. People flooded the pavements and even in the cold, customers sat outside bars and bistros eating and drinking. This was a Parisian rush hour and citizens were drinking or snacking before going home. He passed a heaving brasserie, outside tables under a typical red awning with faded unreadable gold letters announcing the establishment's name. The smell of garlic, Gauloises, Gitanes, alcohol, and cooking food in the air. He then arrived at the station.

Pigalle Metro station was packed. Several armed policemen stood about, but obviously they knew nothing about the five deaths nearby and the fugitive. There was a queue to the ticket office. Better get out of here quickly! Many young and agile Parisians never paid on the Metro. They vaulted over the barrier. Trent copied them. He just managed to catch the train to Champs Elysées-Clemenceau, and he sat back as it vanished into the blackness of the tunnel.

It was obviously a waste of time going to Avignon or Marseilles. All now seemed to be a bit of a red herring, or what had Hitchcock called it in his films, a McGuffin? Trent's mind was set; he'd get back to England and get to this island in Wales where he was sure many questions would be answered.

Back at his hotel, he managed with a mix of schoolboy French and English to inform them that sadly he needed to return to England.

'There was an illness in the family, comprenez? You understand?' He retrieved his passport from reception and went to his room. No time to catch his breath. He packed his few toiletries and clothes. His passport in the name of Stephen Brown he hid in a compartment in the suitcase, and he took another one from one of the hidden pockets in his leather coat. This was in the name of Mark Whittle.

It was highly unlikely that the police would trace him to here, but best to be careful. He would not use his plane ticket to get back but go another route. So Mark Whittle left the small hotel and headed for the Gare du Nord and the night ferry, the international boat train back to London. It would take over eight hours to get to Victoria Station, plenty of time to recharge his batteries and think through the events of the past few days.

At the Gare du Nord, he purchased his ticket. He had some time to kill and made three calls to London. Battling with the overseas operator, a lack of French, and the exorbitant cost. The first call was to the prof via the secured line. Inevitably, the colonel was not there. He briefly told a shocked Prof of what had happened in Paris and he arranged to meet him in the morning. Away from the Outfit's HQ.

Trent was now distrustful of the place.

He also phoned a contact in London to meet tomorrow afternoon. He would supply a few interesting things for Trent to be used over the next couple of days.

Finally, he briefly phoned Camille and arranged to stay at her place the next evening. His flat was now probably besieged by press. He also told her an edited version of events in Paris.

He slept on the train journey to Calais. The sea journey from Calais to Dover was particularly stormy. A seaman told him that this was the worst crossing he had ever seen, before turning to be sick over the side. Good job he was downwind! Trent noted several other crew members being sick, it was not something that bothered him, travel sickness.

The boat was nearly empty of passengers. He no longer felt tired with the rain and wind lashing the vessel. Didn't fancy the tiny bunks in the tiny cold cabin either. There was little in the way of refreshment. He managed to scrounge a cup of weak coffee from one of the stewards. God, it was vile! He flung it aside and sat sheltered by one of the lifeboats, smoking.

He stared out at the waves rising and falling, caught by the ship's own lights. The rain fell heavily. His thoughts mulling over and over, the mayhem and conspiracy that he had been caught up in; a picture slowly forming in his mind and the semblance of a plan going forward.

A lone seagull nearby sheltered from the storm. Buffeted by the rain and gales, he looked sad and lonely. Trent knew how he felt.

Chapter Twenty-One
London, 1 November, Meeting at Kew

Trent arrived at Victoria Station early morning. His passport was stamped at the desk at the end of the platform. Feeling a bit dishevelled, he made his way to the station public conveniences and paid the attendant to enter the Gents. There he had a perfunctory wash and brush up and changed his shirt. Feeling slightly better, he took the tube to Kew to meet the prof at the pre-arranged venue.

The meeting was at 10.30am in Kew Gardens of all places. Hardly the centre of espionage, but maybe that was the point. After the stormy night at sea, it was a pleasant sunny morning, but still slightly chilly. Sitting on the pavement by the tube exit was a young lad with what was supposedly Guy Fawkes. 'Penny for the Guy, Mister?' The urchin looked imploringly at Trent.

'Shouldn't you be at school?' He asked, but threw a few coins into his collection anyway.

With a wry smile, he paid and entered the gardens.

He strolled through Kew past the Temperate House with its collection of rare species from around the world. Then past the Palm House, and the King William Temple (built for Queen Victoria). Finally, he met the prof down by the Kew Lake. He was examining some flora or whatever it was called and Trent remembered there being similar stuff in the prof's office.

'Royal Botanic Gardens, Kew, opened in 1840 and has the largest and most diverse mycological collection in the world,' was the first thing the prof said. 'Co-come on, let's walk,' and he took Trent by the arm, and they walked towards the pagoda.

Outside the Outfit, there was something different about the professor. For a start, whilst his white hair was still unruly his normal scruffy state was covered by a surprisingly smart/expensive-looking raincoat, and he wore thick leather gloves to keep out the cold. He also carried a smart briefcase. In fact, compared to Trent, unshaven and rumpled, he was a picture of sartorial elegance.

It was more than that. Away from the office, he seemed more relaxed, more human. Although he still had a nervous stutter, it was not so pronounced.

'What's that word, myco-myco something?'

'Mycological; it's the study of f-fungi, something of great interest to me.' He looked sharply at Trent. 'It's…it's good to see you safe and sound. My, you have been in the wars. Scarcely believable. Are you OK?'

Trent nodded and the prof continued. 'Sorry to h-hear about Monsieur Jourdain. Did you know him well?'

'Not particularly.' Trent thought about the larger-than-life character that was Alphonse. He would miss him. Shrugging his shoulders, he asked: 'Where's the colonel?'

'Well, f-f-irstly he was shocked by Smith. Handpicked him! But at least the traitor has now been found. And secondly, he was not too pleased to see you back in England. Partic, with the news and so on around you. It's actually on Panorama this evening. Also, reporters have now found your flat, and the news people know about Paris and the deaths; these leaks…' He gestured impatiently. 'Smith I suppose.'

He continued. 'Anyway, the colonel and Sir Richard are very very busy with all sorts. Meetings with the P-PM and the cabinet. S-Scotland Yard and MI5. Trying to bring home the seriousness of the plot against our country. And all your reports to me were written up and have been very useful background to all this.' He looked at Trent again searchingly.

'I bet they have,' he replied.

'The colonel and the boss are still asking for emergency powers to combine all forces—military, police, etc., etc., and take on this communist threat. Although,' he mused, 'strangely, the robberies, bombs, strikes have all gone quiet. Lull before the storm, eh? Something in the air?'

Typically, the more he talked, the less he stammered.

'Let's continue this at a nearby café I frequent.' So they walked past the Palm House towards the exit. 'You know, I come here as much as I can. So relaxing. Not far from where I live in Ealing. Of course, I've only a small garden, but I love it here. My hobby. All these plant and fungi specimens. All the volumes of books with prints and drawings…excellent, lovely—and I bet you thought my only interest was work.'

Before Trent could reply, they were outside their destination and the prof was pointing at an old-fashioned looking café, "The Maids of Honour".

'I often call here for tea and cakes after a walk round Kew. It's pretty quiet Monday morning, we should be able to chat in peace.'

Trent noticed his stammer had completely gone, he seemed more confident. Was his nervous demeanour an act? The thought went through his mind. This almost seemed a different person.

There was something "old-maidish" about him now as he continued to waffle. 'Family-run bakery here, famous for their teas and cakes, but do sandwiches as well. Maids of Honour, they're dainty little tarts, almond-flavoured curd cheese. Henry VIII's favourite. Would you like?'

'No, thanks.' Trent thought of Alphonse and his Parisian afternoon tea with gateaux. He looked at the menu and ordered Welsh rarebit with a pot of coffee. Prof ordered his tea and cakes.

Trent noticed the "No Smoking" sign with disgust.

The food arrived and Prof became business-like. No stutter, the old maid abandoned. He produced from his case an envelope and taking photos out, he handed them to Trent.

'These were taken yesterday and show this Welsh island from a distance. Various angles and then some close-ups. These have also been presented to cabinet with your transcribed reports.'

'Who took these?'

'Jones, from our place. You know him?'

'Yes, we've met, vaguely.' So he couldn't have been out in Paris with Smith then!

'The island, Yns Penglog, the locals say it looks like a skull; can't see it really myself. It's about a half mile from the coast, several miles north of Aberystwyth, and a mile from a place called Wallog.'

Trent looked at the photos. 'It looks like a large rock with a building and lighthouse on.'

'Yes, it does. There are the remains of an old Napoleonic fort there. It was built in 1797 shortly after the minor French invasion of Wales. Napoleon's troops were defeated at the Battle of Fishguard. The government of the day in panic proposed to build several of these forts along the Welsh coast. This was the first. There'd always been a lighthouse there and the fort joined onto it. A white elephant really, stuck out in the Irish Sea far from major sea routes.

'Anyway, it remained empty until the 1950s when an eccentric millionaire erased much of the fort and built a dwelling there. The magazine below the fort still remains and part of the ownership means the lighthouse has to be kept in working order.

'Jones took the photos with a telephoto lens and we also had them blown up. You can see the landing point with what we think is Khan's super-yacht anchored. There is unbelievably room for several boats in the sheltered harbour. The other one there brought in some guests for Khan, the smaller boat.'

There was a lull as the elderly waitress brought their food and drink. Dressed olde-olde world, in black and white. Her dress corresponding with the black and white beams all round the café. It was very tranquil; a couple of pensioners in one corner, a Japanese tourist, with camera, in another. No one could overhear them.

Prof pointed at further photos. 'See, the group on the landing stage.' He handed him a magnifying glass. 'Jones took these from a coastguard helicopter we borrowed for the occasion. He'd tracked the other smaller boat from Aberystwyth.'

'Yes, these are really interesting.' Trent studied the photos.

'I can see Khan and an attractive blonde woman in the background greeting several characters, and yes, yes, there's this Zombie, Mueller. His scarred features and height, you can't miss him.' He felt the excitement bubbling in his chest, although his expression and tone did not change. 'Oh yes, and that's Khan's man, Ayub. Who are the others?'

'That's Khan's wife, Gemma. Obviously Mueller as you say. There seems to be some guards hanging about and the men he's greeting…' He paused and ate one of his dainty cakes. Trent also finished his lunch, realising that he'd not eaten since yesterday afternoon in Pigalle. The prof continued.

'The small man in glasses is XXXXXXXXX, a leading member of the Communist party in Britain and ringleader of the strikes. The larger man next to him in the beret is XXXXXXXX of the IRA. And finally, XXXXXXXX of the Angry Brigade. Not sure who the other two are.'

He let this sink in. 'Seems to be a gathering of the leading figures in this plot. Khan, we believe, also represents militant Muslim groups.'

'Are they still there?'

'They were earlier today.'

'Is Jones still out there?'

'No, he's sort of assistant—aide de camp—to the colonel and he's with him and Sir Richard at a cabinet meeting.'

'You know, don't you, that I'm going to Wales, come what may.'

'Yes, the colonel expected you to say that. What he does say—in fact, orders you—is to observe the situation and only act if absolutely necessary.'

Trent made no answer, so the prof continued. 'Look, Sir Richard and the colonel are trying to get the PM to agree to an army assault on the island. They believe that there's a massive armoury still there in a large magazine deep in the rock. So he asks you to try and wait for this.'

'Does he?' was all Trent could say. More tea and coffee were ordered and the prof produced further documents from his briefcase.

With his normal efficiency, he showed Trent copies of Land Registry details and original architects' plans for the renovations on the island. He even produced charts showing currents and the rocks surrounding Yns Penglog. And then, the address of Khan's warehouse in Aber.

A potted history of the place followed: A multi-millionaire called Fred Blakemore had purchased the place in 1959. Mad Fred he was called; he'd made his fortune in brewing. Some said that he had then over-sampled his own product. His plan was to renovate and build a retreat off the Welsh coast where he could hide from the world.

A fortune was spent and the fort replaced with a thirties-style house next to the lighthouse. The magazine below acting as a storeroom cellar. He also tried to create a garden in the area by the magazine. There were steps down from the house to the garden and then further steps to the harbour. These were improved. There was a long pathway through the garden, which was now very overgrown with weeds.

Mad Fred didn't have long in his retreat and in 1961, he somehow fell from his paradise and was never seen again; presumed drowned.

Some years passed before he was declared legally dead and his estate put the island up for sale. Purchased in 1970, Land Registry advised, by a Miss Gemma Smart, Mrs Khan's maiden name. Obviously, a front for Ajmal Khan.

It was now suspected he used the island for his drug racket. The smuggled raw drug brought in from Marseilles and then refined on the island to make pure heroin. The west Wales coast not so well watched by the coastguards as the east of England. Also, few walkers used the coast path as it was too precarious and so the island had privacy. The drugs were then transported via Khan's plastic business.

The drug smuggling of late replaced by smuggled guns and ammunition.

The prof finalised: 'As I say, Khan and the others are still there; the local coastguards have kept a discreet eye on them.'

Trent thanked the prof for the extensive background, then asked: 'Why all this info if I'm to do nothing but watch?'

'Just in case, just in case. Here, take these papers in the briefcase.' He handed it over and returned to his plate to finish the "Maids of Honour".

The Prof knew, the colonel knew, and Trent knew that the chances of him doing nothing were less than minimal, in fact, zilch. They shook hands and Trent set off for his next rendezvous.

Chapter Twenty-Two
Still London, 1 November

Leaving the Kew area, Trent took the Underground again to Heathrow, where he picked up the hired Cortina. He filled it with petrol and then drove on to Hounslow.

Here, he visited Lloyds Bank, cashed in his last remaining francs for sterling, drew out further cash and paid for a banker's draft. It was now a nice autumn early afternoon with the sun shining and the temperature reasonably moderate. He drove out of Hounslow past Osterley and his flat. He wasn't going there with the reporters hanging about. Up to Kensington, then past Regents Park, north to Camden. He certainly was getting about on this mission!

His next meeting was with "Bomber" Harris. John Harris was his real name and the nickname came from his dubious field of business. "Bomber" supplied arms and accessories to his discerning clients. These were mainly mercenaries and others working abroad. Fiercely patriotic by his own lights, he would never supply anything in the British Isles that would arm gangsters or terrorists. What happened abroad, he didn't care about; a dubious moral stance perhaps.

Trent used him from time to time when the Outfit's supply of "equipment" did not live up to expectations. He always paid from his own pocket. The Outfit and the colonel did not go for modern gadgets and Bomber could also supply any of these. They met at Bombers lock-up under a railway arch near Camden Town. Trent had ordered a pile of "equipment" from him the day before, whilst at the Paris rail station.

He was somewhere in his early to mid-fifties and he shouted "spiv" to the high heavens. He reminded Trent of George Cole as Flash Harry in the St Trinian's films, with his dyed black hair in a Teddy boy quiff and a too-long overcoat with wide shoulders and trilby hat. Always a ciggie behind his ear and he spoke with a strong Cockney accent. This all finished off with an untrendy pencil moustache. He operated from a lock-up under a railway arch in the back streets of Camden Town.

Absolutely nothing was known of Bomber's background. If anyone was an enigma, it was Bomber. Although he would always deny knowledge of such a word if questioned.

"Major" Bob had introduced Bomber to Trent. Bob had been with Trent in Aden in the SAS and, eventually, had been cashiered for excess drinking. When the British Government withdrew from Aden in 1968, he'd become a mercenary for the Yemen Arab Republic, fighting the partisans.

Bob had tried to get Trent to join his happy band but Colonel Stewart had beaten him to the recruitment. "Major" Bob had stayed in touch and pointed him to Bomber. 'Should you ever need anything better than rubbish HM Government supplies.'

Trent asked after the Major and Bomber informed him that he was in England at present. 'Between jobs, you might say.' He continued: 'See you're a bit of a hero, Mr Trent, a celebrity—VC/SAS mixed up in murder and communists—on the telly.'

Trent gave him a stifling glare that Bomber took as an order to desist on the subject.

'Have you got the stuff?'

'When have I ever let you down, Mr Trent? There's a small matter... hmmph...'

'Yes, of course, payment.' He handed Bomber the banker's draft, who held it up suspiciously.

'Cash, Mr Trent. Tut. Always deal in cash.'

'That's as good as cash, Bomber, and you know it.'

'But the taxman...'

'You've never paid tax in your life, all those bank accounts of yours. Hidden away.'

Grumbling, Bomber stuffed the draft into his pocket. Then they loaded equipment into the car. This included firearms, explosives, timers, climbing, and underwater gear. He'd taken time to show Trent how to work the explosives and set the timers.

They shook hands and Trent asked him before he left: 'Have you in your...er... professional capacity, come across any of these bombs going around, the ones being set off all over the country? Do you know anyone involved?'

'No, Mr Trent. Must be from abroad; bloody foreigners!'

Trent said OK, said goodbye, and drove off. He parked in the next street and entered a phone box (why do they always smell of urine?). He phoned the prof and updated him. Prof also confirmed the boats were still moored off the island. In fact, a third one had joined them. The coastguard was still keeping tabs. Somehow the third boat arriving didn't surprise Trent.

One part of him wanted to rush to Wales and finalise matters. The more sensible side reasoned that he needed to rest and plan. He was certain they'd all still be there tomorrow. He set off for Camille's.

Chapter Twenty-Three
London, 1 November Continued,
Camille's Apartment

Eventually, Trent drove down Baker Street to Grosvenor Square to a hidden corner of Mayfair. Camille had an expensive apartment in amongst a group of Mews houses, a typical quiet back street which only the locals tended to use.

He parked the Cortina in an underground car park beneath the apartment block. He noted Camilles' 1965 Chevrolet. He also noted there was no longer an Outfit operative keeping an eye on things. He gave a rueful smile at this, not surprised again.

Trent had only been here a couple of times before and felt faintly uncomfortable in the apartment; the elegance against his bare, minimalistic flat in Osterley.

Camille greeted Trent with a kiss and very few words. She knew he would open up in his own good time. She poured him a brandy and even said, 'Have a smoke (smoking was normally banned in her abode!).' He thanked her for the brandy and declined the cigarette. Camille guessed he'd be hungry and went to prepare food.

'We can watch *Panorama* in a bit, and then if you want to talk…' Trent said thanks; he'd go and shower before dinner.

Showered, shaved, freshened up, he sat there with the brandy, the smell of cooking filling the room. It smelt nice!

He looked around him. All very old-fashioned, tasteful, and expensive.

He knew very little about décor, or houses, but Camille had told him the block was built in the 18th century.

If he did know about such things, he'd have known that the bookcase taking up half the wall was by Franco Albini. It was filled with classics, contemporary fiction, and biographies, all with her catholic taste, and she would actually have read them, not just for show.

There were early editions of Dickens, Tolstoy's *War and Peace*, and in the middle, a copy of the Kama Sutra. 'Not a patch on us,' was her comment, when she'd seen him once looking at the controversial tome.

He'd been brought up on comics, and Just William and Biggles from Thimblemill Library. Camille had improved his reading material and introduced him to a wider range of literature. Although in truth, he preferred something like Alistair Maclean.

The lighting design was by Lindsey Adelman with a Venetian glass chandelier on the ceiling. All turned down low except discreet lights lighting up several 16th century pictures on the wall (all originals). Everything set off by a roaring fake log fire. None of it really a sixties or seventies style.

The flooring was chevron dark oak and the sofas and armchairs were covered in deep yellow chintz with marigold yellow cushions. Very comfortable, not masculine! A Ukrainian rug lay in front of the fireplace.

There was a small bar, champagne on display. An expensive TV and hi-fi, and a dinner table covered by a white silk damask tablecloth.

But Trent knew hardly any of these details. Typically Camille though, stylish. God knows what it costs (wages of sin?).

At the end of the living room were the doors to the bedrooms, bathroom and kitchen, where there was the rattling of pans.

Camille brought his food on a tray and opened a bottle of Chianti.

'I don't really cook, live on salad or go out. One thing I can do is spaghetti bolognese. I thought you'd want something substantial. I've eaten.'

She poured a glass of ruby red Chianti, glinting in the light of the fire. '*Panorama* will be on in a minute. Do you want to watch?' Trent grimaced but said yes.

She turned the TV on and the famous music filled the room. Trent watched, eating his meal on his lap.

It was the same old rubbish—an exposé of the so-called communist plot to destabilise the country. The Birmingham murders, as they called them. Khan, the Zombie; the strikes, bombings. An assault on civilisation!

And at the centre, Philip Trent, the VC hero who uncovered it all at the loss of his friends. There was an old picture of him accepting the VC at Buckingham

Palace, in uniform and thankfully barely recognisable. There was even a mention of Alphonse and Paris and further deaths. Where is Trent now?

One light moment came when the BBC reporter stopped Mrs McDougal outside Trent's flat with typically inane questions. She told them off sharpish in an almost impenetrable Aberdeen accent and threatened to set Tess on them.

Trent and Camille smiled at this and he asked her to turn the TV off. 'Can't stand any more of this!'

She turned it off and slowly turned to him. 'So, so sorry, Philip, about your friends.'

Sometimes things are so difficult to put into words—sympathy, loss, facing up to mortality of friends. Trying to say the right thing, sometimes whatever was said it fell short. He grunted in response.

'I know you like your privacy. Must be hell all this publicity. At least no one will recognise you from that photo.' An attempt at humour, to change the subject, to move away from death.

'Good job there's no photos of me about,' he said.

'I've got one.'

'Have you? Please don't show me, or anyone! I prefer anonymity.' He sipped his wine.

'It was taken when we had that seaside trip out, when you weren't looking.'

He remembered the trip well, to Dorset. An enjoyable memory of the type that was so rare to him.

'Good break and none of those posh places you drag me around.'

'I think you've adapted admirably to the high life.'

'Maybe, maybe; well, sometimes.'

'Well, I've been to your football games, you misery.'

'Yes, and you enjoyed them; hot pie, Bovril and all. You're more socially adaptable than me.'

'Let's just say we enjoy each other's company wherever we go.'

There was a lull, a reticence that was rare between the two of them. He looked at her blonde beauty as she stared into his eyes and held his hands. Another strange, unfamiliar sensation. He loved this girl and trusted her. Golden locks falling over brown eyes, Slavic cheeks, curvaceous. She was wearing an expensive catsuit—with a tempting zip up the front—accentuating her figure. Theirs was a love story without too much sentiment.

Suddenly, the dam between them broke and he felt the need to unburden himself. To tell this delightful woman all. She continued to hold his hands, her brown eyes on his face searching.

So he told her everything, left nothing out. The death of his friends, of Alphonse. His suspicions, theories, the treachery of Smith. The question, why was he still alive? His tears, anger and thoughts of revenge on this Z, Khan, Smith, and the whole rotten crew.

He outlined his thoughts on what was happening and the vague plan of vengeance he'd thought out on the boat from France. What he proposed in Wales and at Yns Penglog (He still refused to call it Skull Island). Also his collection from his private armourer, Bomber.

As the evening drifted into night, they went round and round fine-tuning Trent's plan, fortified by coffee and wine. Camille agreed with many of his suspicions and aims, and in the end, they came up with a final plan.

She was sympathetic, supportive, without judgment, and by the way, gorgeous. She also helped him to collect his thoughts and focus. When this was all over, he was going to give it all up. Run away, get married in Amalfi or Venice, and live happily ever after. Even have kids!

Camille brought him out of this fantasy and back to earth.

'Do you really have to go to Wales?' Even as she said it, she knew the answer. 'If you do then I think I ought to come, you need support.'

'You know I do; it's kismet if you like, to use one of your cultured words.' He smiled back into her eyes. 'Also it's too dangerous for you. It's what I'm paid for. Better alone.'

'But Phili…'

'No buts,' he interrupted, and took hold of her hands and stared into her eyes, daring her to argue. She backed down knowing it was of no further use to press the point.

'So off to Skull Island in the morning. Sounds like a children story, doesn't it? I still worry…'

'Well, don't, it's bread and butter to me. And anyway, with all that planning, and with our masterplan…' He gave a smile. 'Can't fail.'

Camille gave a look that said she wasn't entirely convinced, but said no more. A shadow passed between them and Trent misread the sign.

'Don't worry, I know Colonel Stewart wants you to report on me. It has never bothered me.'

'Nothing to report. You never give anything away, not even a titbit. Just that bloody dog and football, football…'

'That's what they say. Taciturn.'

'I know, and you take it to the limit.' She sighed. 'Look, there's lots of things I want to discuss with you, but let's concentrate on the Welsh malarkey.'

'Oh yes, and what's that?'

'Leave it, Philip, get the next couple of days over.'

'OK.' He noticed tears in the corner of her eyes and he changed the subject. He'd never seen tears before.

'Right, let's go over everything again and then I want you to put all our thoughts into a written report; you were always a better writer than me.'

'Who's that for?'

'It's for my fat, drunk friend as you call him. Kev Bloomer. The reporter. A sort of view from the coal face, so to speak, of all this malarkey, to borrow your phrase. My side of things, with all the bollocks going around. Let's get the proper version of events out there.'

He rarely swore in front of Camille and she recognised the deep tension beneath well hidden.

'An obituary.'

'No, my side of things.'

She left it off there.

They then spent another hour, and another bottle of Chianti, going over the "foolproof" plan and everything. To try to make sense of the theories and then Camille put Trent's thoughts into a coherent format for Kev Bloomer and maybe others. He then tried on Bomber's underwater gear. Camille laughed at the sight of him! Finally, they finished. 'Oh, by the way, do you need any clothes washing? For your next adventure?'

'No, I'm alright, thanks, packed enough for a week. Anyway, I'm not a total stranger to a launderette.' He smiled. 'Thanks for all your help.'

She looked at him. 'You look tired. Come on, time for bed. Might take some time to get Bombers underwater stuff off.' She took him by the hand and led him to the bedroom. How much sleep would they get? Anyway, a smidgen of sentiment with love perhaps…

Chapter Twenty-Four
To Wales, 2 November

Philip Trent was up at 6.10am, having set the alarm. Camille was still asleep, never an early riser. A shower, a coffee, and he was on his way. He felt surprisingly refreshed after all the recent adventures and a very interesting night with Camille. His mind was now on Wales, the island and revenge.

A quick smoke outside and he set off. He took the Cortina and made for the A40. He estimated the journey at about four hours, traffic willing. He would go via Oxford up to Ross-on-Wye. Then on to Leominster and the A44 into Wales.

The morning was fairly bright, a nice early morning; a nice autumn day. The London traffic hadn't built up yet. In any event, it was coming into the city and he was leaving. He stopped the car in Marylebone Road and phoned the professor for his daily update.

'S-s-so you're off to Wales then?' The stutter was back.

'Yes, on this nice sunny morning.'

'Remember what the colonel said: observe, no action.'

'Yes, I remember.' He was non-committal as normal. The prof told him the colonel had pulled off the Outfit guards from his friends, citing the cost.

Trent again said nothing; he'd already noticed and anyway he didn't think it actually mattered now.

'Well, be seeing you, catch up later.' He put the phone down before anything else could be said, and set off again on his mission.

He put a cassette in the player. Camille had given him a Creedence Clearwater Revival tape. 'Here, try something new, you Luddite.' It wasn't bad in actual fact. With the music and his mind busy on his plans, the journey soon went by.

Finally beyond Kington, he came to Wales. "Croeso Cymru", "Welcome to Wales", said the sign. The Welsh language on signs was a fairly new development to encourage the traditional language and wasn't as yet in many places.

The landscape of fields and low green hills was the cultivated, the farmed face of Wales. There were cows in the fields, sheep dotted on the hillside and every so often a farmstead. In the distance were the dark, snow-capped mountains of the real wild Wales, and typically the bright autumn morning was giving way to rain, with dark, black clouds gathering on the hillside. Trent had always liked Wales and he could remember camping with the cubs near Barmouth so many years ago.

He had also come to Wales in 1969 on a job. He had been to Aberystwyth and Caernarfon at the time of Prince Charles' investiture. Spending most of his time at Aberystwyth, where Charles was at university. He was seeing Camille then and there was no Welsh "Poppy" to entertain him.

At the time, there were rumours that the "Free Wales Army", or whatever they were called, would make some type of attack on the prince. This proved to be all "hot air".

However, Colonel Stewart had dispatched him for several weeks to ascertain if there was a threat to the future Prince of Wales and King of England.

Trent had a nice quiet vacation in Wales and checked everything out. No real threat, beyond some demonstrating and a few holiday homes, owned by the English, burnt down. Everything had fizzled out.

Welsh rain was now threatening, clouds darkening and the hills covered by mist. He remembered a small transport café at Crossgates in a valley beyond Pen-y-bont still on the main A44. He stopped and for once had a pot of tea (he remembered the coffee as foul!) with an excellent sausage sandwich. Camille always suggested he eat more healthily and look after his diet, without much success it must be said. He ate his meal and looked out the half steamed-up windows at the distant shrouded hills and the smattering of rain falling, then smoking a much-needed fag.

He kept half an eye on the Cortina where he had all his equipment stored, except the Beretta which was in his shoulder holster beneath his jacket.

In the café, there were a couple of long-distance lorry drivers, an elderly couple, and a pretty Welsh girl, in her early twenties, serving behind the counter. She was an attractive, very Welsh-looking waitress. The girl was short with dark hair in tight curls and bright blue eyes heavy with mascara. She wore a mini skirt beneath her café-stained apron. She obviously recognised Trent as non-Welsh

114

and had politely asked in English what he would like in her strong attractive Welsh accent. There was noise from the back kitchen, which told Trent there was a cook busy doing something.

The café was warm, too warm. He sat on a hard wooden chair in front of a battered table. On the table, there were sauce bottles—brown and red—and salt and vinegar. Not a place of comfort—faded lino on the floor, paint peeling on the walls. There was a clock on the wall, stopped, and a calendar from last year. The lights were on although it was still early morning. The lights battled with the dark clouds outside.

Not at all inviting, and he thought of some of the meals he'd had with Camille and Colonel Stewart. Still, the sandwich had been rather good and the strong black tea palatable.

In fact, the only real inviting thing there was the young girl serving with her attractive Welsh lilt.

Suddenly, there was a loud roar outside and out of the mist and drizzle, six large motorbikes appeared on the forecourt. There were old-fashioned petrol pumps adjoining the café with a completely separate hut to facilitate the petrol customers. An elderly gent appeared from the hut and started to fill the petrol tanks.

The café door swung open with a ping of the bell. Two of the bikers entered whilst the other four busily supervised the elderly forecourt attendant tending to their bikes. Trent finished his tea, watching the other two approach the girl. His fellow customers quickly made themselves scarce.

Trent knew something of the Hell's Angels following a mission involving drug and arms smuggling to the UK from San Francisco.

The Hells Angels motorcycle club originated in the US in the late forties. In Great Britain, there grew up biking gangs, but they were a pale shadow of their American counterparts.

The first English Hells Angels chapter was thought to have been opened in 1968. This supposedly follows a visit by Californian Angels to the Beatles' Apple HQ in London. A visit at the behest of George Harrison. A strange arrangement by the most spiritual and peace-loving of the Beatles. A visit that ended in disaster.

This crew from South Wales looked like the weaker imitation bikers, although they still wore Angel regalia. They rode Harley Davidson, wore full-face helmets to evade recognition, and leathers with patches which indicated their club location and rank.

The two bikers strode arrogantly across the café floor. Whilst a cartoon copy of the real hard US version, they were still frightening enough to scare off his fellow diners. They had vanished into the gloomy, dull morning.

One stayed behind whilst his larger, uglier (this was relative) companion approached the girl. He had long greasy hair poking out from his helmet and a straggly beard. His leather jacket had Nazi and Satanic inscriptions and his arms and neck were covered in tattoos. Both of them ignored Trent.

'Hey, darlin', teas and full breakfasts for six.' He had a South Wales accent which differed from the girl's local voice. 'Hurry up with you.'

To his comrade: 'She's a pretty bit of stuff, ain't she? Lovely tits. How about showing us what you've got, darlin'?'

The creature then pulled her from behind the counter and started to fondle her as she broke down in tears.

'Get lost, Grandad.' The face of a middle-aged cook appeared from the kitchen and then vanished again.

It was obvious to Trent that they were high on drugs or alcohol, or both. He gave a sigh. Here we go again...

'Let's have a look at yer,' the biker snarled, as he started pulling off her top. 'Whah...'

Suddenly, he was gripped with something like an iron vice and thrown to the floor.

'Get back to the kitchen, miss. Now, you ugly pig.' Trent stepped back and kicked the thug in the face very hard. He fell back to the floor out cold.

A feeling of déja vu—Africa, that girl in Hereford he'd rescued—those Chelsea thugs, even the fight in Paris. Saint George to the rescue, a damsel and a slain Welsh dragon. That familiar flash of light through his head...

The other biker was in two minds what to do, but looking into Trent's eyes, he saw something there he'd rather not see and hastily left the café.

The girl had now reappeared and sniffing; she said thank you. Trent handed a business card and said she had any more bother is there, then to phone the number, and ask for him. He'd written his surname in large letters on the back: *TRENT*.

The card said: *Goldsmith's, Southampton Street, Financial Advisers*, the front for the "Outfit" in London.

He left the café and hurried to the Cortina and drove off. He saw the bikers staring at him and surmised that this may not be the end of the situation.

Much better to get them away from here. He also noted the bikes were not Harley Davisons; again, cheap copycats of America.

The ugly one he'd floored now staggered out of the café. Well, he must have a thick head! This was just what he didn't need when he had to get to Aberystwyth and the island as soon as possible.

The next town was Rhayader and as he drove towards it, he heard the motorbikes start up behind. Let them follow him and get them away from the café and innocent bystanders as quickly as possible.

Making sure he was well in sight of his pursuers, he turned down a rough track off a side road which seemed to lead to nowhere.

Most of the trees down the lane had lost their leaves but there was a copse of evergreen trees at the bottom of the track. No one about, he turned the car round to face the main road, beneath the trees dripping with rain. He then prepared himself for the approaching bikes.

Chapter Twenty-Five
2 November, Journey to Aber

When the six motorcycles came down the muddy track, two at a time, they came upon the Cortina facing them, front doors open, lights on, shining in the muddy red pools on the ground. An empty Cortina!

The first two parked their bikes and approached the car holding crowbars as weapons. One of them—christened "Ugly" by Trent—seemed to be their leader. He looked around and muttered: 'The English bastard, he's done a runner, the chicken shit.'

He looked past the car, beyond the copse, at the fields. No sign of their quarry. Suddenly, out of nowhere, their nemesis appeared, dropping from one of the trees where he'd hidden covered in leaves. Six shots from his Smith and Wesson. The front two had their weapons shot from their hands in a spurt of blood. The other shots smashed into the petrol tanks of the two front bikes. There was no time for fisticuffs he'd been delayed enough already.

Before anyone could recover, Trent had a Beretta in his left hand, pointed at them.

'I'm ambidextrous. For those thickos among you, means I can shoot equally well from left or right.'

The first two bikers were on the floor trying to staunch their wounds and whimpering.

'Right, you four, patch these two up with a rag or something and get them to a hospital.' He waved his gun. 'Go on, move those bikes.' He pointed at the punctured machines, now useless.

'Hurry, I haven't time to mess about, get out of here. Oh, by the way, if any of you try to harm that girl, I'll come and kill you. Got that, Ugly?' The now completely demoralised leader nodded.

The four bikes rode off with two wounded soldiers on the back of two of them; a sober, cowardly bunch who had met briefly the Angel of Death. Hardly Marlon Brando and the Wild Ones!

Trent waited until they'd gone. He didn't think there'd be any reports to police with that massive dent in their pride. He then came out of the lane and swung the car in the opposite direction towards Rhyader. He could have done without the interruption to his Welsh odyssey. The real dragons to be slain were at that island.

He stopped outside Rhyader at a small post office with an antiquated public telephone (still with obsolete unused A and B buttons!). It was next to a GR phone box. There he phoned Camille.

At first, she tried again to talk him out of his plans, but she knew in reality that it was useless. More importantly, she had found a place in Aberystwyth which would provide all his seafaring equipment that they'd decided he'd need the night before. In fact, the only place in the area.

'It's all ready for you, Philip, as soon as you get there.'

'Thanks, where do I go?'

'White's Aber Angling Centre at the harbour, only place there is. Ask for Captain White.'

'Captain?'

'Yes, apparently, he runs boat trips as well during the season.'

'How much do I owe him?'

'He had to be paid before he'd get things ready. Don't suppose you've a credit card; no, too old-fashioned. I used my Barclaycard.'

He mumbled his thanks again. 'I owe you.' Then with a reluctant "I love you", they said goodbyes. (Still no good at this emotional stuff!)

At Rhyader, he left the main A44 to Aberystwyth. Instead, he took the ancient mountain road route. This went through the snow-covered Cambrian mountains and passed the Elan Valley, with its reservoirs and dams. Providing water for Birmingham a hundred miles away.

He knew the area as he'd visited the dams when the Welsh nationalists threatened to blow them up in '69, but it had all come to nothing.

The road was narrow and precarious going between the white snow-peaked black mountains, showing through the dark rain and misty clouds. Lower down was a land of grass, rocks, heath and bog, all covered with scattered ice. Some of the ice and snow also drifted across the road and he drove with care. Occasionally, out of the mists, a sheep lumbered into the road.

He passed a ruined stone cottage and then an old shepherd's hut—all abandoned—victims of the inhospitable elements in this wild place. He could see the rough road through the low clouds, snaking ahead, and then a red kite appeared, swooping high in the air.

About halfway down this treacherous road, he stopped and parked in a small layby. A mountain stream next to the parking spot was frozen solid; he pulled his large leather coat around him. Then collecting some of the equipment provided by Bomber Harris, he ascended the hillside, taking care on the slippery grass. The wind howling around him.

He reached a height well away from the road and he had a fairly good view of the area through the patchy mist. There was nothing or nobody in sight.

In a dip in the hill between large rocks, he took out the equipment. The Smith & Wesson he'd already tested with the bikers but fired it again. He then tested the Beretta and various other bits and pieces in a large holdall. The loudest being a selection of explosives.

The noise echoed in the valley below but there was no one about to hear and the wind at this height deadened the sound. Only some startled sheep were witness to his actions.

Satisfied that what Bomber had provided all worked, he returned to the car. Luckily without slipping and falling down the ice-covered gradient.

A couple of miles on, he approached the ancient Cwmystwyth mines. The crumbling skeleton of the abandoned mines standing in front of a black hillside—blackened by thousands of years of mining—silver, lead, slate, zinc, and copper.

A desolate ruined place of ghosts. A sad place where no birds sang and the locals rarely visited. A place where you could feel the ghosts, the shadows of people who lived, worked and died there over the centuries.

Trent slowly passed the place and suddenly, he could see in the mists the spectres of all the people he had killed and maybe of all the people he was going to kill. All lined up in the mines of Cwmystwyth, staring at him through the murk. Including his friends, recently added to the list of death.

He wasn't, what you would call, a superstitious person or someone with a conscience, but the events of the past week were now changing his perspective on everything.

The deaths of his friends and Trent somehow at the centre of things, were darkening his thoughts. This old mine was reflecting that. Cold shivers, cold thoughts. He put his foot down and quickly moved on.

Chapter Twenty-Six
2 November, Aber, Wallog, and Beyond

With a shiver, Trent shook off these maudlin thoughts as he approached the aptly named Devil's Bridge. Here, he swung north back to the A44. As he approached Aberystwyth via Llanbadarn Fawr, he stopped at a newish industrial estate where Prof had said Ajmal Khan had a unit.

Identified by signs, "Khan Import and Export" and "Zombie Plastics Ltd", he approached the building. All alarms and cameras were off, and the door tore down and hanging by its hinges. He kicked it aside easily and it was obvious, as the police in Birmingham had said, that the unit had been abandoned.

Like the one in Birmingham, there were a few empty boxes about together with a couple of injection moulding machines, but a search revealed nothing else.

So on he went past the new Aber university up on the hill; the November sun shining weakly, it not raining for once. He made his way to the south of the town and the harbour where White's Angling Centre was situated. The time was 12.50 pm.

Near the old harbour in the water, colourful buoys, red, white green, were bobbing up and down in the choppy waves. A few fishing boats were moored, and there was a ringing, tingling of the masts in the wind. Other boats were piled up on dry land, sheltered for the winter months. The water muddy grey, blackish green seaweed at the base of the harbour wall. In the distance, gulls were shrieking in the cold air.

Fish heads and tails lay about amongst piled-up lobster pots, and two gnarled, sea-beaten fishermen sat working, mending nets, staring suspiciously at Trent.

In the corner of the harbour, there was his destination—a run-down brick building, open iron gates at the front leading to a yard with a shop and workshop at the rear. Next to the yard in the water, there was a moored boat proclaiming "White's Aber Boating Trips".

They sold everything from fishing tackle, bait, nets, to dinghies and small boats. Also advertising "Boats for Hire" and also for the holiday season, boat trips. He parked in the yard and approached the shop.

Camille had ordered with her "new-fangled" credit card a small dinghy, which could be used with oars, or the outboard motor at the back. Also importantly, a small trailer to transport it.

A pimply lad with fashionable long hair was behind the counter smoking a cigarette, dressed in obligatory flared jeans and a flowery buttoned-down shirt.

A symbol of modern, albeit Welsh, youth. He hurriedly put the cigarette out.

'Diwrnod da,' he said politely.

'Good afternoon, is Captain White here?'

The lad switched to English. 'He's tied up at the moment; who is after him?'

'Can you get him untied please, my name is Trent. My friend, Miss Camille Morris, has ordered some nautical items for collection this morning.'

Trent's voice was polite, quiet, but the Welsh lad recognised *that* something behind it. Something the biker in the café had seen earlier.

'Yes, yes, Sir. I'll see if I can find him now.' There was a lot of grunting, cursing (in Welsh) from the room at the back of the shop. Then Captain White appeared.

'Prynhawn da.'

'Good afternoon, Captain White?'

'Ie, it is Mr Trent?'

He had a high sing-song Welsh accent, which didn't suit him at all. Captain White, the old Welsh sea dog. He was anywhere between sixty and eighty, whitehaired, white-whiskered with a weather-beaten, red-veined face. He was smoking untipped Senior Service, and his slightly tottering gait more to do with a bottle of rum in his pocket than his years at sea.

On his head, there was a sea captain's cap, in faded blue, with an anchor to denote his station. He was also wearing an aged battered sou'wester coat. Although called captain, he'd never been in the Navy, Royal or merchant. In fact, he'd rarely been outside Aber and the local sea routes.

'It is all ready for you, see.' He looked at Trent through watery eyes, a waft of rum in the air. 'Dafydd here will set you up.'

Then with a large belch, he sat down on a chair in the corner of the yard sheltered from the sea wind. His eyes narrowed as he watched Trent.

Dafydd wheeled out a trailer and started to fix it to the rear bumper. Trent suggested he stop smoking, mindful of the explosive content in the boot, covered by tarpaulin and blankets. (Bomber had told him that the stuff was harmless without proper detonators, but you never knew!)

'There's petrol canisters in the boot, don't want you to blow us all up.'

Dafydd stubbed his fag out and carried on with his work. Finally, he brought out a dinghy and affixed it to the trailer. Then handed Trent the oars.

'There's a storm coming, can feel it in the wind.' The captain now swigging from his bottle. 'You be a fool, indeed, to go out in this. Anyway, what you be doing? Is it a bet?'

'Yes, captain, it is,' Trent said with a blunt finality to close the matter.

Captain White was certainly drunk, but something shrewd and appraising in his rheumy eyes said there was perhaps more to this man. However, Trent's instinct was he was a man not to be trusted and in all probability involved somehow with the shenanigans on the nearby island.

Trent also noticed the expensive walkie-talkie hanging on the wall in the shop.

He then thanked the captain and his assistant, Dafydd, and drove the Cortina and its load out the yard, and out of the harbour.

It was now early afternoon, the weather still reasonable for the time of year. The sea looked calm but Trent was mindful of Captain White's words. There were dark clouds gathering over the sea and mountains. Yes, a storm was approaching.

He drove out of Aberystwyth and towards Bow Street in the A487 north. He stopped at the small hamlet of Bow Street, going into the local shop he asked about Wallog.

When going through his plan with Camille, she had sketched out a map of the area. From Aberystwyth going north, there was Clarach Bay and then the next stop was a lonely deserted beach called Wallog, with an equally lonely old house. A few miles further north were Borth and Ynyslas sands. Wallog was earmarked as the best site to launch his expedition.

In the shop, Trent bought a couple of packets of cigarettes and a newspaper. He opened up a conversation with a very chatty lady behind the counter. He said he planned to walk over the cliffs from Clarach Bay to Borth, bird-watching. He also asked about Wallog and the house; casually asking if it was inhabited or empty.

He then received a lengthy history of Wallog, who owned it, their names, etc., etc. There were two houses joined together and an old lime kiln there. Also, when the tide was out, there were deposits of glacial moraine which stretched miles out to sea as a shingle spit, also known as Sam CynFelyn. She said you could get to the beach either via clifftops or a rough track from the nearby B4272.

The upshot of the conversation, and the bit Trent wanted, was that the house was boarded up and closed for the winter. Which made it easier to utilise the beach for his setting-off point to the island.

He thanked her, drove towards Clarach and picked up the B4272 towards Borth. After a short drive, he turned down the small road towards Wallog, or should he say muddy rutted track! The car bounced up and down for about half a mile when he saw a small isolated side track leading to a dead end. The nearby fields were empty and now churned mud surrounded by bare trees, the golden leaves gone into the sludgy ground.

This was ideal; he reversed the Cortina into this turning and undid the trailer. He then hid the dinghy, trailer, and other items deep in the bushes there, to be collected later. He kept the wetsuit and Beretta. Pretty certain the items would be safe there; it also assuaged his conscience about leaving firearms and explosives about in the town (whatever Bomber said about safety!).

Driving a little further, he parked at the back of the old house. The sun, now gone, the wind was getting up, the promised storm was in the air. He'd better get a move on (cursing the bikers who had held him up). He got out the car with a pair of powerful binoculars in their case (also via Bomber).

The tide was out and he could clearly see the spit stretching out to sea. Now wearing strong walking boots, he set off towards the cliffs and the path to Borth. There was no one in sight anywhere, thank goodness.

He walked along the beach, through driftwood lining the level of high tide. There was a mixture of flotsam, detritus, including a large tree branch, a wooden box, old fish bones, feathers, and the skeleton of a gull. The wind was now whipping up sand into his face.

He then passed the old lime kiln and went over a wooden bridge. There was a stream running towards the sea and a small waterfall. He then was on the cliff path and a very steep slope. There were lots of ups and downs on this route making it a very strenuous walk and the cliffs were little used. On one of the ups he could see, despite the darkening weather, a fabulous view of the Cardigan coastline. With the wind getting up, it was blowing into the grassy slope, which vanished into the black nothing of the steep cliffs and sea below. Occasionally, he could see seals on the rocks, lazing or diving in the sea.

Restless waves crashed into the jagged black rocks far below, gulls circling and crying. Although darkening, the coastline was still visible, some remnant of sun shining down onto the sea and land. This created an ocean of black with grey patches, topped off by white-tipped waves.

The different light patterns creating a distant land of brown, green and black, with some autumn gold still persistent. Far-off random sheets of rain falling from the sky; distant scribble. Rain now constantly threatening everywhere.

The isle was about a mile from Wallog and a half a mile from the coast. He could now see it, the turbulent waves surrounding it. There was now a lowish tide, and he could some small caves at the island base, which gave him food for thought.

Then, suddenly, he was adjacent to the island. He knew the harbour was on the right side of the island with the boats anchored out of sight. He studied it through the binoculars and could just make out a couple of guards wandering round what he assumed was the garden built by "Mad Fred". He kept low in case someone there also had binoculars. He could also make out the house and lighthouse, gulls and evil black crows circling above.

And at last, he could see why the locals referred to it as Yns Penglog. There in the rock facing the mainland, the buildings above it, was the sinister shape of a human skull. Formed by years of wind, waves and driving rain—Skull Island. For the second time that day, there was an involuntary shiver up his spine. Yns Penglog, the place of revenge and destiny.

Chapter Twenty-Seven
2 November, Still Aberystwyth

After checking over Skull Island, Trent returned to Aberystwyth. He pulled up at the National Library of Wales next to the university. The Cortina now a rather mud-spattered careworn car. Up on a hill, overlooking the town, Trent took in the view of the bay below. There were now dark clouds gathering, precursor of a storm to come.

To the south, there was the old ruined castle then the harbour and beyond, a hill with a monument on. To the north was Constitution Hill with the ancient funicular railway to the café on top of the mountain. Then the river, Aberystwyth, mouth of the Ystwith. The whole town grey in the rain and with thoughts of the bikers and what lay ahead; welcome to Aberystwyth, Croeso Cymru; welcome to Wales indeed!

It had been Camille's idea to come to the library (what a girl!). He checked out old maps and admiralty and nautical charts, along with books on local currents and tides. This he cross-referenced with the data provided by the prof.

He then drove to the Belle Vue Royal Hotel on the seafront. He had been here on his last visit and he knew it had a small car park at the rear. Parking the Cortina, he booked in for one night.

After a quick wash, he went out onto the old Victorian promenade. A need to refresh and clear his mind of the night to come, of revenge, of the Zombie and further death. He breathed in the sea air, needing to calm down and save the adrenalin for later.

Like many British seaside resorts, the town had seen better days. A decline is seen with cheap, overseas package tours growing. Trent looked out at a rougher sea, the tide now coming in, and the rain increasing.

Along the front, desultory lights flickered as if embarrassed to be there at all. He passed the King's Hall with old posters on the wall, advertising old bands, some long gone. The Mindbenders, the old 60s group was the only one he recognised.

The pier had been wrecked by a fire and storms many years before and only the front part was operative, the rest falling into the sea.

There was an old naval mine nearby, a remnant of the Second World War. Painted red, it was now a large collection box for the RNLI. Trent pushed some coins in, always a sucker for a good cause.

The walk over the clifftops had built up an appetite. There was a Chinese restaurant opposite the pier; he remembered it from last time. Chicken fried rice, which he liked, with the bonus of cockroaches. He'd accidentally touched a cheap print of Hong Kong hanging behind him and the little blighters had scurried out, running up the wall of peeling paint. Happy memories; he'd give it a miss.

He then recalled a good chippie up by the castle and went up a road called Heol-y-wig to the chip shop. Trent then sat in the old ruined castle grounds in a shelter and ate the delicious fish and chips with his fingers. Aber Castle in ruins, the mine in ruins, everything he touched in ruins. A state he hoped to bring to Yns Penglog later.

Edward I had erected the castle, along with castles in Flint, Rhuddlan and Builth Wells. All part of his campaign to keep the unruly Welsh in order.

After various battles, and the castle changing hands from the English to the Welsh and back again, it fell into disrepair. The final nail in the coffin was in the civil war. Aber was Royalist and when defeated by Cromwell, he destroyed the castle in his ruthless policy of slighting.

It was now about 5.45pm, there was a nice little Banks' pub he remembered from before. This was the Nags Head in Bridge Street where he had two pints of mild with a smoke. Good job it was not Sunday, dry in Aber! (Although the locals would continue drinking at hidden booze dens). Then he phoned Camille with an update but not this time the prof, no more reporting back to his superiors.

Now nice and calm, he walked back to the hotel along Marine Terrace. The storm was building and waves were crashing over the promenade wall. An excellent night for taking out a dinghy. Not! Now high tide, he hoped to catch the low tide later. Before preparing for bed and some early rest, he flicked through his notes to get his head round things then checked an inventory prepared by Camille.

Inventory

- dinghy, trailer, outboard motor
- oars
- wetsuit/face mask/climbing boots
- diver's watch
- guns
- explosives/detonators
- grappling hook gun and climbing rope
- binoculars
- face camouflage
- water flask
- waterproof backpack for guns, etc.
- torch
- Commando knife

Totally relaxed, he put the alarm in the room on for 11pm. He listened to the sea outside. Now calm inside, outside a storm before the coming storm of the assault on the island. He fell into a deep sleep.

Chapter Twenty-Eight
2/3 November, to Skull Island

Nearly midnight, he was back at Wallog beach, the tide going out. He checked the time on his large illuminated diver's watch. The alarm had woken Trent at 11pm; he'd got ready with his wetsuit under his long leather coat. The puritanical hotel was locked up at 10pm and he had to get the owner up. He revisited the ruse used in Paris—an ill relative, had to leave, so sorry. He then paid in cash. In the car under street lights, he applied face camouflage. This would stop any light reflecting off his pale face. Light that could come from the moon or the lighthouse on the island.

The storm had subsided a little (thank goodness) and the tide was receding. It was a chilly night, no stars, but the moon was shining brightly on the water. He parked the Cortina at the back of the old, deserted mansion and picked up the equipment from the hiding place in the bushes. Would he see the car and trailer again?

He then carried the dinghy down to the shore over his head. In the dinghy were the grappling hook gun and rope and oars. The other items were in the waterproof backpack, except the luminous diver's watch on his wrist.

Trent then pushed the dinghy into the waves, the lighthouse flashing its beam out to sea acting as a beacon. A storm was still lurking; lightning flashed down the coast lighting up the blackened headland.

From his afternoon studies, he knew the currents should be favourable going out to the island (but not so coming back; if he actually did!). He switched on the outboard motor; it would never be heard above the sea, but he had planned to row the last bit anyway. Bouncing over the waves, he set off. He was not over-concerned with the trip; he'd done something similar in the SAS, both in training and in action. And in rougher waters he seemed to remember.

Trent let the dinghy chug along with the currents, the moon shining on black waves, the black island, the lighthouse on the other side, slowly looming. His mind drifted slightly to the only trip out of London he and Camille had ever had, which she had alluded to the night before, the trip to Dorset, a fine two days in the sun…and rain.

A large wave brought him out of his reverie and he then decided it was time to switch the engine off and paddle the rest.

The waves were boisterous and crashing against the base of the rock. He'd have to be careful. Around the bottom of the island, there were the series of small caves. These he'd seen earlier through his binoculars, and they were particularly noticeable now with the low tide.

He secured the dinghy in one of the caves where there was still room for it to float when the tide came in. He pulled on his face mask and waterproof shoes and slipped into the sea. God, it was rough!

Then he eased his way round the side of the island, gripping the rocks or swimming. He'd chosen that particular cave as it was near the harbour but still not visible to any of the guards. He swam round the corner to the boats, taking great care not to be swept onto the rocks and a watery grave.

There were now four boats lined up in the harbour. One further very familiar one, "White's Aber Boat Trips", no surprise there then! Swimming out to the larger one, Khan's yacht, he could see silhouetted against the flashing lighthouse two guards with sub-machine guns at the top of the steps.

He took in the view, treading water in the choppy sea. The steps from the harbour went up to "Mad Fred's" garden, where the bottom part of the old fort, the magazine, was. Then there were further steps up to the totally refurbished house, next to the lighthouse, overlooking the open sea.

The guards couldn't see him in the dark and he hauled himself up onto Khan's super-yacht. Then removing his backpack, he took out Bomber's explosives and set them up in the main cabin. He set the timer for one and a half hours, he then dropped over the side, finished his preparations, and swam gingerly back to the hidden cave.

He took off his mask, changed into climbing boots and took a few moments to catch his breath. Then taking the gas-powered grappling hook gun from the dinghy, he fired the attached rope and hook up the side of the cliff. From studies of the plans and his earlier observations, he knew the garden had a path to the side where 'Mad Fred' had constructed a sort of balcony to sit on at the end of the garden. This was well away from the house and out of view of the guards.

From his time in the library, he knew it was roughly 110 feet to the very top of the lighthouse and 20 or 30 feet or so to the garden. The fired hook caught on the balcony wall and testing that it was secure, he started the ascent.

Whilst the storm had abated, he was still climbing a wet, slippery surface, with a strong wind blowing him about. There were not any safety devices with this climbing tackle. Using full strength, he pulled himself up using both hands and feet. Finding crevices and ledges in the rock, slowly he made his way up.

Dangling from the rock face, he could clearly see the lights of Aberystwyth to the south and Borth and Aberdovey to the north. Lightning was still flashing along the coast.

Suddenly, a crevice gave way under his feet. Down he stumbled and slipped a few feet, banging his knee and elbows on the rock surface.

Damn! He regained his footing, still cursing, he rectified and pulled himself up. Only a few feet more…there! Got there!

Climbing over the balcony wall, he pulled the rope up, then checked his injuries. Only minor cuts and bruises, although there were rips in his wetsuit in the left elbow and knee.

Again taking time for a breather, he surveyed the layout in front of him, which was lit up occasionally by the lighthouse.

The path and the garden were now a mass of entangled weeds. A particularly virulent, strong and nasty-looking stinging plant seemed to be the most prevalent weed growing. A very appropriate plant for Skull Island.

He retrieved his Smith & Wesson from the waterproof backpack, and then gun in hand, he made his way through the entangled garden, dripping water.

On the walls round the garden, the old cannon placements could be plainly seen. A white elephant, the prof had called the place, and Trent could see his point; what was it guarding out here in the Irish Sea? Even taking into account the story of the French invasion some two hundred years ago.

In the fortress wall below, what was now the converted house, there was a rusted pair of iron railings which formed a gate, and they were wide open. Behind this was a modern steel door, also open. Either side of the door were small windows with iron bars in. Cautiously, he approached the doorway. Next to the door was an old worn-down staircase leading up to the house.

He knew that this entrance was to the ancient gunpowder magazine and shell store. Entering slowly, gun first, the place was completely empty and yawned at him.

The large room was in the shape of an arc and had been thoroughly modernised, the walls gleaming white with strong fluorescent lights. There were a couple of dozen boxes which on examination revealed automatic rifles and ammunition, and at the rear of the room was a setup that reminded him of the chemistry lab back at school.

A long wooden desk with technical and chemical paraphernalia on. This was obviously Khan's centre for producing the finished heroin. As before, he planted his explosives and set the timer as he had done on the boat.

Stepping back, he suddenly noticed in the right-hand corner, a little darker than the rest of the room, a massive tarpaulin covering a large pile of something.

Intrigued, he went to the corner and lifted the covering. Astonished, he took a step backwards. Quickly recovering, he returned and pulled off the whole of the sheet.

Bodies; a pile of bodies! By the look of it, all machine-gunned and by the lack of smell, he would say recently, no decomposition yet.

He recognised some of the corpses. There was Ajmal Khan, his wife, Gemma, and his aide, Ayub. From the photos the prof had shown him also the IRA man, the union man, and various other terrorists. Finally, on top of the heap, Captain White.

Nothing. Nothing surprised Trent any more and the only reaction was a slight raised eyebrow. He left the drug den/mortuary and breathing in the sea air, he took a moment, looking out at the distant dark coast. On the wall next to the magazine entrance, he noticed that it was riddled with holes from the machine guns and the black patches in the dark were the blood stains. The place of the mass execution of the supposed conspirators.

He felt no remorse for Khan and his motley crew and pushed them out of his mind. He started on the stairway up to the house above, taking care on the worn steps with the water still falling from the wetsuit. Upwards to meet the people behind all this and if, as planned, to wreak vengeance.

The house on top of the steps was a testament to Mad Fred's eccentricity.

He'd more or less demolished much of the old fort and built a thirties mock Tudor-style suburban house on top of the rock island. Built of pale red bricks, now faded in the salty sea air, moss growing on the roof. There were large bay windows and an Art Deco front door.

Trent came up the steps. At the top, there was a large privet hedge forming a tunnel up to the front door. Most incongruous, but there you go! The hedge looked in remarkable condition, until Trent realised that it was in fact plastic. So crazy; Alice in Wonderland land! Had he fallen down a rabbit hole? Holding that thought, he approached the door and then cursing, he slipped and stumbled into the hedge.

Getting up and continuing, he then reached the front door, all glass partitioned and stained glass windows; was it suburbia? The front door was wide open and he approached with caution. Suddenly, the hall lights came on and there were three guards in front of him, machine guns raised. Behind them stood Smith, smirking, pistol in hand. 'Drop your gun, Trent, and hand over your backpack.'

So, into the trap, the spider and the fly.

'Hello, Smith, long way from Paris.'

'Shut your mouth; in fact, I'll do it for you.' He swiped his gun across Trent's face, leaving a red mark on his cheek and a bloodied lip.

'Come with us.'

He was frogmarched to the back of the house where there was a sitting room, again in a thirties style. There was a wind-up gramophone, a wireless, a sideboard, a heavy wooden table and chairs, and a ticking grandfather clock. The only modern things in there were a bank of TV screens and a radio set for transmitting and receiving. Equipment of a much higher quality than what the average radio ham would have.

On the wooden table, there was a pile of belongings. Wallets, spectacles, a woman's handbag, and other bits. Retrieved from the corpses no doubt. In the middle, a pile of papers with green writing on them. By the side, a fountain pen and an inkwell with green ink.

Behind the papers, face to the wall, was an erect figure. It spoke.

'Welcome to Zombie's abode.' The figure turned round. Trying to create a nightmare within a nightmare! The figure was wearing a Zombie mask.

A familiar, well-spoken voice said: 'Sorry, I really couldn't resist that.'

He pulled the mask off to reveal the supercilious, sarcastic face of Colonel Alec Stewart.

Chapter Twenty-Nine
3 November, Yns Penglog

'Sit down, Trent.' Smith ordered and one of the guards gestured with his machine gun and Trent sat down in front of the colonel. With three machine guns and a pistol pointing at him, now was the time for discretion not valour.

'You don't look surprised?' Colonel Stewart looked disappointed.

Trent sighed. 'Nothing surprises me any more. I keep saying that. May I have a cigarette?' The colonel nodded and one of the gunmen lit a cigarette for him and handed it to Trent. The colonel also lit up one of his expensive cigars.

'Look, Colonel, I guessed it was one of you.' In fact, Camille had helped him come to this conclusion in her flat. Was it only a day ago?

The colonel's eyebrows raised. 'One of us?'

'You, Sir Richard Abbott, the prof, or all three of you. But mainly, you, I think.'

'Well, hmmph...not the prof, you got that wrong.' He continued from behind a veil of blue smoke. 'Well, so very clever of you, Philip.'

Strange; he never called him by his first name, only Trent.

'When did you first suspect, then, and why come here if you knew? All that palaver across the water, swinging from ropes like Tarzan. All a waste of time, you know.'

He pressed a buzzer on the table and two more of his henchmen appeared, carrying the explosives he had hidden in the boat and the drugs lab.

'You see these TV screens on the wall? Khan had cameras installed all over the island and on his boat. Very security-conscious. Now as you know, I'm not up on gadgets and technology. Just like yourself. But these were useful; we saw you planting the bombs. Evans here is an explosives expert and he has defused them.' He waved to one of the men.

Evans looked vaguely familiar; he could have been the one on the Paris roof with Smith. It had been getting dark though and Trent couldn't be sure.

'Yes, you have seen him before.' The colonel, laughing, read his thoughts.

'With Smith in Paris, believe it or not. Evans is also an expert shot.'

Evans up close would not be forgotten. He was short, stubby, a Peter Lorre lookalike in extra-thick glasses. He was like the assistant to Frankenstein in the Hammer film.

The thugs standing with Smith were skinheads from central casting. Followers of the fascist Adrian Joyce no doubt, who Trent surmised was up to his neck in this conspiracy. He had to admit though that they looked really professional, with an obvious military background. No easy escape then!

The colonel broke through his thoughts. 'We expected you, of course.'

'Captain White I suppose.'

'Yes, one of Khan's men. Knew you'd disobey the prof's orders to observe and it was probable you'd go to White's place for the stuff you'd need to get here. Only place in Aber. He radioed in on his walkie-talkie when you'd bought the dinghy. We then told him to join the party and then waited for your arrival. Would you like a brandy? You look a little chilled in your wet gear. Get him a brandy, Evans.'

'No, thanks.'

'We're not going to drug you.'

'I'm alright.'

'Those bombs—what were you planning? A suicide along with the rest of us?'

'I always thought it 50:50 myself.'

'Yes, well, if anyone could escape from the explosion, then I suppose you could. By the way, we're not going to let you, escape I mean.'

The colonel walked over to the brandy bottle on the old sideboard and helped himself. He took a drink.

'See, not drugged. I've always admired your tenacity; why I rescued you from the court-martial. Always thought you a little crude, perhaps. Must admit, I never thought you'd spot our subterfuge—'

'Who's we?'

'We'll come to all that in a bit. Now please tell us how you cottoned on to our plot?'

Trent went through all the thoughts that had crossed his mind in the last couple of days. What he'd discussed with Camille in her apartment. No harm in playing for time with this dangerous maniac.

'In Berlin, Ernie Johnson was shot by that harpoon, very specifically. My first niggle. Why not me? He also, on further consideration, seemed very nervous and stood by the window and wiped his forehead. Almost sending a signal to his killers.'

He continued through the chain of events as he saw them, and as he'd outlined to Camille the night before.

'Firstly, that bloody intelligence committee, stupid questions. Questioning my politics, my patriotism. My grandfather! Designed to wind me up no doubt, to confuse…Along with your green ink sarky comments on that report. All…all psychological to get in my head. Which worked to a degree.'

The colonel nodded his head and smiled, almost like a teacher to a pupil getting top marks, but he didn't interrupt.

'You then sent me to work with Steve, an old friend as you knew, in Birmingham. We then went up against this Khan, a most unlikely terrorist. Another one of your dupes, no doubt. Questions, questions kept niggling at me…That oh-so-convenient clue of Penglog in the warehouse. Why did Khan and his wife flee? And why burn the papers? It made no sense.'

Trent paused; he looked round the room at all the ancient furniture, and the grandfather clock, it had stopped; then with a groan, it started again. He swallowed and picked up the theme, the most difficult bit. He stared hard at the colonel.

'So the death, the senseless death of my friends, by you bastards. If it was to scare me off tracking Mueller, it would have the opposite effect. Killing me would have been the answer. But no, your intention was to drive me on in anger and make me the centre of the story exposing the so-called commie plot. Then all the convenient leaking of my past and encounters with Khan. I should have known at this point…'

'When did you first realise?' The colonel was genuinely interested; he flicked his cigar ash across the table.

'Not just then. Firstly, there was all the shenanigans in Paris. Alphonse pointed me to Wales, and then his death. Smith and his buddy shot Alphonse and the attackers, but seemed to miss me on purpose. I first started to be suspicious then.

'It was on the long trip on the boat from France that everything began to click into place. All my reports to the prof seemed to be leaked, the papers, Nationwide TV, it was all unreal. I thought possibly the prof may be involved, but I was certain at that point that you were. I realised, for some reason, you wanted me to come to Wales and I wasn't going to disappoint you.'

Trent paused. He'd not spoken this much for years. If ever! 'I'll have that brandy now please.'

The colonel nodded and Evans brought him the drink.

The colonel also had another brandy, relit his cigar, and turned those ice-cold blue eyes on Trent. 'Well done, well done, you've surpassed yourself.' He gave a mock handclap. 'And to what end was all this Machiavellian scheming about?'

Trent collected his thoughts, extinguished his cigarette, and continued: 'You needed a patsy, a war hero, with that damned VC. Someone trusted, above suspicion, who could first make all these reports about the supposed communist plot to destabilise Britain.

'A plot that involved funding a united group of terrorists and unions, and they were patsy's as well. You and your plotters then had all this backed up with the bombings, robberies and strikes, riots and such like. My reports to the prof were leaked to the press. Then the murder of my friends made me a focus. Sympathy from the country, what evil I was fighting; what a bloody hero.'

He looked at the colonel with disdain. How could he ever have trusted him? He knocked back the brandy. 'I guess that all this was to enable you to make some sort of coup against the government, as a right-wing group saving the country against the so-called communist/terrorist threat and a weak government. Though why you enticed me to Wales is probably beyond my range of thinking.'

Stewart smiled, an unpleasant sight. 'Well done. Camille always said you were cleverer than I thought, not just a brutal soldier who blindly followed orders. I should have listened.'

On hearing him use Camille's name, Trent started to rise angrily from the chair.

'Steady, sit down, easy.' Smith waved a pistol in his face, the machine guns also moving closer. He sat down.

The colonel continued. 'No one could ever call me a sentimental man but I've always had a soft spot for you, almost fatherly. I was against using you but was overruled by my comrades in arms, shall we say, and in the end, I saw the sense. You became the star of the story and that almost let's say romantic/ human element helped sell the story to the press, the public and the government.

'Going back to your earlier question, the "we" of course is Sir Richard, myself, Jones, Smith, and our man in parliament, Sir Adrian Joyce.' (Sir Adrian there was a surprise, not!)

'Smith is a thug, aren't you, Smith? But Jones is a real asset. Great intellect. He helped us put all the details of this project together. You...ha...can thank him for that! He linked up with Adrian Joyce whilst dabbling with Tory politics in Oxfordshire. Found they had similar right-wing views despite all that Latin! Then he went to work for Sir Richard and it all fell into place, so to speak.

'Sir Richard is the main thrust of it, and as you say, you and the prof, the dupes. Now if you're sitting comfortably, I'll tell you the full story, and you are so very privileged to hear it. Although, the last thing you'll hear.'

Chapter Thirty
Still Yns Penglog

Outside the storm was getting up again. Rain lashed against the suburban windows, the wind roaring and distant waves crashing. Far off thunder could be heard. The room full of oppressive, stifling heat.

In the strange thirties living room, there was a pause whilst Colonel Stewart readied himself. The only sounds inside were the ticking of the grandfather clock, the rasping of the colonel's cigar, and the heavy breathing of Smith in Trent's ear. Four guns were pointing at Trent, the colonel smiled at this, took a sip of brandy and then he began:

'We needed to show the world and the PM that there was an imminent communist-backed threat to our way of life. So we got Khan on board with a promise of a million pounds and our support to flood Europe with his heroin. We told him: no drugs in this country! He, with our help, then built up a network of scumbags—terrorists, republicans, left-wingers, the lot. He was then provided with funds to ferment anarchy and chaos. Supposedly, from East Berlin.'

'Where did these funds come from?'

'A mix of wealthy supporters, then later, the proceeds from the robberies. We still have piles of the money hidden away to fund our aims. Khan didn't know the political aspect; he was blinded by money. Just a common crook, dealing drugs.

'No, that's unfair; his smuggling route was clever, using this bleak Welsh coast where not much is watched. He brought the raw opium into Marseilles and sold it to suppliers across Europe. For this country, however, he brought it to this island and converted it to heroin himself. Then with the late Captain White's help, got the drugs over to the unit in Aber. Then distributed it with the drugs hidden inside the plastic masks and novelty toys. Latterly, we used the same route to smuggle arms into the country. We've built up a massive arms cache for our plans.'

'To what end?'

'Patience, patience; never your strong point, hey?' The colonel had taken to pacing the thirties living room, his eyes now fanatical as he warmed to his theme, the cigar and brandy abandoned. Trent yawned and affected an indifference, which he didn't entirely feel.

'So we sought to create a reign of terror, aided by the press and TV, and some sympathetic newspaper editors, with a hint of Irish and Islamic terrorism. The bombs sorted by our explosive genius Evans here and your friend Z, or Mueller whatever, masterminded the robberies. The left-wing unionists weren't averse to a bribe either and they stirred up strike actions, as it also suited their aims.

'Then the fake microdot you brought back allowed the prof to put together his report on the plot and everything happening, which we fed to the PM and the cabinet. Bolstered by your reports and the publicity surrounding you. Independent agent, you, and independent intelligence analyst, Prof, helped to keep things moving nicely. Both of you totally above board, beyond reproach. Ha ha!'

Trent had half an eye on the gunmen, all focussed on him, professional, no chance of escape there.

'So how did you get Johnson to bring me that disinformation from East Germany?' He asked.

'We gave him all the info and microdot. Told him a cock and bull tale about you being a suspected traitor and we were testing you out. Also money talks and we gave him a small bonus; Johnson came cheap.'

The storm outside grumbled on, the lightning flashed closer and thunder was heard above the sea and rain. All very appropriate. All very hackneyed.

'So then you had Mueller kill him?'

'Yes, he was told to make a signal that when he was safe and had handed over the dot; it was a signal for his death.'

'I assume he was killed so he wouldn't give himself away?'

'Absolutely.'

'How come this Mueller/Zombie works for you and where is he now?'

'Mueller works for money—mega, mega-money, which is what he gets. We knew of him for a long time and recruited him from Cuba. His scarred face, the Zombie nickname, Khan's masks, it sound amusing to put together. Something for the press to latch on to. Oh, and in answer to your question, where is he? Mueller is working on the next part of our project.'

'So you then moved on to sending me to Birmingham.' Trent uncomfortably adjusted his seating position, the Zombie guns went immediately in his face.

'No movement,' Smith spat, waving his pistol.

'My God, Smith. You're ugly up close and your breath stinks.' Trent tried to get a rise out of him.

Smith angrily raised his gun to deliver a pistol-whipping. The colonel gestured him to stop. Smith sulkily nodded and the colonel returned enthusiastically to his theme.

'Yes, Birmingham; you were to find the Penlog clue, all a bit OTT, all a bit Boy's Own, but it seemed to work. Point you towards here.'

'Why did you get Mueller to kill Steve and Jackie?' Trent's face did not move a muscle. He wasn't giving them the satisfaction of his true feelings.

'I was against it but I was again overruled by the others. It was Jones' idea. You would be driven by rage and not raise too many questions, and it worked, up to a point. (If he ever got out of here, Jones would get his comeuppance; all his ideas, the Latin-spouting bastard!)

The colonel continued. 'Also, we were going to leak to the press. You became the narrative. The brutality of the murder and the VC hero tracking down the enemies of the country. Great news story, great report to the PM, which with the publicity hoo-ha, he couldn't ignore.'

Ignoring the guns, Trent took a drink of the brandy. 'Then I suppose you got Alphonse involved to tell me more lies?'

'Yes, Alphonse would point to Khan as the focal point, with his smuggling operation bringing weapons into Britain via Marseilles. He would highlight Wales and also Khan meeting communist agents, all rubbish of course. Alphonse wasn't happy to go along with this. So we blackmailed him with his penchant for girls below the age of consent, also with photos. Also, money helped. As it does. Shame about Alphonse, a useful agent.

'We killed him, again in case that mysterious elusive thing of a conscience surfaced and he told you the truth. Again good copy for the papers and Prof's reports. Knew once he was killed, you'd come back to blightey and go to Wales for your revenge. We also had the photos of Khan and his men on the island, which we obviously organised. These we used in conjunction with the Number 10 reports.'

Trent asked for another cigarette. The colonel nodded and he was given one. He drew the smoke deep into his lungs and it helped him relax. He said: 'So with all that happening to me and the problems in the country, you had enough to convince the government that you and your kind should take control.'

'We're nearly there with the cabinet, nearly there.' The colonel briefly looked at the storm outside then continued. 'You were right about a couple of things as well. I showed you that report on you, let you read it upside down to unnerve you and also to show that you were beholden to the Outfit and to me, in the right job.

'Also you continually asked why weren't you killed if you were the threat. We hoped in your sorrow and rage, you wouldn't think too clearly. We underestimated you there, however, you still turned up here.'

'Yes, why did you want me to come here and obviously expected me to?' Trent eyed him through the cigarette and cigar smoke, hanging in the air.

'Yaas, interesting; gets interesting now. We need to push the PM to sign that order for Sir Richard to take control of a combined military, intelligence and civil force to save the country, and we're nearly there. Your final report will be the icing on the cake.'

'My report?' Trent stubbed the cigarette out.

'The story that will be told,' Colonel Stewart continued, his fanaticism glaring out. 'You came to Wales and the island in pursuit of your investigations. And again, you reported to Prof before you set off. You were to follow up the Khan links and his contacts with the terrorists. There at his drug den, you discover further things about the plot and as is your wont, you escape and make it back to the mainland.' The colonel permitted himself a smile.

'You then report directly to me as the info is so important. On the top-secret line direct to my home. I then submit the final report to the PM and again, it's leaked to the papers. Then sadly, you will be killed.'

He paused for effect, looked at his watch. 'In fact, you've already "escaped" from here, the report's gone to the PM and the morning papers will carry the story: "VC hero saves the country, now missing, believed killed in the line of duty", or something like that. Then later, you'll be found dead. The tragic hero....ha ha. The PM is ready to sign the order for Sir Richard's combined forces and nothing can now stop us. We'll take over the country and run it as it should be run.'

Chapter Thirty-One
Yns Penglog

Another pause, a deep sigh, and the colonel continued.

'Your body will be found later today on the sand dunes near Borth, at Yynslas, your dinghy nearby. A half-hour telephone call from an isolated phone booth near there was made last night to my number, supposedly from you. Evans went and did that. This was your supposed report to me. If anyone ever checked, which I'm sure they won't, it'll look as if you contacted me. Then it'll look as if you were later caught and shot. We'll get the police to check the dunes later.'

'Fascinating; you must all be totally doo-lally to come up with that. Seems all so over-complicated, like all your plotting. Can't you keep it simple?'

'Maybe, but the PM has come to trust your reports and with the press looking on, he'll now sign. So complicated or not, it's working. Again thanks to Jones.'

'What did my final report say then?'

'Simply that all previous fears of a widespread communist plot are true. That Khan is overseeing all these anti-British elements and following their campaign of terror, they now plan the final coup de grace.'

'Which is?'

'Ay, yes, the coup de grace. Well, it's 5 November, the day after tomorrow, so you can probably guess...'

'You're going to blow up parliament and blame Khan and his mates.'

'Well, that's what it'll look like following your report. But if you knew history, and nobody ever properly does, the Gunpowder Plot was actually to kill King James the First. A Catholic plot. Parliament happened to be the location of the king.'

Trent was incredulous as it hit him what was planned. He stuttered: 'Y-y...you're going to kill the Queen?'

'Absolutely, old boy. Excuse me, all this exciting talk makes me thirsty.' Stewart refilled his glass and also topped up Trent's. The guards stood still around Trent, like Madame Tussaud's statues.

'You really are mad.' He drank some more brandy; God, he really needed it! Madness everywhere!

The colonel continued. 'As I say, your report just sent to me…ha…will point them towards parliament, but we will actually kill the Queen.'

'But why? I thought you were patriots doing this for the country. She's your Queen! For God's sake!'

'I'll come to that but…'

'And why kill Khan and his gang, had they outlived their usefulness?' Trent interrupted as the thought struck him about the pile of bodies in the drug den.

'Happy to put them out of the way; also we were finished with them. Khan was scum, a drug dealer and the others a blight on humanity. We enticed them here for a final strategy meeting on the "Red" plot and then executed them…no loss. Under a new regime, all such dregs as him will be eliminated. Also got rid of some potential left-wing threats to our plan going forward.

'We will shortly bury them far out to sea with weights. But I digress.' He'd been pacing as he told his story, but now the colonel suddenly seemed tired. He rubbed his eyes, yawned, and finished up his drink.

'I've really enjoyed telling you all this, Trent, Philip. It's a shame that you'll soon be leaving us; now then…er to the final part of our story.' He looked genuinely sad; the hypocritical bastard.

'We go back to the failed coup of '67 against Wilson's government. Sir Richard and myself brought in to sniff out any future plots; joke, ha. Sir Richard had sympathy for the plotters and was peripherally involved, and so was I. So to some extent our plot was an extension of '67. We'd learnt from that, and needed to show a threat to the nation, that we'd then overcome and our coup would gain public support.'

The tiredness gone, his fanatical glint was back. 'You talk about the Queen, about patriotism.' His voice rose, spittle in the air.

'Queen Elizabeth II has presided over the dismantling of our empire and our way of life. She is a symbol of failure. So she will die, to the country, at the hands of our enemies, but in reality to true patriots.'

Trent still couldn't believe what he was hearing. He shook his head, unable to respond. All lunacy!

The colonel continued. 'We will replace her with the Duke of Windsor, Edward VIII. Although frail, he will become a symbol of our new nation. People will forget his abdication, years ago.'

'What? He'll never agree. Replace his niece?' Trent finally found his voice.

'He will. We have been in discreet discussions with contacts of his wife, Wallis Simpson; she would love to be Queen. As far as Edward is concerned, he will replace a queen murdered by terrorists. This may only be temporary. We look at the strong men of the hard right, dictators. Men like Franco in Spain, Salazar in Portugal, and other South American presidents. Also South Africa; particularly South Africa. This may be the future model for our leadership. Look at what's happened to our country since the war…'

Colonel Stewart then expounded in detail what was wrong with Great Britain, to the background tick-tock of the old grandfather clock, to the background swish of the sea.

'The greatest empire the world has seen now, lost, except for a few outposts. Patriotism, and except you, I must say, sneered at derided, old hat passé whatever. And so it goes on: A quasi-socialist government, weakening of our armed forces, strikes, drugs, hippies.' He stopped for breath, his gimlet blue eyes daring Trent to contradict.

'The devaluation of pound sterling, cosying up to the…' He spat on the floor. 'EC/Europe to join their club. The growth of republicanism…

'Immigration. Small things, like not standing up for the national anthem. Decimalisation (and even you hated that!), the satire on TV, mocking our institutions—no respect, no pride!' He shouted the last bit, then went quiet, almost of whisper of regret. 'So you see, it's all got to change, and it's a shame you couldn't join us—an excellent soldier, but we knew it would be too extreme for you and your world view would be too narrow.

'Still,' he cheered up. 'You've played your part—yes, an excellent part.'

Misty-eyed again. 'We can erect a statue to you—the hero, the martyr, outside parliament…ha.'

Trent finally interjected: 'Madness, it's total madness. You can't believe it'll work. You can't turn the clock back!'

'Oh yes, we can.' His misty eyes were gone in a flash. 'You don't realise how much effort and planning we've put in. The PM will now sign the authority for Sir Richard to lead the combined force against the plot. Sir Richard will then have a final briefing at his place, the Manor House; tomorrow, yes, hmm…that's fourth; losing track.' He continued, 'This briefing will consist of all our leading supporters—judges, Lords, police chiefs, civil servants, generals, editors, Uncle Tom, and all.

'Sir Adrian Joyce will be there and some of his private army, his militia recruited via the National Socialist Party. Fully armed via our friend Mr Khan and trained. New name by the way: Great Britain National Party. Very snappy…as these moderns say.'

Trent shook his head. 'Sounds like a load of deluded fascists; Nazis!'

'No, not Nazis, although some of their ideas were good. No death camps, no pogroms against the Jews, no Adolf Hitler. Although homosexuality will be banned and a few other undesirables. Maybe gipsies; we'll see.

'Back to the story…following your "report", we will put extra security in parliament to pull the wool over everyone's eyes. However, our real target will be at Swindon, where Her Majesty will be opening a new library on 5 November; fireworks, that'll be. Ha!

'That will be the catalyst. Our new forces will swing into action to avenge the Queen's death against the red devils. We will control the armed forces, intelligence services, the judiciary, and police, then the press. What do you think so far?'

Trent couldn't answer. His head was whirling with the detail. It was so audacious, they may pull it off. All he could do was shake his head again. He beckoned for another brandy and drank it back in one.

The colonel smiled one of his smiles. 'Yes, hard to believe, left you speechless. In fact, my voice is tiring, read this. I scribbled down a few of our next moves as we swing into action and some of our long-term objectives. Thought you might be interested as you've helped bring them about. Here's a copy.' He handed over some sheets of paper and then refilled his glass.

As a captive audience, Trent couldn't argue as Colonel Stewart handed him sheets of paper. 'This will form the basis of the meeting at Sir Richard's place; he and Sir Adrian will present. Jones is getting everything ready now.'

Trent again shifted in his seat, the gunmen still eyeing him warily, and then he read the most incredible and concise piece of writing—the destruction and then rebuilding of the UK—all written in Colonel Alec Stewart's trademark green ink.

Chapter Thirty-Two
Actions Following Assassination

(The colonel's notes)

- Spirit Prince Charles away for his own "safety"
- Arrest PM, Cabinet and many MPs (unspecified charges at this point)
- Close parliament
- Take over civil service, local councils, etc.
- Take over armed forces, police
- Take over TV, radio stations and press
- Arrest potential opponents
- Including any in the police/armed forces, etc.
- Move army into cities to support the police
- Arm the police
- Further support from Sir Adrian's armed private army
- Put Navy and Air Force on alert; war footing
- Put strict curfew in place
- Set up interim government, Sir Adrian's new GB National Party

Party
Long-term objectives

- New Great Britain for the future
- Police/ military state
- One-party system: GB National Party
- Run by central committee and dictator
- Local government also run by committees

- Interim king a puppet for continuity; Disband Communist/Labour party
- No strikes
- Crush crime/drugs/hippies, rock & roll!
- Introduce apartheid system
- Copy South Africa
- Create second-class system for inferior races
- Move away from Europe
- Bring back pounds, shillings and pence
- Retain imperial measures
- Ban homosexuality
- Ban women working
- Build up army from conscription
- Wipe out by force Republican strongholds in Northern Ireland
- Reclaim by force the Republic of Ireland

'Once the assassination of the Queen happens, and a mix of our security, the armed forces and Sir Adrian's militia take control, then as you can see from the agenda we take over the reins quickly.' He waved the paper in the air. 'It is actually very easy to organise a coup in this country when you control the right elements.'

Another pause and he continued: 'We'll then arrest Prince Charles for his own "safety" of course. This followed by further arrests—the PM, the cabinet and many MPs. The charges will be unspecified at first. Parliament will be closed and then we go from there.'

Trent shook his head in disbelief. He had nothing to say but could only listen in horrified silence. The colonel was obviously delighted to have a literal captive audience.

'We have built up in the past few years a network of sympathetic supporters in the police, civil service, army and local councils. This agenda I've shown you is for the main players in our group at this final briefing tomorrow. They will then galvanise and organise our people below them.

'We are then poised to take over the armed forces, police, and all the machinery of government, with our militia acting as support. The militia will take over the TV, radio stations and press, and arrest anyone on our list of potential opponents.'

'A long list, I would guess,' Trent spoke for the first time.

'Yaas, a very long list.' The colonel looked annoyed at the interruption, lit another cigar and continued: 'Including some in the police, armed forces, trade unionists, church people. All types with soft, left-leaning, liberal attitudes. Collected lots of info on these people over the last year. We then move in the army to support the police and our men in all the major cities.

'We will instruct all chief constables that the police to be armed. We will then put the army, navy and air force on a war footing.'

The colonel knocked cigar ash to the floor. He still looked like an ordinary English ex-military gentleman, but a tic had appeared in his right eye. He wiped his mouth of spittle, fanatical eyes staring.

'Our next part of the plan is to put a strict curfew in place and set up an interim government—Sir Adrian's new National Party with no opposition. All supposedly a temporary measure following the Queen's death and the threat of the communist plot.'

'But it won't be temporary, will it?' was Trent's only comment. The old-fashioned room faded, the storm blanked out. He was back in the Outfit's offices in Southampton Street where the colonel had sent him on many missions. Trent had been loyal and obedient, and his reward: treachery, the deaths of his friends, and his death imminent.

The voice he knew so well, sarcastic, patronising, now something else— zealous. Trent looked at him with narrowed eyes as he took up his topic again. The room was over-hot as the storm outside raged. Claustrophobic—with the gunmen close, and the colonel now a hazy shape through the cigar smoke. Looking at his notes, staring at Trent, he resumed.

'Our longer-term objective once we're in control is to create a new Great Britain for the future. And I emphasise the word great. Total central control, with a one-party system in charge and effectively a police/military-controlled state. All run by the GB National Party.'

The colonel was now on cloud nine as he imagined his utopia. They'd run out of brandy and he gestured to Evans for another bottle.

'Any comment, Trent?' Trent said nothing, as he had nothing to say, so the colonel sort of nodded, filled his glass and went on.

'The government will be run by a central committee with a president. Probably Sir Adrian. All local government will be by committee, but all subservient to the central one.

'We will have an interim king, a puppet, but no constitution. In due course, we'll get rid of the monarchy; too cumbersome. As you can see from the sheet, all opposition parties will be disbanded, strikes banned, dissent banned. No say from the uneducated proletariat. All power in the hands of those born to it.'

'You mean you and your ilk; your public school cronies.' Trent also signalled for his glass to be refilled and he took a swig.

'And why not? We were made and educated to rule.'

'What about democracy?'

'Democracy is inefficient and the ruin of many a country. It will cease.'

Trent raised his head. 'Rock & roll. What's wrong with that?' He said flippantly.

'Music of the devil, saps morality in the young.'

Still astonished, Trent continued: 'This Irish thing, what will the US think of that? All those Irish Americans?'

The colonel laughed. 'Well, that's the clever thing. We've been liaising with some extreme elements of the CIA and if we promise to support Nixon on the Vietnam War—military and vocal—they say he'll support us whatever we do. At least that's their promise, we'll see. Well, at least our armed forces would help there. Got no problem with fighting communists, they're our real enemy.'

Trent said: 'What are you going to do with Prince Charles and the PM?'

'In due course, the courts will find them complicit in the plot. The PM, a traitor. Charles desperate to be king. Complete tosh, of course. But they'll be tried and executed.'

Trent looked at his diver's watch; dawn would soon be approaching. Distant light could be seen through the windows across the sea; the storm was abating. 'Well, a very interesting fairy story. You're all completely round the bend. If you think you can achieve this, you're delusional.'

For the first time, the colonel showed anger. 'And you're a bloody nuisance! I felt that you should understand what we will achieve as you help. But you're too weak to want to be part of it. Now we have to deal with you. We won't tie you up or handcuff you, you weren't held captive, remember our narrative. You "escaped" and went to Borth to report to me. However, we are going to incapacitate you.

'Read this spy thriller, one of Fleming's, I think. Something from there I wanted to try. In the book, the villain breaks the index finger on the left hand.

Too charitable. We'll do it correct. We'll break it on your right hand, I noted long ago you are right-handed. That'll slow you down…Smith…'

The guns still pointed at Trent; Smith said with an evil grin: 'Pleasure.' Two of Stewart's men held Trent down, the others still keeping guard. Smith bent the index finger right back. Trent swore. 'F…'

'Now, now, Philip,' tutted the colonel.

Sweat poured from him as the pain increased. The whole thirties room becoming hazy.

Snap—crack—his finger broke and he briefly passed out. His anger at the colonel and everything bringing him around. He grimaced and tried to ignore the pain.

'You are tough, tougher even than I thought,' observed Stewart. 'Thought you'd be out for the count. Smith…'

Trent was hit from behind and he fell into blackness.

Chapter Thirty-Three
3 November Escape from Yns Penglog

Trent could hear far, far away the sound of the sea and wind interrupting his sweet dreams as he lay unconscious. Dreams took him back to Dorset with Camille. Their only holiday together and that only for for two days.

Memories drifted—cream teas, pub lunches, clifftop walks, April showers, their thatched cottage B & B.

They stayed near Bridport and on the second day, walked by the sea between Hive Beach and West Bay. A swim in the soft rain, making love in the sand, waves crashing. *From Here to Eternity*…almost…

Suddenly, the colonel was there, standing in the sea, no, walking on water; typical of him! Smoking his cigar, drinking his brandy. 'Hhmmph, Trent, up to your old tricks. Can't keep your mind on the job…ha ha ha ha.'

What was he doing in Dorset? Why were those horns growing out of his head? Why was he holding that machine gun—rat-a-ta-tat! And then Trent was back at the haunted Cwmstwyth mines; the ghosts still there, and there with them was himself—Philip Trent, staring back—forever damned.

Sweat rolling down his back, in his armpits. Dripping! The heat, blazing sun…mosquitos biting…the jungle surrounding the clearing. This wasn't Dorset, this wasn't Wales; he was in Central Africa.

The blood, machine gun fire, sweat in his eyes, couldn't see, the flash from the guns. Comrades down, a swerving run, more blood—blood, blood, blood…

Trent jerked awake, sweating, the pain in his ruined hand jolting through him. Where was he? Where was this miasma of despair? He had that recurring nightmare of Africa alongside mixed memories. It took him a minute to come around. He was in the magazine below the house, Khan's converted drug lab. He was on an old sofa—there for the lab workers he supposed—with an old blanket slung over him.

The pain was insufferable. And even worse, there was an ache on the back of his head where Smith had hit him. There was a bathroom in the corner; he staggered to it.

He washed as best he could and found a first-aid box. He strapped his finger with plaster and bandages, and applied iodine to the gash on his head. It really stung but he'd survive; his nan had always said he'd got a thick head!

There were a few aspirin, which he gulped down, and returned to the sofa. Someone (the colonel?) had left the remains of the brandy on the floor, which he drank to wash down the tablets.

Also by the sofa, some "saint" had left matches and cigarettes (for the condemned man). He lit up and started to smoke looking out the small barred windows at the dawn breaking over the sea. He looked at the diver's watch, nearly 9.00am; been asleep a couple of hours or so anyway. He fiddled idly with the watch, thinking about his next move.

The magazine door was flung open, breaking into his thoughts.

'Morning, Trent, Philip.' It was a smug, self-satisfied Colonel Stewart standing in the doorway. 'Excellent day for a revolution to start.'

He held up a newspaper, *The Times* (no *Daily Mirror* for him). Headline read:

"VC hero uncovers plot; now believed missing".

'Sorry, no breakfast in bed, but read this.'

Trent flicked through the paper—nothing new—all that the colonel had outlined earlier. By the colonel stood Smith, Evans, and four other "Zombies" (Trent had decided to call them that; seemed appropriate), guns at the ready.

Stewart gestured him to go outside.

'The gullible PM has signed off the state of emergency declaration. Sir Richard now heads the combined forces to combat our enemies.' The colonel was almost gleeful. 'Our little coup d'état is underway.'

It was a grey cold morning, a sea mist coming down and, salt wind blowing.

Trent could hear the water breaking on the rocks now. A gull crying in the wind. Crows cawing. He took a deep breath of clear air. 'So, what happens now?'

'I've been up for a few hours fine-tuning the speech for our followers tomorrow, the 4th, which I've faxed to my colleague, Jones, and he can add to it. With oversight from Sir Richard, when he's back from number 10 and Adrian Joyce, of course.'

'What's faxed?'

'A Xerox fax, new to me as well. You can send documents via the telephone line. I should really get up to date…' He paused, thinking. 'Anyway tidied up here whilst you slept.' He seemed almost accusatory. 'I'm now going with these two on Khan's yacht,' he gestured at two of the men. 'Smith and the others to bring the rest of the ammo, dump you on Borth Beach, and when he's dealt with you, he'll then get rid of all those other bodies at sea.'

Two of the "Zombies" (great name) stood now with machine guns on the steps up to the house. Smith brandished his pistol in front of him and Evans stood at the top of the steps down to the harbour. Trent eyed them; with the colonel and his two acolytes now to go to the boat, he had four left to contend with. All heavily armed.

Before he left, the colonel concluded: 'Now, sadly, truly, must say our goodbyes. I was your mentor, introduced you to London, arranged the mortgage on your flat and showed you the fleshpots, and of course, introduced you to Camille. You were a good agent, the best, but you must now die.

'Smith wants to shoot you slowly, give you maximum pain; the sadist. He'll kill you and put you on that over there.' He pointed at a stretcher lying by the magazine wall. 'I won't stay and watch.' A shadow passed over his face, some form of guilt perhaps. 'They will then take you to the dunes at Ynyslas and dump you not far from the phone box where you…hmmph "called" me. With your last crucial report…hah brilliant! Killed in a hail of bullets when the supposed communists track you and execute you.'

There was almost a tear in his eye, the old lunatic. 'So, brave comrade, soldier, I salute you.' And he did. Then he spoilt it. 'I'll send your love to Camille, ha ha. In person…'

Internal rage burnt. Trent clenched his fist on his good hand. He then steadied himself, still ignoring the pain in his right hand. The colonel and his two men went down the steps to the harbour, the boats and large yacht still visible; the mist thinly floating around the vessels. The other four remaining guns bristling.

'Right, Trent, finale time,' Smith, the bastard, snarled.

Trent could see the colonel and the two men below get onto Khan's yacht.

He looked at his watch.

'Seems to have stopped.' He fiddled with it with his left hand.

Smith raised his gun.

BANG! Explosion!

Blast at the harbour below, the bottom steps collapsed.

The massive detonation ripped through Khan's yacht and the nearby boats, flames in the air.

Black smoke rolled across the ocean, burnt driftwood drifted.

RIP—the colonel and co, buried at sea. Good riddance to insane rubbish. For Steve, Jackie, and others.

Smith, shocked, reacted. 'What the f...?' He spluttered. 'What have you done?'

'Me, nothing. Must be a fuel tank or something.'

Another twiddle of the watch. Bang! Another explosion!

The two guards on the steps up to the house blown aside in the eruption.

The parochial, pastiche, the mockery of suburbia—tottering, rocking.

Debris was falling; Smith, astonished, took his eyes off Trent. Evans, still in shock from the colonel's demise, his gun pointed down.

Another bang!

Trent and his Glasgow kiss hit Smith with his forehead on Smith's chin. With one quick movement, he grabbed Smith's gun in his good left hand, shot him, swivelled and shot the befuddled Evans.

All done in seconds, automatically, no time to think.

'I'm ambidextrous! That wasn't in the colonel's records, was it?'

A loud crack behind; the house was collapsing and falling into the magazine below. Flames and smoke were billowing.

Burning stuff was now falling into the drug lab. God, there was all that ammo in there!

Flinging the gun aside, he jumped over Evans' body and sprinted through the garden of weeds, the garden of death, and reached the balustrade on Mad Fred's terrace.

Left-handed, he vaulted over the railing, the sea far below, the ammunition exploding in a tsunami behind him.

Chapter Thirty-Four

The colonel loved to say that he couldn't be bothered with new-fangled gadgets. 'Stuff of the spy movies,' was his derisive sneer. Should now be his epitaph.

Trent banked on this when he obtained the explosives, also the fact that the colonel did not know about Bomber, his extra curricular armourer. Two of the bombs and detonators were meant to be found as decoys. The other two—the surprise—was a limpet mine device and the other disguised as a dead animal, a rat.

These were ignited by a complicated electronic mechanism hidden in the diver's watch (beyond Trent's technical knowledge, though he trusted Bomber's expertise). The watch workings were apparently only a small part of the inside, the rest being the remote detonator. This was set off by an extra button on the side of the watch. Held in for ten seconds and then turned three times. It was set up to explode two sets of devices, and one set he'd blown up on the Welsh mountains to test and to make sure he could operate.

At Camille's apartment (how long ago was that?), he'd told her all his suspicions of his employers and his plans. She had followed his logic and agreed with his conclusions. She knew the colonel well and whilst appalled at his actions, she recognised his ruthless and devious streak, and his obsession with the British empire. She'd then helped tidy up his plan, even if she wasn't over keen on him going to Wales by himself. She'd then typed up a report on all their suspicions for Kev and his newspaper.

What he hadn't said in the plan was that if it came to it, he would blow everything up including himself.

A vague suicide mission, in fact, although he didn't think it'd come to that. If Camille guessed his thoughts, she didn't say anything. Not really keen on the whole plot, she didn't press the issue however. She knew nothing would change his mind and that this was his profession.

He guessed that Khan would have new modern cameras on the boat and all over the island, as he had in his other establishments. Even if he hadn't, he was sure they'd find his "dummy" bombs. As it happened, the cameras were there, easily spotted, and he placed the explosives in full view of them. He then dropped over the side of the boat and secured the limpet bomb on the underside, out of sight.

Likewise in the gunpowder magazine, he'd set up the bomb in full view of the cameras. Then after he pretended to stumble into the plastic bush by the front door, he deposited the "rat bomb".

Finally, when the colonel and the crew boarded the yacht, he'd set off the detonators and they worked! Also killing the remaining Zombies on the island, but the ammunition store exploded causing more damage than envisaged.

Whilst studying the island's maps/charts, he'd ascertained that the water below Mad Fred's garden was very deep and no hidden rocks. He'd earmarked a potential escape route, so when he'd leapt over the balustrade, he knew he'd have a good chance of survival. (More than the 50:50 he'd stated to the colonel.)

It was not an Our Man Flint-like dive, dignified and elegant, he'd dropped like a stone into the sea below, trying to relax to mitigate the impact.

He shattered the cold grey sea and didn't know how far he'd shot below the surface, nearly losing consciousness in the deep water.

Ears roaring, nose full of water, he surfaced. Coughing, with bloodstained eyes, spitting out salt water. Damn! The cliff had collapsed covering the cave entrance and obliterating the dinghy. As he bobbed up and down in the choppy waves, he became aware of the crashing noises, and rocks and burning wood hit the water around him.

He grabbed a piece of passing driftwood and clumsily pushed his way through sea and debris, and away from the doomed island. God, it was cold!

It was difficult with a broken finger and blood flowing from the back of his head to swim. He clung to the wood and kicked out his feet and awkwardly moved through the waves, the current biting.

Moving away from Skull Island, he could make out the remains of the house and lighthouse on fire. Screaming gulls and black crows followed the black clouds billowing to the sky. There was a further crash and much of the remaining buildings fell into the sea. The turbulence rocked him and he held tight to the driftwood as a tidal wave washed over him, soaking him even further. Somehow he kept going.

Freezing and tired, his finger aching, blood oozing into his eyes, he turned and looked at Yns Penglog just visible through drifting mist and smoke. No longer Skull Island, the rocks making up the "face" now disintegrated and the buildings completely gone. One of the boats drifted out from the harbour on the other side, burning as it floated out into the Irish Sea.

He looked at the lethal watch, no longer telling the time, and he flung the useless timepiece into the sea. He could see the nearer shore, the cliffs black and shrouded in mist, giant waves crashing on the ragged rocks. There was no way he could approach those turbulent waters, he'd have to continue on to Wallog beach. He took a deep breath and pushed on through the pain and battled against the raging sea.

Another colossal explosion and nearly all the rock island returned to the seas clutches. Further waves hit the bedraggled wreck that was Trent, he spat out salt water. It wouldn't be long before officialdom from Aberystwyth came to investigate, he needed to get clear of here as soon as possible, if he could.

Trent soldiered on, but didn't know how long he could last. Yet another mouthful of sea water! He could feel the strength ebbing out of him, a watery grave awaiting him. Wallog was still a long way off, steady, steady—must keep going!

Through the sea mist, there came the sound of an engine—phut, phut, phut. Was this a boat from Aberystwyth? No, surely it was too small. A pin point of torchlight could be seen sweeping over the water, then a dinghy appeared through the murk, heading towards him.

Who was it? He could make out the shape of the helmsman, a gun now clearly visible, replacing the torch. Was this another of the colonel's men come to finish him off?

Trent wasn't sure if in the mist and noise of the sea he'd been spotted. He abandoned his driftwood safety net and grabbed another small piece of wood floating past and took a deep breath. Dragging up some strength from god knows where, he dived beneath the waves and under the dinghy, the wood a weapon in his good left hand.

He came up out of the sea like Poseidon in Jason and the Argonauts, a nemesis from the deep.

Chapter Thirty-Five
3 November, to Rhayader

'You're not going to hit me with that, are you?'

Trent dropped the wood, fell back into the water, deflated and exhausted.

It was Camille, sitting in the boat, gun in hand, sardonic smile on her lips—calm, serene and as beautiful as ever.

'Someone's got to rescue you, Philip, been in the wars again?'

Dressed in bell-bottom jeans, a polo neck, white mac and wellingtons, she still exuded class, if a slightly damp class. She tutted. 'You've got me all wet, and look at the state of you. Can't take you anywhere.'

She took in the mess in front of her, holding on the side of the dinghy—soaked, his wetsuit torn and tattered, cuts and bruises showing. A broken mangled finger and blood dripping from his head.

'How's the masterplan going?… Mmm? No, don't tell me. Come aboard, try not to tip us over.'

She held out a hand and he manoeuvred himself into the boat, trying not to capsize it. 'Thanks, Camille, you're an angel. How, how come you're here?' He fell into her arms and they awkwardly and wetly embraced. Her nose wrinkled—he smelt of sweat, salt, blood and smoke. They kissed. The craft bounced up and down.

Suddenly, through the gloom, there was the sound of sirens and they could just make out a lifeboat and a police launch making their way to the cursed island. Presumably from Aberystwyth to investigate the explosions. 'I'll explain later.' She pointed at the rescue crafts. 'Let's get away from here, quick.' She pocketed the gun, a Beretta model 21 he noted, and started up the engine and turned the dinghy round in the direction of Wallog beach.

Camille rode the dinghy at full pelt through the rough sea and up onto the pebbly beach, tearing the underside and mangling the outboard motor. They disembarked, dodging the waves bursting around them, and made their way up the shingle beach. Trent barely able to walk and Camille holding his hand.

The remains of the island, the cliffs, the Wallog mansion, all shrouded in the smog of the sea mist and smoke from the explosion. Trent stopped for a breather by the old lime kiln.

'Not now, let's get out of here before someone comes. You're missing, presumed dead, remember. It's in all the morning papers, your potential demise, so it must be right! Bought a copy in Aber, you can read it whilst I drive.'

The faithful mud-covered Cortina was still behind the Wallog house and amazingly, the key was still in a wetsuit-zipped pocket. He made for it.

'No, don't.' Camille grabbed him by the hand.

'Got a change of clothes in there and some first-aid bits.'

'No, best if everyone continues to think you're dead. Particularly, your enemies. Don't touch the car. I've got you some clothes from your flat; you gave me a key, remember? Also bought some first-aid stuff.'

'I love you, Camille,' he blurted out.

'I know, I know. Now come on. I'll explain everything in a bit.'

Already there was the sound of distant police sirens heading in the direction of Borth. Had they been tipped off from some other of the colonel's co-conspirators that his body would be there? The waves crashed onto the lonely beach, the wind roaring, Camille's wrecked boat floating out into the foam-filled sea.

Still holding his hand, she led him to her car—the sports Chevrolet, normally spotless, now also mud-spattered—parked in the lane. A similar trailer to the one he'd used lay next to the car abandoned. She handed him a torch. 'In the dashboard, there's a flask of coffee and brandy. Now let's go.' Camille turned the ignition, pressed her foot down and sped down the rutted muddy track.

They drove some miles down a minor road; Trent was too tired for questions, too tired to read the paper. They parked near Penrhyncoch in the wilds, surrounded by snow-covered mountains, a fog descending; a real pea souper, not the thin sea mist he'd battled through earlier.

At Camille's behest, he took off his wetsuit, shivering as she rubbed him down. They buried the suit deep in some bushes and then Trent put on jeans, shirt, jumper, and an anorak. Then she bathed his head wound and put a plaster on it, and bandaged his finger. He then took some painkillers with the coffee.

'OK, let's get moving.'

'When did you get so bossy?' (When did she get so efficient?)

Camille then drove, very fast, down the back road towards the A44. Trent was feeling half-human, but they said nothing as they drove through the mountains.

The silence was finally broken. 'How come you came to my rescue?' He asked. The car, expertly handled by Camille, sped along the Aberystwyth to Rhyader road, taking the twisting bends in the mountains a little too sharply for Trent, whilst following the river Wye. Grudging admiration, however! He always drove carefully, no car heroics despite his VC, gunplay and other adventures.

'Listen, I saw your mate, Kev Bloomer. Yesterday late evening, he told me about the headlines coming out—your supposed message, then you missing believed dead.' She took another bend at top speed, Trent winced, then she continued: 'I know you weren't going to that island until midnight, yet that story was going to the printers before that.' She paused.

'I also gave him the account of things we put together for his editor, all of what we believed the colonel and his merry men were up to.

'But there was a "D" notice out forbidding any further news on the story. I knew the news story to be printed was all lies, so I came down here to see what was what. Knew I shouldn't have let you come here alone.'

'Thanks, Florence Nightingale, you're an angel of mercy. Y'know it would have been OK but for all that ammo there exploding, wrecking the dinghy. Hadn't planned to swim back with this bust finger. A flaw in the plan? Perhaps…' He was desperate for a cigarette but that could wait; he respected Camille's views on the wicked weed. Instead, he asked a few questions that had been bothering him.

'Camille, I didn't know you had a gun. Also, you turning up in another boat, how did you do that?' He was beginning to realise just how resourceful Camille was.

Slight pause; slightly evasive, she concentrated on the road ahead. 'Had one for some years, for protection. My mother encouraged me to have one; her Russian background. Also, I er…broke into White's boatyard and stole another dinghy and trailer, it was in the early hours and no one was about luckily. Thought I might need a boat…er…but was making it up as I went along. Then drove to Wallog took…er…twenty minutes. Was considering my next move when there were the explosions. You know the rest.'

Trent looked at her quizzically. 'How did you break into White's yard?'

She continued. 'Wasn't that difficult? The yard gates were open anyway and they'd left the key in the boat motor. Seemed to have left in a hurry. So easy really. Improvising; Ad Hoc as I said.'

A very impressed Trent commented, 'Well, White won't be bothered.'

He then explained everything that had happened on the island, including the bodies of Khan, White and others. The death of the colonel and also the plot to overthrow the government and introduce a far-right regime.

Staring ahead at the road and the mist topped mountains, she nodded in the right places and when he'd finished, made no immediate comment. After a moment, she turned and looked at Trent. 'What's our next move then?' He noticed the "our". 'We'll book a room at a local hotel in Rhayader, you need a rest. We both do. Also must get you to the Cottage Hospital there, get you fixed up properly.'

Trent had been thinking about what to do next as they drove along. 'This meeting at Sir Richard Abbott's place, the Manor House near Marlborough, for tomorrow, the 4th. This is the final briefing with all their main supporters before the assassination of the Queen. We need to find out what time this is going on and break up the party.'

'Why can't we warn the authorities?'

'Well, with Sir Richard in control, no one is going to believe a rogue agent, me, who's now supposed to be dead. With their plan to dump my body on Borth Beach literally up in smoke; they'll probably think I died in the island explosion. Best to keep it that way.'

'What are your thoughts?'

'I'm going to call up a few friends and make arrangements. A meeting at your place this evening if that's OK?' He scratched his head. 'Yes, that's it, and we'll first organise someone to watch Abbott's mansion place, before we get there.' His thoughts tumbled out. 'We'll need some way of recording the meeting, get proof of it all and then destroy them all. In the meantime, let's rest and sort out details at this hotel, but first some phone calls.'

Camille then drove into Rhayader, the cataract of the Wye, a historic livestock market town sheltered by the Cambrian mountains. Known as the gateway to the Elan Valley and the reservoirs there, and it was also the centre of an important local tourist trade.

They pulled up in the centre by the town clock and Trent then "borrowed" coins from Camille to make several phone calls for a meeting later that night. They agreed to meet at the clock in about an hour and then Camille went to find a hotel and booked in at the White Lion.

Trent phoned a few contacts quickly using up the coins and then having to reverse the charges, he came back after about fifty minutes and met Camille.

'All set up at your place for 8pm. Had a devil of a job at first convincing them that I'm still alive but they're all coming.' He pondered: 'Could really do with someone watching Sir Richard's place as early as possible. The colonel said the fourth but that could be any time after midnight; let's think about that.' He noticed the time on the town clock, 11.55am, nearly lunchtime. Camille noticed his glance.

'Yes, I'm hungry too. Let's get you to the Cottage Hospital and whilst they tend to you, I'll go and organise something to eat. Then we'll nap for a couple of hours and then leave for the meeting at my place.'

So a little while later, they were in their hotel room in the White Lion. Trent's finger was properly strapped up, stitches in his head, antibiotics and strong painkillers taken.

Camille had provided bread rolls, cheese, pork pies and crisps, and most importantly, a small bottle of whisky. Also feeling sorry for the invalid, she purchased some No 6 cigarettes and matches. 'Not in my car, though,' she admonished with a smile.

They fell upon the food and had a picnic in the hotel room. Trent swilling it down with whisky. Camille stuck to water. 'I'm driving; don't drink too much with those pills.'

'When did you become a right nag?' But Trent was also smiling. They decided he needed a wash the most and he went off to the bathroom; no shower, only a bath. Feeling about 75 per cent normal, he sat on the bed smoking whilst Camille had a bath.

After a while, she came out, a blaze of golden blonde beauty. She was dressed only in a bra and pants, and Trent despite his injuries, felt his heart racing.

'How about some personal loving care for the invalid?'

'You should rest; it can't be good for you, painkillers and whisky.'

'How do you know what's good for me? I need something not prescribed on the NHS.' He held his arms open, good and bad.

'You'll have to be careful with me.'

Camille slipped out of her underwear and got into the bed. 'Don't know about that. Hmm, not bad for a dead man.'

He woke with a start in bed, alone, some time in the mid-afternoon. There was Camille sitting in an old rocking chair looking at the mountains through the window. The fog now gone, they were clear and snow-capped. There seemed to be tears in her eyes.

'Are you OK?' He asked.

'Yes, been for a bit of a walk. I let you sleep.'

'What's the matter? You seem distracted.'

She looked at him, brown eyes, with sadness.

'What is it?' He persisted. 'You know I love you.'

'Yes, I do.' She paused. 'No easy way to say this, Philip...' Another pause.

'I'm also a spy, a double agent. In fact, technically, you could say a treble agent...'

Chapter Thirty-Six

He'd kept saying that nothing now surprised him. Well, this did.

He picked his chin up off the floor and a gamut of emotions flashed by. Trent went to the window and stared blankly at the Welsh snow-topped vista.

'Philip, please say something.' Camille reached out for him. Stony-faced, he pushed her aside.

'I suppose the gun comes with the job.'

'I know it's a bit of a shock, please come and sit down. Let me explain.'

She was obviously very upset and even the hard-hearted, tough guy, Trent couldn't bear to see her so. Her normal cool now banished.

She sat on the bed and he sat beside her; she reached for his hand; he didn't recoil.

'So tell me, Camille, Mara Hari. I know you did a bit of work for the colonel and spied unsuccessfully on me, but what else? And I'm going to need a cigarette I think.'

She didn't demur, so he reached for the packet on the bedside table and lit up.

'And so, let's have it.'

So she started. 'As you know, my mother was a Russian emigré; she escaped the Communists in the 20s.'

'Yes.'

'Well, about ten years ago now, mother was unwell. She was getting on and basically, we were fairly poor. So I took up, let us say, my current role to provide a decent life for both of us. Really, despite what you think, it's nearly all proper escort work. Being a companion for rich, elderly gents. Most of them are incapable of the physical side, or too drunk, or sometimes homosexual, using me as cover.

'So I built up a network, a reputation. It was then that the Russians approached me. They threatened to kill my mother if I didn't do some work for them. And I believed them.'

She stopped, walked to the bathroom and returned with a glass of water. She took a sip.

'Go on.' He took a long, blissful drag.

'I was already doing my job with top politicians, ministers, MPs, civil servants, lords, you name it! What they wanted was me to inveigle (and that was their word) information out of them. Any bits of gossip I could muster. Into Christine Keeler/Mandy Rice-Davies territory. I was so angry with them—threatening my old mother—that I approached the US Embassy. Finally got through to the CIA and offered to work for them as a double.'

'Why not for the British?'

'I think the country was only just getting over the double agents working for British intelligence—Burgess, Philby, Maclean, and others. I didn't trust the British as safe at this point, so I went to the Americans.'

'So what did you do for our cousins?'

'Basically, I fed disinformation to the Russians. All carefully prepared by the CIA people to look realistic but actually to do the Reds some damage. Sometimes they fed something that was real to make it all look bona fide.'

Trent interrupted. 'You've been doing this for some time now but your mother died some years ago. Why did you carry on?'

'I felt sort of trapped on a treadmill. But also, to be honest, I suppose I liked it and with the Americans and the Russians, and even the colonel sometimes, paying me, it was also useful. You know the lifestyle I like. The escort stuff doesn't pay that well; well, to the amounts I need for my lifestyle anyway. So I just went on with it and I guess it suited me.'

Trent, who hadn't been looking directly at her, now raised his eyes and stared straight at her.

'What about Colonel Stewart? How come that came about?'

'Somehow he gravitated to me in the clubs. Someone in the CIA let slip something of what I was doing. The colonel was always well-connected; anyway it amused him. He also liked to be seen around town with me. I was his vanity item.'

'Did you sleep with him?'

Camille gave her throaty, sexy laugh. 'God, no, the colonel wasn't interested. As I say, it boosted his ego to go out with me.'

'Is he—was he I mean—interested in men then?'

'No, I don't think so. I think he's what's called asexual. Not interested, period. Must have been all those cold showers and bromide in the army.' Another throaty chuckle.

Trent stubbed out his cigarette in a big, old-fashioned, metal, battered ashtray on the bedside table. 'Didn't affect me.' He interrupted, then carried on.

'So what did you do for the colonel?'

'He introduced me to you. To become friendly. At first on a professional basis but…you never gave me anything anyway.' A big, big pause. 'Then I fell in love with you…'

Both Trent's eyebrows went up and he felt the hotel room shake and move. She only rarely said this and usually in a wry way, this was more heartfelt and sincere. Despite this admission, he recovered and pressed further.

'So, you were to keep an eye on me for him, which I guessed anyway. Anything else?'

'I did one or two mundane jobs for him, chatted up potential traitors, as he saw it, went out with people he was interested in. As I said, working for three parties, a triple agent. The Russians, the Yanks, and the colonel.'

'What do you think of Stewart now?'

'Despite his stuffy military bearing, I actually found him good company. I think you did as well, if you're honest.'

Trent lit another cigarette, chain-smoking now. He thought of the introduction to the London nightlife, the fancy meals, wine, the clubs. A world away from Smethwick.

'I did; he helped me, how to put it, find a new way of living. Gave me a job I was good at (loved?), sorted out my flat and he introduced me to you.'

Another No 6 drag. 'He was a sarcastic old bastard, but I can't believe he got involved in all this, can you?'

He remembered the remains of the whisky and finished it off.

'You know,' Camille mused. 'In answer to your original question, I'm absolutely stunned at what he's done. However, he was always obsessed with an idealised view of Britain and the empire. He wanted the past back and this plot he must have seen as a way of achieving it. I also think that boss of his, what's his name, Sir Richard…?'

'Abbott.'

'Yes, him. I think he led the colonel astray on this one. I met him once in a club—smarmy git—tried it on. Gave him short shrift. There were two people the colonel sort of revered—this Sir Richard and you...'

'Me?'

'Well, not actually worshipped. He thought highly of you, was jealous of your exploits and almost loved you. Not in a sexual way, more paternal. "Best agent we've got", he'd say.'

'And then he killed my friends and tried to kill me.' He flung his stub across the room with some violence, missing the waste bin. 'Best agent be damned...'

'Yes,' Camille agreed, 'that certainly does put a different slant on things; good riddance!'

'Absolutely.'

Camille changed tack. 'Philip, do you forgive me?'

He thought briefly. 'Nothing to forgive. You did what you had to do. And never anything against me...' A pause. 'Wish you'd told me though.'

He held her; they kissed. He looked out the window. It was getting dark, the mountains disappearing.

'We'd better go; need to be at your place for 8pm.' He thought of Camille's driving compared to his. 'I'm sure we'll make it.'

'Yes, and we can talk further on the drive.'

So shortly after 4.00pm, they left the hotel and leaving Rhayader, they passed a sign, in English and Welsh. "Bonfire Night at the Park...Fireworks... Food for all...an exciting, explosive event".

'Yes, I think it will be,' Trent muttered as they swept past into the Welsh late afternoon.

Chapter Thirty-Seven
Back to London

Dark now, Camille hurtled down the A44 away from Rhayader. The rugged Welsh landscape behind them—the hills now softer and smaller—their dark shapes just discernible in the late autumn afternoon.

She drove past the small track where he'd tangled with the bikers; how long ago that seemed now (and something he'd not mentioned to Camille, yet!). She then motored on towards Kington. She flicked the radio on for the news, no mention of mysterious explosions at the island near Aber. No further mention of Trent and his actions, missing in action.

'They must have used a "D" notice to shut the press up. No way the press wouldn't have been all over your misdemeanours.'

'Trying to think up a story. Something that ties in with the rest of their narrative to the world I suppose.'

Camille then took a sharp bend suddenly, changing through the gears with efficiency. They drove through a small village; street lights temporarily lighting up the inside of the car. Trent could see his battered reflection in the dashboard—staring, grimacing back.

Leaving the village, he stared at the road ahead, the headlights catching the countryside's dark shapes. They caught an animal running across the road, it managed to escape and flee into the woods. He continued:

'The friends I phoned earlier to meet up later were Major Bob and Bomber Harris. Not sure I told you about Major Bob. I was in the SAS with him. He was kicked out.'

'Why?'

'Drink.'

'I'd have thought that knowing you, it would have been de rigueur in the forces.'

'I admit a few drinks were taken but not when on the job. Bob took it to an extreme and was drunk too often, on and off duty.'

He frowned, remembering. 'Good soldier though. When he left the force, he set up a very successful mercenary group, and he wanted me to join at one point. They're not working at present and he's agreed to provide assistance—not sadly just for old times sake—he and his men will need paying.'

Camille looked over at him, then returned her eyes to the road. 'You know some interesting characters, Major Bob and this Bomber gentleman.'

'You might meet Bomber later as well; he's bringing over the weapons we need to your place. The major is ordering them.'

Trent had told her about Bomber Harris when they'd discussed his plans for his trip to Wales and the island, and his suspicions of the colonel. He'd described Bomber as his personal armourer and someone he'd kept secret from Colonel Stewart. For reasons he'd never really understood.

'So Major Bob is bringing some of his men to your flat tonight, apologies! He's working on some ideas for a plan of action. Good man. Told Bob to tell his men to mind their manners. Also Kev Bloomer and Bomber. We'll then sort out this plan.' He looked over at Camille, her concentration, her driving gloved hands gripping the wheel.

'Hope it's better than the last master plan!' She observed. 'Anyway how do we pay the mercenaries?'

'I've an idea about that. We'll pursue that later. In the meantime, we need to get someone to Marlborough to keep an eye on Sir Richard's place, so we know when this big meeting starts. On the fourth the colonel said, but could be dead just after midnight tonight. Also, we need to set up some sort of recording device. We need to get evidence, proof of what they're up to. Proof we can give the PM.'

Camille then had the grace to look embarrassed as she said: 'Don't know how to say this, but, but following your mention of the need for evidence, I asked my "friends" at the Russian Embassy to already keep an eye on the place. Phoned them whilst you slept. They'll provide the latest in spy monitoring equipment.'

Trent was once again speechless. Didn't know whether to laugh, cry or show anger. Instead, he could see a problem potentially solved. Pragmatic, he said:

'Are they OK with that? Can we trust them?'

'Philip, when you told me the other night what you suspected Sir Richard and the colonel were up to, I approached the Americans for help. Although wasn't sure how we could use them at the time. Now they didn't seem interested and more or less told me not to be a silly girl and run along. Of course, I didn't tell them of your planned assault on the island. Don't really trust them.'

'Good job,' Trent said. 'It ties in with what the colonel told me. Some in the CIA gave tacit support for their project. Subject to future support for Nixon's Vietnam War.'

'Oh, I see; now it makes some sort of sense.'

'Then you went to the Russians.'

'Yes, at first they were sceptical, but finally came round. They were already annoyed and concerned that the press were blaming the Eastern Bloc for all the troubles. The last thing they wanted for Britain was a right-wing coup. Wanted it to swing to the left if anything.'

She swerved to miss a wandering sheep and continued:

'So they agreed to help when required, but not direct action. So I phoned them whilst you were snoring away.' She gave a small smile. 'They agreed to put one of their men on watch at Marlborough and also set up surveillance equipment. He's not one of their action guys; he's a watcher, a ghost. He'll show us how to work the equipment when we turn up. Make sure it records the main meeting hall; he'll help, but mainly an observer.'

His admiration for the woman he loved rose even further. He grunted an acknowledgement. He then realised he was dog-tired, not had much proper sleep since God knows when. Camille in contrast was still wide awake, almost fresh; not affected, she drove on.

He collapsed into sleep as Camille put her foot down towards London.

Chapter Thirty-Eight
London

Trent and Camille arrived back in plenty of time for the 8pm meeting. Wash, brush-up and cup of coffee. Camille then phoned her contact at the Russian Embassy. They had agreed that some of Major Bob's men needed to be with the Russian observer as soon as possible. Trent didn't think this "big meeting" at Sir Richard's house would start bang on the start of the fourth, after midnight. His money was on sometime the next evening. But better to be safe…

Camille had made the phone call in the bedroom; she came back with a smile on her face. Trent felt a sharp unusual tightening of his chest. How beautiful she was; how lucky he was. Was this really love?

She laughed, deep and throaty (and sexy?), and stray blonde hair fell over her eyes.

'I've told them to expect some help later. Their man is their top observer, spy, called "Dukh", the ghost, believe it or not, in Russian. He's in Poachers Wood overlooking the mansion, the Manor House. They wanted a password. I gave them one, Chanel No 5.'

They both broke down in laughter at the thought of the soldiers and *that* password.

Major Bob, his sergeant, Des Williams, and three soldiers turned up shortly after. They came in a Matador military truck and a Jeep. The truck they put in the underground car park, the other they found space for outside.

Kev also arrived at the same time.

*

The last time Trent had seen Major Bob Wootton was in his club, Whites, St James Street, London. The oldest gentlemen's club in the country.

Bob was fiftish, small moustache, blinking watery eyes, hair going white. He spoke staccato and very loud. His appearance was military smart, spoilt by broken veined nose and slightly shaking hands. When he ordered a round of drinks, it was as if he was in the mess, giving orders.

At that time, he was full of bitterness about his discharge from the SAS, and the way he considered he'd been treated. Conversation was all one-sided and full of bile. He was also very drunk.

He had been an excellent officer until drink had taken over, but he always said: 'Never on duty, old boy,' but then hadn't lived up to that maxim. It was the time he'd tried to persuade Trent to join his mercenary group when the colonel had already recruited him.

'Let's have another one for the road, Trent, let's have another.' It was always one more for the road with Major Bob, but Trent had had enough and declined.

At that time, the major looked a sad character; he had no family, his "marriage" to the service had been curtailed. Trent watched him stagger down St James Street in the direction of his flat in Kensington. 'There but for the grace of God…'

*

His sergeant, Des (Desmond) Williams, in contrast was the model of sobriety. He was second generation West Indian, of Jamaican origin. His widowed mother had come to England in the Windrush boat in 1948 with young Des. She was a nurse and after the Second World War, she and others had come to help the severe labour shortage at that time.

He was roughly the same age as Trent, but at 6ft 4ins, towered over him.

Very strong and muscular, he was also what was known as a gentle giant.

He had been a private in the Staffordshire when Trent was a corporal. There had never been any problem with his skin colour, then he was very popular with his peers. When Trent had left, he heard that a new strongly racist sergeant major had picked on Des incessantly. In the end, Des snapped. One punch and the sergeant major was hospitalised for a month.

For this, Des received a dishonourable discharge and joined Major Bob's private army and in due course became his sergeant.

Des, the major, and Trent had that in common. All forced out of the armed forces.

*

'Hello, Corp,' said Des, shaking Trent's hand. 'Have to say, you look dreadful.' He glanced at the cuts and bruises on his face, the plaster on his head and the bandaged hand.

'Better than the other guys, Des, better than them; anyway, corporal no longer. And you're a sergeant in the major's mob.'

Des introduced his comrades—Corporal Poole and Privates Parker and Sale. Poole was a cheerful Stokie. He was in his late thirties and had served in the Staffordshire after Trent had gone to the SAS and was a close pal of Sergeant Des. They'd both joined the major's group together.

Affable and friendly, before the army he'd briefly worked at Wedgewoods in the pottery industry. This had bored him so he'd turned to a life of petty crime, and had never been caught, this had continued until he was called up for National Service.

An ardent Stoke City fan, he had a wife and five kids back in Burslem and needed his mercenary wages to support them.

He nodded in a friendly way at Trent, the complete antithesis of his two colleagues.

Parker and Sale were of particular professional interest to Trent. He recognised them as born killers, in the mould of the late, but not lamented, Smith.

So miserable looking, he'd call them the Doom and Gloom twins. Sale, Doom, Parker, Gloom. But equally, they could have been called the Laurel and Hardy of death.

Sale was small and cadaverous, so gaunt and thin, white-faced and bloodless. His grim poker face, almost vampirish. His hair cut very short, a buzz cut, American military style. His eyes were dead, his demeanour cold. His military fatigues hung loosely from his frame.

Parker was larger, heftier, running to fat. He was Hardy to Sale's Laurel. There was not a flicker of humour or humanity in his expression. His narrow eyes in his puffed-up face constantly moving, searching for his next victim perhaps. He had a similar haircut to his comrade, but his uniform was well filled, straining. No one knew where they came from, they'd appeared fully formed in the mercenary group—angels of death—no one dared ask about their pasts.

Good men on your side in a fight but not good men in the general scheme of ordinary life.

Major Bob had remained aloof and silent, looking at Camille's impressive art collection. He now erected a flip chart against one of the walls for his plan of action.

Kev helped Camille open the bar and lay out some snacks. They shared a bottle of Chablis whilst the four soldiers assaulted cans of beer which Camille (surprisingly) had found and they laid waste to an assortment of cheese, biscuits, nuts, and crisps.

Trent took Major Bob aside and told him about the Russian assistance and the audio equipment. He didn't bring up Camille's association with the Russians. He said he'd arranged it all, that over the years, he'd built up some surprising contacts and had called in a favour. He also said that they needed to get a couple of the men over there ASAP, to liaise with the Russian "Dukh", the Ghost.

The major didn't look over-thrilled at this Russian involvement but he could see the need for the recording equipment. They also agreed that Trent should give an overview of the situation and that the major would then give his military assessment. After Trent, he would dispatch Des and one of the privates to Marlborough and the Manor House. Des had already hastily prepared a map of the area, the Manor House, and surrounding area.

Trent then gave him the password, leaving the major spluttering: 'So there's a Ruskie called Duck and his password is a perfume; God! What is the world...'

Meanwhile, in Camille's elegant, expensive apartment, the lights were low, except for one wall where the flip chart was lit up. The fake but effective log fire casting light and shadows around the room. Outside, rain was now beating on the apartment windows; the changeable autumn weather, still changing.

Kev was talking to Des: 'Not entirely sure why I'm here. The whole thing seems incredible, and I only know half the story. If that?' Kev scratched his head, knocked back his wine and helped himself to nuts. 'Incredible,' he repeated. 'Do you know anything more?'

Des shook his head. At this point, he knew next to nothing and guzzled at his beer without a word. Kev, never one to miss an opportunity to chat with a tall, strong soldier, soldiered on. Camille thought Kev was wasting his time; she'd noticed the look of appreciation Des had given her earlier.

The soldiers were on their best behaviour, despite the cans of beer, and they were also very taken with Camille and kept her entertained with tales of derring-do. She eventually excused herself and went to ask Trent and Bob if they wanted drinks. They both declined. 'Clear head and all that,' said Bob.

The intercom buzzed from the basement garage and they all looked up, startled.

'Don't panic, that'll be Bomber Harris with all the arms, ammo and equipment that you ordered, Major.' Trent turned to Bob. 'Do you want to come down and check?'

'No, you, the sergeant and Parker have a look-see. Williams knows what we want.' Now the commanding officer in charge, he then turned to Camille. 'Yes, I think I'll have that drink please.'

Trent was momentarily concerned, knowing the Major's penchant for alcohol, but as he left he was relieved to hear him asking for an orange juice. The major had said, 'Never on duty,' and was true to his word, these days.

In the large garage, there were only a few cars about and the army truck and Camille's car. In the middle, there was a rusty old van. For safety's sake, Trent managed to secure the doors to the flats above and the entrance to the garage. Bomber then climbed out of the van.

'That's good, no prying eyes,' Bomber said. 'Mr Trent, glad to see you still alive, battling against all our enemies, hey. Though surely, you can't believe everything you read in the papers, can you?

'Everything is here as ordered, at short notice you might say. Please check, be my guest. Also got your replacement guns, Mr Trent—Smith & Wesson and Beretta.' Des and Private Parker climbed in the back and several minutes later emerged.

'Seems fine, Bomber, thanks,' Des said, and then the two of them quickly unloaded the truck. Trent was surprised to see that one of the boxes was a bumper box of Standard fireworks, including rockets.

Whilst the soldiers were loading, Bomber, the "Flash Harry" lookalike, combed back his greasy, dyed quiff, took the perennial cigarette from behind his ear and lit it.

Trent said: 'I'm afraid we can't pay you today, Bomber; should be able to in the next few days. But thanks for your efforts.'

'Normally, as you know, I'd want payment upfront. But I can see things are topsy turvy at the moment. I'll wait. I know your credit's good, Mr Trent.'

There was then hammering on the outside garage door; an angry resident wanted to park their car. They'd finished loading into the Matador so the soldiers went back upstairs, everything well-hidden in the vehicle.

Trent asked him up to the flat for a drink. 'Won't come up; the missus will have my supper ready. Thanks all the same.' He stubbed out the fag and put it back behind his ear.

Trent unlocked the garage door and a rather large, middle-aged lady was waiting outside by her car, looking peeved.

'Sorry, there seems to have been something wrong with the latch, my apologies.'

'Latch indeed. Hmmmph,' she snarled with a glance that could kill. Luckily, then Bomber's van swept past and vanished into the night. Trent also took the opportunity and also vanished.

He went back to the "party" above with the astounding thought in his head. *Missus? Bomber?* Kev was now chatting to the major, Camille watching with an amused smile. Trent said: 'Let's go then. Battle orders…'

Chapter Thirty-Nine
Briefing at Mayfair

Trent, not used to public speaking, took a shot of whisky and proceeded the best he could to give an overview of everything that had happened to him and the plans of Sir Richard Abbott and Sir Adrian Joyce, the fascist.

He finished with mentioning the Russian called the Ghost, apparently Dukh in Russian. 'We need to get a couple of you over to meet him.' He nodded at the soldiers. 'And then work with him. He's going to help record this meeting to get us this proof we need. Sergeant Williams has a map of the area to locate him. This Dukh is hidden in Poachers Wood, overlooking Sir Richard's mansion, the Manor House. Now, any questions?'

There was a stunned silence in the room as the enormity of what they'd heard sank in. The major, the professional mercenary, asked: 'In effect the action we propose is totally illegal, that doesn't worry me. But with all the risks despite the good cause, the men here will want to know how they're going to be paid.'

Before Trent could answer, Des Williams interjected. 'Major, Sir, Corporal Trent, from what I hear about this plan for apartheid in this country, I'd do this for nothing. And gladly kill them all. Also to kill our Queen. God!'

The gentle giant abandoned, the anger and rage in his 6ft 4in frame visible. Camille hastily poured him another drink and pushed it into his hands. Kev stepped slightly away, his eyes popping. Des brought his emotions under control.

Trent continued. 'I believe that there are wads of cash held in the target house…thousands…from those so-called Zombie raids, used to help fund this revolution. Also feel free to ransack the place. I've been there a couple of times and there's plenty of gold and silver objects and works of art. Help yourselves. Spoils of war you may say.' He allowed himself a grim smile.

He looked around Camille's normally immaculate apartment. Empty beer cans, wine bottles, glasses, ashtrays overflowing; smoke filled the air. Camille, laidback in the middle, seemed not to care.

The major asked another question. 'This lunchtime when you phoned, did a little homework, studied the Ordnance Survey map, dug up a stately homes of England book, read up on this Manor House and also looked at Who's Who. Abbott's got a family. I don't mind killing all these revolutionaries but I baulk at the idea of his wife and children.'

Camille answered: 'Don't worry; in effect, Sir Richard and his wife are estranged. His family are in the south of France at present. Colonel Stewart told me a few weeks ago.'

Trent agreed with this, common knowledge at the 'Outfit'. He said: 'Major, I think your blokes should get off to Marlborough now and liaise with this Russian, the ghost. And remember the password.'

Major Bob gave instructions to Des and Private Parker to go to Poachers Wood and make contact with the Dukh, "and don't start a world war!". They were to hide the truck in the woods. Then he pointed out a track to the centre on the map where they were to set up base camp. Then they were off to observe the Manor House until he and the others arrived. He gave them the password: Chanel Number 5.

As the two left, there was much hilarity around the name Dukh and the perfume. They closed the door to much "quackery" and "ee oop me duck" from Corporal Poole.

At that moment, the phone rang and with a glance at Trent, Camille went into the bedroom to answer (could it be the Russians?).

With the vanguard gone, the major had further queries.

'Do you think there'll be much opposition to any attack?'

'This Sir Adrian's new GB National Party have been training some sort of militia. Well armed, I would say.'

'How many do you think will be there?'

'Difficult to say, but I'm sure there'll be some sort of guard. We can assess when we're there.'

'Calibre?'

'Again a guess; some may be ex-army, and the few I've met were tough, but most inexperienced, I'd say. The National Party plan to control the regular army after the coup, but they won't be involved at present.'

Camille came back into the room, stifling a laugh. 'That was Mrs Freeth from next door. Complaining about strangers locking her out of the garage and then the ruffians parking their lorry in *her* car park. Then the noise next door, us! Having a party! I've smoothed her over, promised her afternoon tea at the Savoy, bought off so cheap.'

Still laughing, Camille poured herself another Chablis.

As everyone else was smoking, Trent lit himself a cigarette and inhaled luxuriously. 'We need to cut off the head of this, whatchamacallit Camille?'

'Hydra, Greek mythology, need to cut off all its heads, actually; had more than one.'

'Yes, and destroy this bloody evil conspiracy.' Sharp intake of breath. 'OK, Major, now over to you…'

Kev interrupted. 'Before we go on, why am I here? Can't print your story y'know. This D notice…'

'Kev, we're going to record this meeting/seminar, whatever it is. Your job will then be to deliver the recording to your editor and the PM. The most important task of the lot. You have all the contacts to do that.'

'Oh, OK, then. And I thought it was going to be something difficult. Huh! But yes, you're right. I do have a special contact who can help.' Kev retreated back to his corner and his glass of wine. His face now whiter than white.

Trent went to one of the armchairs and took another sip of well-earned whisky. Major Bob Wootton, swagger stick in hand, stood in front of the illuminated flip chart, cleared his throat and then began…

Chapter Forty
Still London

On the flip board there was a roughly drawn map of the Manor House, near Marlborough, and the environs.

Major Bob was like a professor at university giving a lecture. Slightly pompous, long-winded and waving his swagger stick. He was in his element.

He first gave a talk on the property itself gleaned quickly from his research that afternoon. He was nothing if not thorough.

All were now sitting down politely. Trent's eyes closed, he could feel himself nodding off again.

Camille wore an expression of total interest. Kev busily polished off the wine. The two soldiers inscrutable, obviously used to their CO's little ways. The rain still thrashing down; the distant whoosh of a firework exploding in the sky.

Using his stick to point out areas of the property, the major commenced.

The Manor House was a 17th century country house. A few miles from Marlborough and north of Axford. There was the main hall, landscaped gardens, parkland, stables and courtyard, a small lake, and some farmland.

At the back of the property, there were modern, recently built facilities: a conference centre and an adjacent canteen. Overlooking this was Poachers Wood, which did not belong to the estate. Ownership unknown.

Bob continued: 'The estate had been in Sir Richard Abbott's family since the 13th century—he is a Baronet and has a hereditary title—and his present house was built in the 1600s. The family had then supported the king in the civil war and after were lucky were to retain the property and only be fined by Cromwell.' (Maybe too much information, thought Trent, still, Bob was always thorough.)

He concluded this bit. 'Trent, you're right, the book I read on stately homes says it has one of the best art and sculpture collections in the land. And the wine cellar is one of the finest in Europe.'

He left unsaid the looting of such treasures by his men.

'Poachers Wood here,' he stabbed at the board. 'I expect this Ghost, the Ivan, to be somewhere here with a full view of the back of the mansion and the conference centre.

'Our lads will find him and then when we get down there, we will have a rota to watch the place. The men will bivouac down in the woods with all their arms. The truck will be at the end of this track well away from the nearest road.' He again pointed at the map.

'There are no farms about for some miles. If anyone is in those woods, and God knows why they would be in this weather, we'll detain them on a temporary basis. The men know what they're doing. Also, the sergeant booked four rooms at the Marlborough Hotel in the High Street. For you civilians—Trent, Camille and Kev, and myself. 'Fraid you'll have to pay up later.' The major then started on his strategy, walking up and down and gesticulating with his swagger stick.

'Gentlemen and, er, lady, there are four main objectives to this operation. I'm, er, sorry to say that I would have liked more time to prepare, but needs must, work with what we've got and so on…hmmmmph.' He waved his swagger stick at his audience.

'The first thing we've to do is record this conference in full and the bally Russians are helping us there. The sergeant and Parker have already gone to liaise with our communist friend.' The major grimaced. 'Who is to supply the surveillance equipment.

'Then we're to get this recording, as I understand it, to the PM or the powers that be; that's right, Trent?'

'Yes, that's right. Kev here knows people, so he'll do that.'

The major continued. 'We'll set up a base camp in the woods as I said. Then once the recordings have gone, we'll attack the Manor House and destroy this whole conspiracy at root. Obviously, we'll get the lie of the land and work out the opposition and where this militia is located. Any casualties, tough—they declared the war—right, Trent?' He was in his stride now.

'Thirdly, whoever survives, we'll imprison and I think Sir Richard's wine cellar will do admirably. Looking at the info on the place, plenty of room there. Do you concur, Trent?'

Trent nodded; he remembered the impressive wine cellar, proudly shown off by his superior.

'Fourthly, our aim must be to stop this assassination of Her Majesty in Swindon. Again, I concur that with this Sir Richard commanding all security services, we'll never get anyone to believe these plots without the proof.

'We'll have to do this ourselves and I may say…' He paused here and looked at his sparse audience. 'I feel offended that people of responsibility are planning all this, and it is…it is our duty to stop them.' His indignation surfaced and he had a fit of coughing. Camille handed him a glass of water.

'Thanks, dear…hmmph.' He cleared his throat. Camille gave a wry smile and pulled a face at the "dear". He continued: 'On an operational point, I propose to only use a selection of my men, those I brought tonight. They're all highly trained and we'll cope with whatever strength this militia has. Bomber has provided us with plenty of arms, etc.

'Now, I've sent the sergeant and Private Parker off to meet the Russian, with this dubious password!' He pointedly stared at Camille. 'Hopefully, they'll get this recording device understood and up and ready.' He pointed his stick at the map.

'We'll set up base camp later here in this wood; there's a clearing set right back from the Manor House. We'll carry out field reconnaissance and analyse what our opposition is, and our plan of attack. We'll split the group into teams to watch the place for when this meeting starts. Everyone will be issued with pagers or bleepers provided by Bomber to signal action stations. The tapes will be taken off by Mr Bloomer, and then we'll attack the building, and cover up the attack with a fireworks display.'

'Ah, that explains the large box of Standard fireworks Bomber delivered,' Trent interrupted. 'Clever.'

The major glared at Trent. 'As previously stated, we'll imprison the surviving plotters in the cellar, and er…' His first hint of a smile. 'The men to take recompense for their efforts.' (He meant looting, Trent assumed.)

'I'm afraid all this is a bit off the cuff, ad hoc, but once we're bedded in the woods, we can evolve things in a proper, orderly manner. Right, any questions…no, good,' Major Bob concluded. 'So I think we'll get off there now and get started.'

He looked at his watch. 'Just over two hours to midnight, when it's the 4th.'

He beckoned to his men. 'Corporal Poole, Sale and myself will get off in the Jeep. I'll see you later at the hotel.'

Trent smiled at the thought of the troops in the rain-sodden woods, while their CO resided in luxury. It was ever so!

Camille packed a few things to take; Trent already had further clothes picked up by Camille from his flat in the sports car. Kev went off in his vintage Jag to get some clothes together. They would meet later at the hotel.

Then off Camille and Trent went in her car. With her driving, they should easily get there before 12am. Plenty of time for 4th November and Sir Richard Abbott's "Big Day".

Chapter Forty-One
Marlborough, 4 November

The Marlborough Hotel, a cosy 15th century establishment in the middle of the High Street. Unlike the hotel in Aberystwyth, luckily they had a more flexible view of closing times. Trent and Camille had made it in plenty of time before midnight despite the M4 section from Maidenhead to Swindon not opening until December, Camille's driving so fast!

Despite the lateness, the manager was happy to see them (quiet this time of year). They had to pay with Camille's well used credit card again and they booked for four people for two nights.

'Sorry two of our friends will be here later,' said Trent.

'Not to worry, I'm on duty all night.' He looked outside at the wet night. 'And when you're settled in, if you want a nightcap to warm up, the bar's still open.' He had a strong, rural Wiltshire accent.

'Thanks,' said Camille, and then inspired: 'One of our party, Major Wootton, is on night manoeuvres out on Salisbury Plain. He'll be still in military dress and soaked, I should think.'

The manager took it all in his stride and after signing the register, they went upstairs to their room. Trent advised him: 'We'll be back for that nightcap, thanks.'

Their bedroom was old-fashioned—panelled walls, an old blocked-up fireplace, and a low ceiling. The bathroom was out in the corridor and shared by residents on that floor. In the middle was a four-poster bed which Camille sat on and jumped up and down to test the strength.

'May need to be strong, later,' she said enigmatically.

'Too tired for all that,' Trent replied, although in truth, he was now wide awake, second wind. 'Sorry we had to use your credit card. I'll sort you out later.'

'Don't worry; if we pull this off, the Soviets will cover expenses and more.'

In the background, the wind rattled the windows and the rain still teemed down. The room suddenly seemed cold and draughty.

Trent shook his head in amazement. 'The Soviets! God help us! Oh, that was genius as well about Salisbury.'

'I thought we'd better have a reason for the major, no suspicions raised.'

'Good thinking. Let's go and get that drink.'

A cosy, old-fashioned hotel; a cosy, old-fashioned bar/lounge. It was similar to the bedroom except there were beams in the low ceiling. The fire burnt in the grate, warming the room and lighting up a fairly modern-looking bar.

When they came down, Kev had arrived with a small valise. He'd not bothered with his room, straight to the bar, and he had a large vodka in front of him. Scruffy as ever, he waved at them, cigarette in hand, scattering ash everywhere.

'The drink's on me; what a handsome couple. Even if one of you is a little battered. If I may say so. Have a look at this paper whilst I get them in.'

He handed over a copy of the *Swindon Advertiser*. There was the Queen's route in Swindon laid out. Trent would study it in depth later.

Camille ordered a white wine, Trent a pint of Wadworth bitter. Kev returned with the drinks and flamboyantly bowed. 'Sir, your Ladyship.' The manager had discreetly withdrawn from the bar and the three huddled around the fire to have a further talk about events.

Trent lit a cigarette. He eyed Kev, who still looked somewhat shellshocked with all this a new alien experience. Camille, who hadn't slept for over twenty-four hours, still looked radiant in the firelight. Outside, there was no let-up in the storm. God help those soldiers out in the woods.

His voice low, his over-the-top campness subdued, Kev asked: 'How, how do they think they can get away with it? This madness?'

Trent inhaled cigarette smoke. 'It's very easy you'll find when the government gives you command of all security and armed forces.'

'The press, you people, have been clamouring for action against these terrorist attacks,' Camille continued. 'Sir Richard getting control is in answer to that. If the Queen is killed, there'll be mob frenzy, and it'll be easy for Abbott and his men to strike. Using the assassination as an excuse for martial law.'

Trent walked to the bar to make sure no one was listening. He returned, sipped his beer, and picked up the conversation. 'A lot of organisation and planning has gone into this. Incredibly, there seems to be support from all parts of the establishment.'

Kev said: 'Unbelievable.' He asked a question asked earlier. 'Why can't we just warn the PM now?'

Trent stared Kev straight in the eyes. 'They'll never believe it without proof. Sir Richard is beyond reproach. We need that recording to prove to the PM and then we'll wipe 'em out—only way.' (Steve, Jackie and others flashed across his mind. What he didn't say was that word: Revenge.)

Camille said: 'The only thing we don't know is when their meeting starts.'

Trent said: 'The watchers up there will know when all the followers turn up.' He looked out the window at the incessant rainfall. 'We're lucky in here.' The major still hadn't arrived and he went up in Trent's estimation, out there leading from the front. 'Poor bastards.'

Camille stood up and also looked out the window. She shivered. 'At least they should be well paid.'

'As long as Abbott hasn't hocked all his treasures and spent all that cash. Although I doubt that.'

Camille yawned, stretching her arms. 'Been a long day, I'm going to bed.' She looked at Trent. 'Don't be too long.'

They watched her leave. Kev downed his vodka and helped himself to another from behind the bar, throwing some coins down. 'What a charming girl; could almost fall for her myself. You make a wonderful couple. When are you going to get hitched?' He took a large gulp of his drink, picked up his cigarette from the ashtray and waved it about, scattering further ash everywhere.

'Y'know, when this is all over, I'm going to run away with her, get away from all this crap. Start a new life. Don't know about marriage though; step too far? Perhaps.'

Kev gave him an appraising look. 'Have you asked her? Is it what she wants? Seems sort of…what is it? She seems very independent and comfortable with her life.'

Trent finished his beer; he hadn't thought that far ahead; get the next two days out of the way. He changed the subject. 'Kev, pull this off and it could be the scoop of the century for you.'

Kev looked thoughtful. 'Somehow I doubt it, whatever happens, I think there'll be the cover-up of the century. Too many top people involved. Oh well…do you want another drink?'

Trent said no, thanks, and Kev again switched tack. He held up the pager. 'What's this all about? Your major gave me this.'

'It's a bleeper thing. It clips to your belt or pocket. When the conference starts up at the Manor House, the men there will send a signal, a bleep to say it's underway. Not used much here but it is in the States. So I'm told.'

'Oh, I see. I hope we can pull it off later. I can see…er…this thing turning into a civil war if Abbott and Adrian Joyce succeed. There's bound to be a fightback against the new regime. People won't just accept it. All end in bloodshed.'

'I agree. We must succeed, and you must get that message to the PM. Absolutely imperative.'

'You do your macho battle bit, not my area, at all.' Kev smiled. 'I'll get it to the PM. I know, if you know what I mean, one of the under-under-secretaries in Downing Street. A dear, good friend. He'll help. I'll get to see the PM and take my editor; he's far from a right-wing supporter.'

'I also may have to involve the prof from the Outfit. I'll think about that.' Trent said obviously reluctant, he didn't know if anyone else there was involved.

On that note, Philip Trent also yawned, shook Kev's hand, said thanks and went upstairs to Camille. He left Kev with his vodka, deep in thought; the rain and wind outside showing no sign of slowing down.

Now where was that four-poster?

Chapter Forty-Two
4 November

An idyllic autumn morning. The rain had stopped, it was only slightly chilly and a bright sun was streaming across Marlborough High Street. It was Thursday, 4 November, and the market town was waking up, shops opening and people were on the move.

Camille and Trent came down to breakfast, holding hands, looking reinvigorated (although how much actual sleep they had was anyone's guess).

There was no Kev in the breakfast room, not a morning or breakfast person. However, surprisingly, the major was there tucking into his breakfast (sausage, bacon, egg, and black pudding). He also looked fresh, spick and span, his soldier's shirt discreetly covered by a thick grey jumper.

Camille ordered fruit and porridge, Trent had the full breakfast. He lit his first cigarette of the day.

'Awful night,' Major Bob said, slurping at a cup of black builder's tea. 'But gave us a lot of cover, all set up for action. Everything is in place.'

A pot of tea arrived (there seemed to be no coffee). Camille as "mum" poured for the both of them. Trent took some of the painkillers from the Rhayader Cottage hospital and drank some tea. 'I'd like to come and see in a bit.'

'Absolutely, old boy.' He finished his breakfast and looked at the two of them. 'That Russian, strange chap. Haven't a clue how he got to the woods, speaks no English. Hope we've got a handle on all that surveillance stuff.' He gave a large yawn. How much sleep had he had?

Camille said: 'I'd like to come as well.'

The major looked at her—fresh, smart—chic, he thought the word probably was. He smiled. 'Not sure, old girl. Terribly wet and muddy, not sure you're dressed for it. Best stay here.'

Ignoring his patronising manner, she said: 'I have wellingtons and old jeans. And there is a good reason for me to come.'

'Oh yes, what's that?'

Trent answered, laughing: 'She speaks Russian fluently, "old boy". She can speak to this Dukh character.'

The major spluttered, he coughed, face red.

'Good God...never. How?'

Camille smiled, charmingly: 'My mother was Russian, left in the 20s. I was taught in the cradle.'

With nothing to add, the major, shaking his head (whatever next?), asked Trent: 'How's your finger wound, Trent? Are you fit for the fight?'

Trent, eyes ice-cold, said: 'Yes, I'm ambi. No, well, I can shoot left-handed. Don't worry.' He thought a week to go until he returned to a hospital to see how it was going (would he ever get there?).

'I'm going then, to see the men,' Major Bob said. 'Do you know the way? A bit...a bit...'

'Round the back of our Bill's mother's,' replied Trent. Camille and Bob looked at him blankly.

'It's what my nan used to say, or round the Wrekin. Never mind, local talk. Yes, Camille took notes from your map. We'll see you later.'

Major Bob left; his Jeep parked down a side street, out of sight. Shortly after, they came down the hotel stairs, Camille suitably dressed. She said to the manager (who was still on duty!): 'Mr Bloomer (Kev) probably won't surface until lunchtime. Not an early person. I'd tell your cleaners to leave his room.'

Imperturbable as ever, the manager replied: 'No trouble, Miss. The gentleman did have a late night with his vodka. We'll see you later.'

Camille had parked further down the High Street, on double yellow lines. An early bird traffic warden had issued a ticket and stuck it on the windscreen.

'Don't worry, I'll deal with that.' Her gloved hand swept the ticket off. She strode down the street and deposited it in a bin.

With that done, they drove off in the direction of Axford and Poachers Wood.

Chapter Forty-Three
Poachers Wood

Poachers Wood, a few miles north of Axford, down many winding lanes. As indicated on the major's map, the entrance to the wood was on the other side of the Manor House. It was well hidden away from the nearest lane. There was an old gate, little used—until now—covered in rusted barbed wire and brambles. A "Private; No Entry" sign had fallen on the floor.

Trent forced it open, closed it, and Camille drove the sports car down a very muddy rutted track. 'This is worse than the one at Wallog,' Camille said as the car bounced up and down. 'Won't do the suspension much good. Have to put it on expenses…'

The rain now gone, the cold blue sky above them was clear, the trees bereft of leaves which had joined the gungy morass below.

Large, white clouds floated by, fringed with black, precursor of more rain to come.

Finally, they bumped their way to the middle clearing. The Jeep was parked there but no sign of the truck, the major, or the others. They got out of the car. Camille gingerly stepped through the sodden ground, churned up by the vehicles' tracks.

Suddenly, some bushes parted, spraying rain, and the major appeared. The army truck well hidden in a man-made shelter behind him, fashioned from the bushes and trees.

'Good, here at last. Private Sale let us know you were on the way. He's hidden by the gate entrance to warn if anyone's coming. With his walkie-talkie. Bet you never saw him.'

Trent agreed they hadn't.

'Rather good at camouflage, my men,' he said proudly. 'Come and look.' He showed them the inside of the truck. All the weapons had been moved, there was a radio set, some small campus stoves, tins of food, and two men in sleeping bags. And oddly, rabbits, partridge, and a deer hanging on the side.

'That's the Russian and Corporal Poole resting after a hard night. Sergeant Williams and Parker are up at the observation post. We're settled in rather well, can't light any fires, but we're managing.' As a strange afterthought: 'Dug latrines out over there in the woods. Sorry, Miss.' To Camille he said, who he seemed to think was some delicate flower (far from!).

Trent said: 'The game there; I guess that's if any officials stopped you, you could claim to be poachers.'

'Yes; Corporal Poole's idea. Done some poaching in his time. Our forager when out on a mission. Your idea, wasn't it, Poole?' Poole and the Russian were waking up.

'Yes, Sir. I have my moments.' He yawned and stretched and leapt down.

'Surely you didn't shoot them? Even in the rain, they might have heard that at the manor.' This was from a surprised Trent.

'Well, Sir, I did shoot them with this.' Pool held up a bow and arrow.

'Proper little Robin Hood, aren't you?' Trent laughed and Camille joined in. It broke the tension a little, a tension palpable in the camp air.

The Russian then appeared and also jumped down from the truck.

He was like a small bull. Stocky, muscular, about 5ft 6ins, with unruly blond hair. A dour, frightened expression, piercing blue eyes, slightly slanting, and a scar on his left cheek. He was Slavic but Asiatic. Dressed in grey military fatigues, his night out in the rain evidenced in the mud and grass stains. He was also still soaking.

The major ordered: 'Corporal, take me and Trent up to the observation post please. Camille can have a chat with the Russian.'

'OK, put this on.' The major threw Trent a green greatcoat. 'Help keep you hidden.' Trent then followed them.

As they left, Camille said to the Ghost: 'Dobroye utro.' For the first time, Dukh smiled, changing his whole personality for a second. He answered in Russian. As they went through the woods, a full conversation was in progress.

'It's about a quarter of a mile through here. We had to carry all the arms there. Under waterproof covering. We're forecasting rain again later.' The major strode ahead, marching. They walked through the wet grass and the autumn brown ferns, rain still sprinkling from the trees.

They came to the edge of the wood overlooking the Manor House. The surrounding trees were now bare, but a mass of thick bushes surrounding the woods provided ideal cover. There was a grassy slope down to the back of the building, 200-300 yards away.

Des and Parker, camouflaged, were watching the mansion. Parker with strong binoculars and Des listening through earphones. Des pulled down one earphone and said: 'Hello, Corp,' to Trent.

'Anything to listen to?' He replied.

'They've got caterers in, we believe.'

Trent had a listen; he could hear the muffled sounds of movement in the conference hall.

'Not too clear,' he agreed.

'Don't think we've exactly mastered the contraption.' He pointed out the portable recording device. The tape recorder was in a large suitcase and it was attached to a satellite dish on a specially made stand. 'Need the Ivan to tell us more.'

'Let's see what Camille can find out.' Trent ignored the quizzical look from Des. He turned to the major: 'Can we get them—her and the Russian I mean—up here?'

'Yaas, don't like too many about but if most of us keep well back, should be OK.'

He instructed Private Parker to go back and to send them up and then to remain with the truck.

'Is it OK if I smoke?' Trent asked Bob.

'Yaas, go back into the woods.'

'Has anyone been down and done a recce of the place?'

'Corporal Poole did in the early hours.'

'Come with me, Corporal, tell me what you saw. You'd like a fag as well I suppose.'

Before the major could say anything, Trent steered Poole back into the woods. He lit them both cigarettes. Poole stamped his feet as he smoked. It was getting colder again. The sun was behind the clouds, the sky was getting dark.

Chapter Forty-Four

They stood in a small clearing away from the others and smoked, the corporal slightly shivering. They were standing in the midst of numerous fallen chestnuts on the forest floor, golden brown, their green prickly shells also lying about.

Keeping his voice low, Corporal Poole said: 'I understand from Sergeant Williams, Des, that you're a Baggies fan.'

Trent took in the corporal for the first time. Potteries accent, and like many from that area, fairly short and stocky. Grey, thinning hair, although probably only in his late thirties, cut short into a crewcut. He had an almost angelic face with a cherubic smile and always seemed laidback and friendly. He held his cigarette inwards into the palm of his nicotine-stained hand.

'Yes, that's right,' he replied, smiling. 'Let me guess, Stoke fan. We're playing you this Saturday.' (Although this seemed another world)

'Beat you 2-0 earlier in the year, didn't we?'

'Yes, but we beat you 5-2 the time before. Not sure how it'll go this Saturday.' He took a long drag on the cigarette and changed the subject.

'You had a look-see at the manor; observations?'

'Went down early this morning. Security very amateurish. No dogs, alarms, searchlights; nothing. There are several guards but they stay mainly round the front. They don't expect trouble.'

Typical arrogance of Sir Richard. He never expected anyone would have the impertinence to burgle, let alone attack his "castle".

'No one had any hint you were there?'

'No, Mr Trent. I was a cat burglar before the army. Never got caught. I should be called the "Ghost", not the Ruskie.'

'Man of many talents—poacher, archer, burglar, soldier. Now tell me more.'

'As I say, no security round the back. In the stables and canteen, there's…oh, about twenty to thirty of their militia. Anything like the slovenly guards, should be no problem. Catering vans were there early on—looks like Harrods—food and champagne to feed the five thousand.

'Anyway, it's all set up in the meeting hall, chairs and the like. Gonna be a whale of a party. There are some small windows to the hall on the side. I climbed up a drainpipe to look in. Got a good view.'

Trent finished his cigarette. 'Nothing but the best for revolutionaries. By the way, did you see a giant of a man there, scarred face?'

'No, absolutely not. I'd have remembered him.' (So, Mueller, the Zombie, where were you?)

'Let's get back then.'

Drizzling now, a low cloud covered the wood with a thin mist. Camille and the Russian were now with the major. The Ghost was now like a puppy, he'd really taken to Camille, as all men did. (*Good job, I'm not a jealous type*, Trent thought.) The major was now anxious and nervous for them to get away as soon as possible.

'Best you civilians out of the way as soon as; no offence. Don't want too many about. May be spotted.

'Now has the lady,' the major turned and addressed Trent, 'got anything out of the Russian?'

'The lady has, Major!' Camille answered, annoyed.

Trent hastily intervened. 'Des, tell her about your technical problems.'

There followed a back and forth conversation as Camille acted as translator to solve the technical issues, which between them they managed to sort out most of them.

'We need to still improve the sound clarity,' Des then said. Camille spoke to the Russian, who with much gesticulation produced several objects from inside his jacket.

'Sil'neye mikrofon.'

Dukh then spoke further and quickly. Camille interpreted: 'The contraption is called a parabolic dish and the antenna picks up sound via radio waves. However, these microphones are much stronger. They send some sort of electronic signal to the receiver here. You need to attach them to the back of the meeting room. Will pick up everything said from the stage on the other side. Much better than the long-range surveillance device.'

The major, exasperated, said: 'Why the hell didn't he do this in the first place?' He looked at the Russian, who now looked scared, shrugged his shoulders.

It was decided that the corporal, the self-proclaimed "Ghost", and the Russian "Ghost" would make their way down to the building and affix the mikes.

'Be careful, Corporal,' said Trent.

'Don't ya worry; if this duck does as I do, we won't be seen.'

After further talk in Russian, the two started to descend the slope on their bellies. Luckily, the mist was now thick and the drizzle turned to rain; this would help hide their progress.

'Off you go,' said the major bluntly to the other two, he wanted as few about as possible until it was time for action. So Camille and Trent left and headed back to the camp and their car.

Driving back to Marlborough, the rain was now cascading down the windscreen, wipers working overtime. Trent asked: 'What did our Russian friend have to say?'

Camille said he'd told her that he was of Cossack origin and his name was Illya Kryvoms; his family had been very affected by the purges carried out by Stalin. He'd only been saved by the coming of Kruschev who had halted the attacks and "forgiven" the Cossacks.

He then felt beholden to Kruschev and Mother Russia and eventually, joined the Red army. He showed a remarkable aptitude for electronics and surveillance and was recruited by the KGB.

They had used him all over Europe, recording and filming their enemies, even though he only spoke Russian. He'd been working in England when they dispatched him to the woods to work with the "English". He had been dropped off in the wilds by two comrades and left to set up the surveillance.

The weather hadn't bothered him, not a patch on a Russian winter. But he didn't entirely trust the English soldiers and was nervous, particularly of the major. That was until Camille turned up.

'Saved the day again.' He pecked her on the cheek. 'Let's get back to town and have a spot of lunch.'

'Yes, and let's have an afternoon for ourselves,' said Camille. 'Before those bloody bleepers go off.'

An unusual swear word from Camille. Trent's reply lost in the sudden roar of the engine.

Chapter Forty-Five

Back in Marlborough, Camille parked her car on the same double yellow lines. Nearby, a young lad with his Guy asked for a penny. (Was it a century ago when Trent had been at Kew and donated pennies for another Guy? No, four days ago.) They gave him some coins, although both agreed and said to him that perhaps he should be at school.

They dashed through the rain, Trent refusing cover under Camille's umbrella (too macho?), and made the nearby Wellington Arms for lunch. It was not long until closing, so just in time. Trent ordered pie and chips, Camille had fish and salad. She had a small white wine, Trent, for once, abstained (with the long night ahead).

Whilst they waited, Camille read a brief history of the pub on the wall. Grade II listed building, dating back centuries. Alleged to be the starting point of the Great Fire of Marlborough in 1653 (Great Fire, really; you learn something new). Present premises rebuilt in the 19th century.

Then they ate their lunch looking out onto the busy market square watching the passers-by in the falling rain, dodging puddles and the spray from passing vehicles.

What followed was an idyllic afternoon in less than idyllic weather.

Following a guidebook found in the pub, they caught a bus to see the Marlborough White Horse on the hill south of the town.

'It's a bit small, isn't it?' Trent said.

'Size isn't everything,' responded Camille. 'You're such a killjoy.'

Back in town, they found an Army & Navy Stores and kitted themselves out in more suitable clothes, including waterproof boots. A "his and hers" military look. Camille collapsed in hysterics at the sight of herself in the mirror, Trent couldn't help but join in; it was infectious. Much to the agitation and disgust of the shop attendant.

Back in the rain—Trent now sensibly also under the brolly—they decided to go to the pictures. The local fleapit, the Marlborough Theatre, due for imminent demolition. You could perhaps see why!

The film was *Carry on Camping* and they laughed at the innuendo, and at Barbara Windsor's bra flying through the air. They cheered when the film broke down, joining in with the locals. Had a choc ice each, held hands, and had a generally British wonderful time in that old, draughty cinema.

Afterwards, back at the hotel, they made love in the old four-poster bed. The coming night was temporarily forgotten. An idyllic afternoon…

*

They came down to the lounge/bar about 5.45pm. It was very dark outside, the clocks had gone back a few days before. The rain was still thrashing down but it was nice and warm inside, the fire roaring, and sitting in front of it, the unique, one and only, Kev Bloomer, all alone. The inevitable glass of vodka in front of him. They sat by him.

'Where have you two been? Up to no good, no doubt.'

Checking there was no one about, Trent answered: 'Up in the woods actually. What time did you surface?'

'Not too late, old thing, felt cultural; took a taxi out to Stonehenge, never been there. Got a bit wet. Got a bit expensive. But hey ho…' He stood up. 'How did it all go up there?'

'All under control, under the major's control.'

'Good; do you want a drink?'

'Just tea for me. Camille?'

She said the same, so Kev went off to sort it out. Trent took out a cigarette, looked at it, and said ruefully: 'Think I'll give up when this is all over.'

'That'll be the day,' Camille responded, smiling. Shrugging his shoulders, he lit up. Kev returned. They talked softly about operations up in Poachers Wood. The tea arrived, and Kev suddenly said: 'God, West Brom on Saturday. Who are they playing?'

'Stoke,' said Trent. 'One of the soldiers supports them. May have a bet with him later.'

'You lose track of time in this game you've dragged me into. Still don't think we stand much chance; your money lost.'

Camille snorted, and swore for the second time that day. 'Bloody football.'

There was a TV on the other side of the lounge, and the familiar music of the six o'clock news started, the sound low.

'Let's turn it up, see if there's anything on about any of this stuff,' Camille said and went to put up the volume.

The newsreader was the authoritative Richard Baker and there was typical coverage of the Vietnam War. Also something on the Pakistan war against the Bengalis in East Pakistan.

And on a lighter note, an item on Walt Disney World, recently opened.

Then suddenly, they said there was to be an emergency newsflash from Number 10. There was much flickering and a BBC roving reporter appeared.

He gave a brief summary on the recent plot uncovered to destabilise the country and the government's appointment of Sir Richard Abbott to command combined forces and combat. He said the following clip was recorded earlier and the prime minister would give a live broadcast to the nation tomorrow evening.

And there he was, Sir Richard, still as debonair as ever. The studio artifice disguising his baldness, pink cheeks, and making him look less overweight than normal. Still looked like Orson Welles however.

He started to speak in the familiar well-bred tones. Camille grasped Trent's arm and he felt her shiver involuntarily. Trent put his cup of tea down and drew heavily on his cigarette. Kev gulped back his vodka.

The speech was short. He had the full backing of the PM and the cabinet, and tomorrow with the Heads of Services, they would finalise the strategy to defeat this insidious attack on this country. The public would be kept up to date as they went along.

There was more of the same and a return to the studio where the viewers were reminded of the PM's address tomorrow, the 5 of November. No mention of that fallen missing hero-soldier, Philip Trent, or the destruction of a Welsh island.

Camille turned the telly off.

In a rather dejected, subdued mood, they finished the tea and had some sandwiches.

These were brought out by the ever-on-duty manager (who Kev had discovered was named Wilf).

Wilf had been watching the news and he made some comment about hopefully this Sir Thingy could sort out the commies. He returned to his hidden lair at the back of the bar.

'If his is the typical public response to Sir Richard, I think they may well succeed,' Kev said, drinking another vodka.

They became even gloomier. So much depended on their operation tonight.

Trent said: 'Let's be optimistic, we have the element of surprise. Try and keep sober, Kev. When we have the recordings, we'll bring them over and you get them to your man and the PM.' He paused. 'I think we'll go and rest and wait to be bleeped.'

Camille, silent, took Trent's arm with some force and they went upstairs.

For once, no ribald comments from Kev, who like the previous night was alone with the fire, the vodka and his thoughts.

*

Trent stepped out of the bathroom. Camille was on the four-poster. He looked her closely. She'd been crying. 'Don't worry,' he said. 'We'll beat them; wreck their plans tonight. This is my and the major's game and we play to win.'

They earlier had a heated discussion about the night ahead. Camille wanted to stay in the woods and help with the assault. Trent argued that she was needed to get the tapes to Kev in Marlborough. Then she should go with him back to London. After a lively debate, she finally agreed to "do as she was told" but pulled a face as she said it.

She gave a half-smile, said nothing, and pulled him to the bed. They kissed; he could taste the salt of her tears. They made love with a passion he'd never known before. As if it was their last day on Earth…

Chapter Forty-Six
4 into 5 November

They were all there—Camille, Kev, the major, Bomber, Mrs McDougall, Tess, the dog, even Steve and Jackie. And, of course, the special guest, Colonel Alec Stewart, deceased. All in that jungle clearing in Africa.

'I thought he was dead,' Trent said to no one. They all filed past a coffin, an open coffin with him, Philip Trent, lying there. RIP... 'Nothing surprises me...nothing surprises me...'

"Beep, beep, buzz, buzz, buzz". The two bleepers/pagers went off and Trent woke from his dream-nightmare. It was 11.30pm; the show must have started up at the Manor House.

Camille slipped out of the bed. 'Me first,' she said and vanished into the bathroom on the landing.

Trent took a couple of painkillers for his throbbing finger; the dressing looking a bit worse for wear. He checked his two guns were in good working order, the Beretta and the Smith and Wesson, and opened the curtain. The street lights were shining down below, blurred in the drizzle now falling. He read the *Swindon Advertiser* whilst he waited for Camille and memorised the Queen's route for the next day.

Both washed, they donned the reject army uniforms and greatcoats. 'Let me look at that finger,' Camille said and tutted. She did some repair work on the bandages and handed him a pair of woollen gloves. 'Here, have these.'

He looked at the fluffy gloves, incredulous. 'What do I do with these?'

'You wear them, of course, keep the cold and damp off that finger.'

Kev Bloomer was still in the same place by the fire and its dying embers. He laughed at their attire but seemed remarkably sober. He was drinking from a pot of coffee (where'd that come from?). Trent said they'd be off to the woods and Camille would get the recordings back when ready. 'Are you alright with everything?' He asked.

'Yes. Wilf organised this pot to keep me awake.' He took a sip. 'No alcohol! I've spoken to my contact-friend at Number 10 and we have got a meeting ready when I have the tapes. Stressed matter of total urgency, etc., etc. But not said why.'

A surprised-looking Wilf appeared, the manager that never slept. He stared nonplussed at Camille and Trent, his mouth open.

'Go now,' Kev whispered. 'I'll deal with Wilf.' With that, they left.

*

Through the drizzle they drove and into Poachers Wood. The headlights were dipped low, although Trent doubted they would be noticed by the Manor House through the thick, dark woodland.

The clearing now resembled a scene from an old film of a gipsy camp. There were oil lamps hanging from the trees with some sort of gauze over them to make them dull.

Private Sale was cooking, or warming up some bully beef concoction on a low-level primus. Sullen as ever. Sergeant Des was playing cards with the Ghost, Dukh (Illya). British/Soviet relations seemingly now thawed. They sat on damp logs. All with their capes pulled round them and trying to shelter beneath the trees, waving in the wind high above. The whole area was now a churned-up, Somme-like, swampy mass.

'Where are they all, Des?' Trent asked the sergeant.

'The major and Corporal Poole are up at the observation place. Parker still watching the gate. He radioed you were coming.' Des returned to his very competitive-looking card game, East v West.

Trent asked Camille if she was coming up to the watchers' place. She elected to stay behind and asked Des and Illya if she could join in their card game. Some version of Pontoon.

Trent went up the dark track. There was no moon, steady drizzle, and the only light from the distant Manor House through the trees. It was now past midnight and the fourth had moved to fifth November.

He was used to the busy traffic of the city, but here there were different night noises. The hoot of an owl, the squawk of some bird or animal, and suddenly loud screeching. The sound of some foxes mating deep in the woods. This he recognised; even Smethwick had foxes in the still remaining bomb sites of his youth, and down by the canal.

He came upon the major and the corporal behind the bushes. In front of them, a slightly eerie sight of the back of the manor and the newly built building bathed in a half-light, casting shadows on the grassy slope.

The corporal was listening, Major Bob watching. The reels in the suitcase weren't turning and there was no light from the spy dish.

'How's the sound now?' Trent enquired.

'Clear as a bell; we put microphones on the wall, some magnetic, some with suckers. Nothing going on at the moment, so we're not recording,' the corporal replied.

The Manor House at the front was lit up like a Christmas tree, the lights blazing into the dark sky, in contrast to the subdued light at the back. Some vehicles could be clearly heard around the front. The major said: 'People still arriving and they are having some drinks served as they come in. Corporal Poole popped down earlier. We think there are about thirty supporters turned up.

'There are lots of posh cars, posh people; although driving themselves, no chauffeurs. Also army brass, scrambled eggs and Navy wallahs too.' The major picked up his earphones and fiddled with them.

'They're miked up down there on stage,' said the major, his breath an icy cloud. 'Makes the recording easier. We have up to four hours of tapes here. Will record when something starts.'

Trent nodded and went further back into the woods. It was now cold. He smiled ruefully at the woolly glove Camille had given him and pulled it over his wounded hand. He lit a cigarette, and smoked it behind a large oak tree, with his left hand.

After a couple of minutes, the corporal appeared. 'Something's happening, some sort of announcement. We've started recording.' Trent stubbed the cigarette out and rejoined them. He'd not had that bet with Poole on the West Brom-Stoke game for—where were we?—yes, tomorrow. Saturday, the sixth.

'We've got an earphone each here,' said Poole and he handed one over. Trent pushed it into his ear. The tape reels now turning, the antenna in the middle of the spy dish now flashing, though hardly discernible. Like something from a sci-fi movie.

As the tapes turned, Trent and the others listened to Sir Richard Abbott's astonishing and frightening speech.

Chapter Forty-Seven
5 November

'Gentlemen!' (There we're no ladies present). 'Welcome, members of the GB National Party, to the start of a new dawn for this country.' Sir Richard's voice boomed over the microphone—rich and plummy—in fact, today, he sounded a bit like Orson Welles as well.

'Please pray silence, a minute's silence for our heroic Colonel Alec Stewart, killed in a boating accident in pursuit of our objectives.' (*So that was the story*, thought Trent.)

Silence, the typical shuffling, coughs and yawns in a minute's silence. All picked up by Sir Richard's mike and amplified though the spy listening device.

Sir Richard then continued: 'Thank you. You are all leaders in your own fields and later today, the appropriate 5 November, you will take control of your particular areas.

'Most of you were part of the failed coup of '67; this one, however, will work with all the planning we've put in. I have complete control over all armed forces, intelligence and law agencies. And when we affect Operation Regicide in the morning, this will be the catalyst for us to spring our little rebellion. The death of Queen Elizabeth the Second, and you can bank, yes bank, on that happening…ha.

'I know a few of you weren't keen on Operation Regicide but…' He paused. 'You are now all on board. A couple of waverers have been, let's say, retired.' He let that sink in.

'Retired, I can guess what that means,' Trent muttered.

There was a loud crash; the three listeners jumped. It was Abbott banging the table to emphasise his point. 'The action is imperative to bring the public totally on our side, and also, as said many times before, to wipe out the symbol of our failed Britain.' Another dramatic pause. 'To misquote Bismarck: An iron fist with an iron glove. Also: Iron and Blood,' he said. 'This will be our motto and we will crush any resistance to our plans.' His voice went up there and now he brought it back to a more measured tone.

'You more or less know your orders. However, Jones here and some of my men will take five each of you to six separate rooms throughout the house. There will be written instructions and my men will go through them with you. Seminars, if you like...

'Then when done, please return. We'll have a final briefing with Sir Adrian and celebratory champagne. Thank you. I'm banking on you. Ha!'

There was a smattering of applause, scraping of chairs, and murmuring. The delegates, for want of a better word, left, followed by Sir Richard and Adrian Joyce in a clearly audible and self-congratulatory mood.

'God, that'll go on forever,' the major said. 'We'll need all these tapes.'

'Well, you can turn them off until they return,' Trent replied. 'Sorry, gents, haven't got your patience to sit and wait. Not my strong point! Still, think of all that lovely loot in there.'

Pound signs buzzed in the major's eyes. 'Absolutely right, what's a bit of cold and wet, hey, Corporal. Anyway, if you're going back to camp, send up the sergeant and the Russian, their turn. Also, ask Williams to send Parker to relieve Sale on gate duty. Thanks, old boy.'

Trent nodded and retraced his steps through the dark woods to the camp. Back at the quagmire, Trent dispatched the sergeant, Ilya and Parker. Camille had retreated to her car to warm up and he now joined her underneath a blanket. They both quickly fell asleep in that strange, dream-like, semi-lit clearing, shadows from the dim lamps flickering around the woodland, ghostly shapes forming...

There was tapping on the car window; it was an ever cheerful Corporal Poole. Trent was awake and Camille stretched and woke up too. 'I think I'll stay in the warm a bit longer,' she said in a sleepy, half-awake voice. They'd been in the car for two hours. Poole grinning updated them.

'They're back in the conference place; the major requests you join us. We've got Parker back from sentry duty, he's in camp, and we're starting the recording and readying for the assault.'

Sergeant Des, Ilya and Parker were back in camp and all smoking. Des raised his arm in greeting. It had stopped raining.

'The major and Sale are listening in. Parker, Ilya, need to get ready, come on let's go.' The sergeant decided to stay with Camille until they were ready to attack. The corporal strode forward, all business-like. Trent and the others followed him up that dark forest path again, a break in the rain welcome. He felt that particular electric tingling run through him, in anticipation of the action to come.

Behind the hedge, on the groundsheet, the two soldiers were listening, the antenna flashing. Trent took the third earpiece. He could hear excited chatter, like school before a headmaster's speech.

Then suddenly: 'Testing...Testing...' He recognised Jones at the microphone in the hall. There was a lot of feedback and he continued: 'Thank you, gentlemen, please settle down now, and pray stand for Sir Richard and Sir Adrian again. Salutant deos...'

There was a slow handclap from the audience heralding the entrance of their two leaders. Trent imagined them basking in the adulation and then Sir Richard beckoned them to finish and sit down.

Whilst the tapes turned, he continued: 'You've all been given your individual assignments, and people under your command in your area.' Pause. 'Excellent. Let's now go over the overall strategy.'

'God, not again,' Trent grunted. He caught sight of the major's watch; it was nearly 2.30am. He gave a sigh.

He went over the same old ground: take over army/police/TV arrests; one-party system. Apartheid; on, and on and on. The tapes were still turning.

One new titbit he mentioned that the militia force put together by Sir Adrian was camped out at an old RAF base at Bovingdon in Hertfordshire. Only used now for occasional film location work. 'They are well-trained and well-armed, and ready to provide support for our coup. We have a small group of the militia billeted here as well.'

Then Sir Richard finished: 'And of course, later Operation Regicide. Our man Mueller is already setting up for that in Swindon.' There was applause.

'So that's where Mueller, the Zombie, is,' said Trent, his anger rising.

'And now over to my good friend, Sir Adrian Joyce, our man in parliament.'

'Thank you...' This was a different Joyce to the one often seen on TV. Gone was any sense of diplomacy or restraint. It was a spittle-spattered speech. An Adolf Hitler impersonation working the followers into a frenzy.

He started reasonably enough. 'Gentlemen, members of the GB National Party. Ruling members I should say. You are now witnessing the birth of a new Great Britain. The return of Empire; well, all the good bits at least.'

He paused. Trent could imagine him staring out over his adoring "acolytes", and then he continued raising the pitch.

'The old empire…all undone by those traitors—royalty, government, the church, all the powers that be. Well, they're all doomed!' This was now a shriek 'The whole establishment…we'll wipe 'em out!' There was a loud roar from his audience. When it calmed, he went on: 'Yes, the greatest empire the world had ever seen—Great Britain—all destroyed.' His voice then softened; he knew how to play an audience. 'So, gents, we'll rebuild—build in our image, a government, armed forces, of our creation. Make our country great again; feared the world over. Crush all opposition—one party, us—wipe out the traitors, the criminals. All these new-fangled liberal ideas. Steer clear of soft Europe.'

His high-pitched screech was back. 'The Irish problem. Finish off what Cromwell started in 1649; suppress the republicans, suppress the Republic…' Higher and higher he went. 'Finally, inferior races. We'll introduce the South African system here, apartheid. What in practice happens in the southern states of the United States? Let 'em do the dirty, smelly jobs.' More cheers. 'Make 'em second-class, non-voting workers in menial jobs. Yes, the white man will once again rule in our new nation. It's all in the bank, as Sir Richard said…'

Joyce built up to a crescendo and finished with, 'Remember our motto: Iron and Blood; Iron and Blood.'

The cheering went on for a good five minutes. The three listeners couldn't believe what they'd heard. 'Fuck,' said the corporal.

'Good job Des is not here to hear this,' Trent muttered under his breath.

The applause and stomping finally subsided; they sang *For he's a jolly good fellow*, which segued into *Rule Britannia*. The corporal swore again and the major's moustache twitched.

Sir Richard came back on.

'Right, thanks one and all. Thanks, Sir Adrian. Work over, now champagne and canapés being served. Please enjoy and raise your glasses to Operation Regicide.' The microphone in the hall was turned off and the background noise of a party could be heard as a distant hubbub.

'Right, recording over, let's get those tapes away and start our assault on these bastards.' Major's eyes shone with the thought of actual battle. 'Corporal, get the arms out.'

Poole went over to the tarpaulin and uncovered the armoury. The major handed the tapes over to Trent. 'Up to Camille to get them delivered, with your gay mate; take them down to her, then get back here as soon as you can and then we're ready for the off.' The major was now firmly in command again.

He jogged back to the clearing and advised the sergeant that things were starting. 'Before you go, however, could you help give Camille's car a push.' The sports car in a sorry state was stuck in the churned mud.

Camille had never been keen on leaving but saw she was the best way of getting the tapes to Kev Bloomer. Trent wanted her out of the way of the fighting.

'We're all soldiers,' he'd said bluntly. 'It's our job; best if you're safe back in London.' He repeated what he'd said earlier and there was no argument this time.

They'd said their long goodbyes earlier under the car blanket. She took the tapes, gave Trent a sad, sad kiss. 'Look after yourself.'

Trent and the sergeant gave the car a push and she was gone into the wet night.

Chapter Forty-Eight

Trent and Sergeant Des Williams arrived back at the top of the hill overlooking the Manor House. Corporal Poole was still listening to the after-conference celebrations. 'Plenty of hangovers after this I bet, won't be in the mood for revolution,' the corporal said to no one in particular, smiling ruefully. The arms were now piled up in readiness and the rain thankfully was easing off.

The major was ready for the off. Trent took him aside and they talked in low voices. The others noticed that the major was obviously in disagreement with Trent and becoming agitated.

In the end, Major Bob shrugged his shoulders in resignation and, exasperated, said: 'OK, blow you! Damn you! But take Corporal Poole with you.'

The others looked on bemused as Trent instructed the corporal, who nodded. They then set off and went down the slope towards the house. They kept very low but luckily, the dark covered them anyway.

Trent's finger was throbbing slightly beneath Camille's glove, he could smell her scent on it. It was now a fine clear night and some stars had appeared in the sky. A cold November night, a frost now forming on the wet grass.

Trent was armed with the smith + wesson in his left hand and the Beretta in a holster behind him on his trouser ammunition belt. He also had a commando knife in a sheath, also attached to his belt. And hidden up his sleeve, a smaller knife for a nasty surprise.

Corporal Poole wore his bow and arrows and quiver. A machine gun also on his back.

They were now running to the back of the conference hall. Dark shadows on dark grass, vaguely lit by the lamps on the back of the hall.

They could hear the voices inside the new building housing the conference. Still in jubilant celebration.

Slowly edging round the building to the older part of the Manor House, they went past a garage to the right, set back from the house.

In a whisper, Corporal Poole indicated there were normally three or four guards at the front. They'd share honours in silencing them.

Behind a small wall at the side of the old house, they crouched. Trent could see three guards lounging about, their automatic rifles leaning against an ivy-covered wall. They were smoking/chatting, just outside the large wooden doors.

In front of them, a courtyard swept out to a large carpark full, as the major had said earlier, with top-of-the-range vehicles. Four Union Jacks swayed in the wind surrounding the carpark.

The corporal held up two fingers. Trent nodded and held up one.

Poole unleashed two arrows from his bow in succession and two guards collapsed dead.

The third, stunned momentarily, made a grab for this rifle.

Immediately, Trent, moving like a cat, was on him from behind, his injured hand over his mouth, the commando knife deep into his back.

Three down. Any more?

They listened; a voice said from inside came. 'Got some booze, chaps, they won't miss it.' The fourth guard!

Poole dodged back behind the small wall. Trent hid behind the open large front door.

'Here you are men…what?' The sentry stared at his three comrades and dropped his rifle.

Trent leapt at him, his knife flashed, left-handed, to his heart and the sentry joined his fellow troops.

'Slovenly lot; shouldn't have too much problem with the others,' the corporal observed.

They stepped over the bodies, their blood seeping, and cautiously looked in on a long, dark hall.

'Right, Corporal, I'll take it from here. You keep guard on this door with your gun, not your bow and arrows! Stop anyone trying to escape.'

The corporal smiled, gave a mock salute, got his gun ready and then sat on the wall, and lit a Park Drive; untipped, bliss!

*

Except for the thugs on the island, it was the first time Trent had seen this militia of Adrian Joyce's. Not too professional but they may come up against a better class of soldier later. Their uniform was all in grey, with a GB National Party logo on the shirt and a small Union Jack. They wore black berets on their heads. Zombies—that's what he'd called Colonel Stewart's men back on the island—and Zombies is what he'd call this militia now.

Trent had been here before on a couple of Sir Richard's lengthy (boring) sermons on joint intelligence (or something?). He moved along the large passage, the sitting room with valuable works of art was on the left. To the right, the dining room, with a table big enough for twenty people.

Then a library, then a study, and a couple of spare rooms, then the stairs to the upper floors and the stairs to the kitchen, wine cellar and stores below. All along the passage, portraits of Sir Richard's illustrious ancestors.

Sir Richard had shown off his extensive wine cellar last time he'd been here. Big enough to hold any prisoners, with a very strong door and lock.

Trent, smith + wesson in hand, then went through a set of doors that took him into the newer section of the building. There was no one about. He passed the conference room, the door was shut, but he could hear the party noises clearly. He crept down the corridor to the canteen and peered through the small portholes in the door. There were about ten "Zombies" in there. Most were asleep in bunk beds, and nearly all the canteen tables were stacked to one side. Their rifles were all piled on the remaining tables. A couple were playing cards.

Trent went back to the conference door. He took a deep breath and kicked it open. Crash!

The party hubbub ceased immediately.

Faces turned in his direction.

The look of surprise on the faces of the two peers of the realm—Abbott and Joyce.

On the stage looking down on their disciples.

The Abbott coat of arms and Union Jack behind them.

He took in the room: two servants dishing out the spread. Jones and three Zombies at the back. The Zombies armed. Incongruously, a bishop in his cassock standing next to a chief constable in his smart uniform. With a start, he then recognised the chief intelligence man who had interrogated him at that meeting by the Thames so long ago. Another crony of Sir Richard.

All stopped in their tracks, staring at Trent, gun in hand.

Sir Richard recovered first, as cool as cucumber. 'Ah, Trent. So you didn't die in that Welsh misadventure, evidently.' He puffed on his large cigar, his jowls wobbling.

'Oh, take that pistol off him, Jones.' He sighed, exasperated, his show spoilt by this oik, this gatecrasher. Sir Adrian looked down over his spectacles like a disappointed headmaster.

Jones, a gun in his hand, and the three armed guards approached him. One guard relieved him of the smith + wesson, another the Beretta and commando knife, but they somehow missed the small knife up his sleeve. The guard then shoved the smith + wesson in his belt and the other gun in his pocket. Jones looked at the large knife covered in blood and dropped it to the floor in distaste.

'My apologies, gentlemen,' Abbott said to his audience. 'We'll deal with this and then continue.'

He turned to Trent. 'Why are you here?'

'I've come to kill you.'

'You and whose army...ha ha ha.'

Abbott and Joyce broke into laughter, followed nervously by their audience. Sir Richard addressed Trent again. 'So you escaped, and killed the colonel...tut. Very clever, but your journey ends tonight.'

For the first time, Trent noticed with distaste the GB National Party logo, alongside the Union Jack and Sir Richard's coat of arms above the stage. A real misuse of the flag he for so long had served under.

Abbott turned on Jones. 'Jones, your plan was always too complicated. All that palaver about reporting to Colonel Stewart and then leaving him dead in those dunes. Should have killed him much earlier. Got rid of him before he went to the island. The PM would have authorised the state of emergency anyway. A refinement too far methinks. Damn...'

The studious, bespectacled Jones blushed under Abbott's gaze. Sir Richard was now standing up on the stage. 'No complications this time; take him outside and kill him, now!'

There was a low murmur through the crowd. Trent had guessed that to many in the audience, the idea of revolution was an academic/intellectual concept and they didn't really want to know about the bloody mechanics of it all. Like the death of Trent.

He was surrounded by Jones and the Zombies. Jones was close, typically he couldn't resist Latin. 'ut vicimus.'

Trent sniffed at him. 'Don't like your aftershave, Jones,' he said loudly. 'Is it Chanel Number 5?'

Further nervous laughter from the hall. Jones snarled: 'Come on, Trent, out.' He would take his embarrassment out on him.

There was the noise of fireworks outside, a rocket, followed by bangers. Then a massive "firework" explosion hit the wall behind Sir Richard and Sir Adrian, and engulfed it in flames. Trent, expecting this, dived to the floor. Another distant explosion, from next door, followed...

Chapter Forty-Nine

Chanel Number 5, the joke password Camille had come up with. Déjà vu, used again in a plot to arrange explosive deaths for Trent's enemies.

The password, a signal for Sergeant Des Williams to fire a bazooka at the back of the conference hall, and then at the canteen and the barn/stables. Fireworks to be set off to disguise the explosions to the distant outside world.

Trent's signal to say that the ringleaders were on stage and in line for a main hit.

His earlier argument with the major was about there being no real need to take the risk. Corporal Poole could climb up to the side window in the hall and signal that way, and then get clear.

There was truth in this. The truth though was Trent wanted to see Sir Richard Abbott, Baronet, Lord of the manor, and for him to know that he, Trent, was the architect of his downfall. Revenge! Sweet Revenge…

Smoke filled the air, debris covered the floor. The guards, the Zombies, were in a daze. Trent had been prepared for the explosion and was still compos mentis. (To borrow a Jones phrase).

Suddenly, from the floor, he threw the hidden knife with force. It hit the nearest guard, the one with his gun, in the neck, in the jugular. Blood spraying, the guard fell. Trent grabbed his smith + wesson back and immediately shot the other two dizzy guards dead.

He stood up, covered in blood, his ears ringing, and took things in. He first noticed that Jones was missing; he'd somehow quickly fled.

Secondly, he suddenly realised that only one other bazooka shot was fired. What happened to the third shot at the stables housing most of the militia?

As if in answer to his question, there was a volley of shots from the side of the manor. A battle commencing between "our" men and the defending Zombies.

The stage had been completely demolished and the two GB National Party leaders with it.

'That army, Sir Richard.' He spat out in answer to Abbott's so-called sarcastic humorous earlier question. 'Good riddance...'

Those at the front of the hall had taken the worst of the blast and were no more, including the Whitehall intelligence man. The remnants of the GB National Party were wandering about, bloodied, among broken chairs, trestle tables, smashed champagne, and squashed canapés. Trent counted thirteen survivors, seventeen dead, plus the two servants. He had a brief twinge of conscience about the servants, but they must have known and be party to all that was going on.

Still in the background, the sound of gunfire and what sounded like large machine guns.

The chief constable approached, his pristine bemedalled blue uniform now torn, and covered in dust, and blood streaming down his forehead.

'Look here—what-what—Trent, that was your name. Do you know who I am? Chief Constable for Wiltshire. I demand you let us go, demand!'

Pompous, commanding, but the effect spoilt by splodges of canapés in his hair.

'Chief Constable, but not for much longer I'd say. We've got your whole conspiracy recorded and the authorities will be here later. Now shut up and get away.'

The chief constable, looking shaken, backed off. Another "gentleman" in uniform appeared; he looked to be an admiral. 'I warn you, let us go. You don't know who you're dealing with.'

There was a sound of consistent machine gun fire from the canteen next door. The admiral and the chief constable ducked.

The hefty Private Parker appeared and sauntered in, a smoking machine gun over his shoulder, an ammo belt wrapped round him, and a half-smile on his lips. 'I asked them to surrender, they didn't; all dead.' It was the first time Trent had seen Parker smile.

It was also the first time he'd heard Parker speak; so he'd killed all the Zombie troops next door. A born killer as he'd surmised earlier.

To the chief constable and admiral, he said, 'You don't know who you're dealing with!'

He then addressed all the survivors, now standing in a huddle in the middle of the wrecked room. 'Right you, behave yourselves, stay here.' To Parker, he said: 'Anyone tries to escape, shoot them.'

Parker saluted. 'Yes, Sir. A pleasure.'

Trent reloaded his smith + wesson and retrieved his Beretta from the dead guard. Now for Jones; he must still be here. He'd never have got past Corporal Poole at the front.

Back in the old building, he switched the hall lights on and he noticed a small trail of blood; Jones must be wounded. Back at the front door, he saw another dead body on the steps, Poole standing over it. It was one of the army generals; he must have escaped with Jones.

Poole echoed Parker. 'Wouldn't give in. Tried to pull rank. Wouldn't reason, so I shot him.' He looked puzzled. 'Never shot a general before.' He looked at Trent. 'Aye oop, Mr Trent, you're covered in blood. Are you OK?' He stopped and listened to the sound of fighting. 'Bit of a battle down at the stables; bazooka didn't go off a third time.'

'Fine time to let us down, Bomber,' Trent said to himself. To Poole, he said: 'Was there someone with the general?'

'Yes, a bloke with glasses, looked like a clerk; scared rabbit. He scuttled off to the right there.'

'Thanks, Corporal. Now go down to the conference place and you and Parker get the survivors down to the wine cellar and lock 'em up. Then join the major and the others.'

'Yes, Sir.' Poole also mock-saluted Trent.

To the right of the main entrance, there was a small passage, some tell-tale blood spots, leading to an even smaller staircase. Probably the servants' back stairs up to the bedrooms.

Upstairs, he passed several bedrooms but carried on following the blood trail, until he came to a larger door. The master bedroom? The blood trail dripped into that room.

There was a vacuum cleaner at the side of the hall. Moving quickly, he grabbed it, ignoring the pain in his finger. He pushed the door ajar and flung the cleaner through, standing well clear.

There were six shots fired—scattered round the door—erratic, no precision. Jones was not any sort of marksman! He pushed open the door, Jones was by the double bed trying to reload. Trent hit him hard in the face and he collapsed onto the bed, his nose exploding in blood.

The room was not as expected in a traditional style. It was sort of feminine 60s taste and must have been Sir Richard's estranged wife's choice. There were orange covers on the double bed, Norwegian wood, cheap-type panels on the wall, and green carpets. An ensuite bathroom was off to the right.

Jones was now lying on Sir Richard's king-sized bed, his nose bleeding and watching the cut on his arm, still dripping blood.

'Jones. Bit out of your league today.' Trent held his gun above him. 'Should have stuck to strategy with the prof. Trouble with you geniuses, delusions of grandeur.' He lowered the gun, pointing below Jones' belt.

'Now I want some information.'

'Not telling you anything, you'll have to kill me.'

'Certainly, I'll kill you, but first, I'll shoot you in the testicles and other bits if you don't talk.'

A sheen of sweat covered Jones' face. He was no hero. 'What do you want?' He stammered.

'Good, don't want to spoil the sheets anymore. Tell me about Operation Regicide. All your idea no doubt. Mueller is going to kill the Queen. But when and exactly where in Swindon.'

Jones said: 'I'm not…' Trent raised his gun, finger on the trigger.

'OK, OK. He's setting up the kill on the top of Woolworth's in Regent Street, Swindon. He's probably there now ready for the morning but you won't stop him.'

Trent remembered the Queen's route from the *Swindon Advertiser* earlier. Approx times and her itinerary. Regent Street was certainly a correct location.

Jones whispered, whimpered, 'Look, I've told you. Please don't hurt me.'

Trent looked at Jones—pathetic on the bed—was it worth it? He looked at the gun in his left hand. An image of his dead friends hit him, sending a shiver up his spine.

'This is for Steve and Jackie. You…!'

He then shot him in the head.

'Villis Ipsum,' he sneered the only Latin Trent had picked up from some of the sixth form seniors when they briefly tried to introduce it at the grammar school. 'Fuck You!'

Chapter Fifty
Battle in the Shires

On the side of the Manor House, near the front, but set well away from the main building, was a group of stables and barns and a courtyard in front. This was where the rest of the militia, the Zombies, were housed. Corporal Poole on his surreptitious walkabout had estimated there were ten inside.

A bitter war was now raging there. The Zombies well dug into their defensive position and well armed. They seemed to have a couple of large machine guns on stands, a Gatling-type weapon.

This, backed up by normal machine guns and rifles, was keeping the mercenaries at bay.

Trent surveyed the scene of carnage. This brutal reality he and his mercenary comrades knew only too well. Who would have believed that this mini-war was taking place in the shires of England? He was surprised that the GB National Party militia was still fighting; they must know it was all over…surely.

- drifting smoke; smell of blood, not just from his clothes…
- exploding shells; noise with its own poetic violence…
- percussive boom; volley of guns in the valley…
- whump, wham, smash, smack
- an indecent assault on genteel countryside

Yes, he knew it well, and it now sickened him, his life of death and destruction. Oh well…once more into the breach…

The major's men were positioned behind what was an old World War II bomb shelter. The underground entrance was blocked up, the top now a grass-covered mound which gave them cover from the incessant gunfire.

Trent, even more dishevelled and blood-covered, crouched down and made for his comrades in arms, bullets whistling about him.

There was Sergeant Des, Corporal Poole, Parker, and the Russian. All returning fire as the shots ricocheted and pinged against the grass knoll. Trent was amazed to see Illya, the Ghost, joining in with other soldiers. But where was Sale? And where was Major Bob?

He knelt by Des, who even in the heat of the bloody battle, expressed surprise at Trent's appearance. A bullet rebounded off the courtyard narrowly whizzing past Trent's ear.

'Where's the other two, Des, Where's the major?'

'Private Sale is on the other side of the stables, keeping them penned in. So they can't escape out the back.'

'And the major?'

The sergeant nodded back to the side of the manor towards what looked like a coal bunker.

'He's behind there, badly wounded I'm afraid. Tried to lead a charge on the stables. Wanted to get closer to throw grenades in. We're too far away to throw them. But that's what's needed to dislodge them.'

'They're better calibre than the others we met, with better weapons,' Corporal Poole gave his pennyworth. Des grimly nodded.

'Yes,' the sergeant continued. 'The major called out for them to surrender. Told us to F-off. Said they'd got food and ammo for months. They don't think they've got anything to lose now.'

The rain was falling down, hissing on the guns as the mercenaries returned fire, futile in competition with the Gatling gun's steady staccato beat.

'I've given the major a shot of morphine but it doesn't look too good.' Des shook his head.

More heavy gun fire, followed by rifle fire—left then right, left then right— white puffs of smoke in the shower of rain. Gunfire flickered, flared behind the stable block, keeping the militia pinned down. The two sides duelled as the night ended and dawn started to awake.

'This is crazy. If we don't get this sorted soon, someone in the area is going to realise that something's going on, and this…this is not a fireworks party.' Trent took a peek over the grass bank and assessed the situation.

'Maybe they'll think it's an early-morning shooting party for the toffs,' replied the sergeant.

'Maybe,' Trent said. 'I'm going to go and see Major Bob, then put some thought into how we can grenade them and smoke them out.'

There was then a lull in the cross-firing. Trent, keeping low, darted to the coal bunker. There was Major Bob, his midriff all torn to pieces and covered in blood.

'I hope I don't look as bad as you, old boy,' the major coughed, blood showing in his mouth.

'I'm sorry it's come to this, Major.' Trent could see he hadn't much time left.

'Could be worse. The morphine's deadened the pain, and this helps.' He held up a small bottle of rum and drank from it.

'I mean, sorry I dragged you into this.'

'Don't worry; this is what I exist for, could…c-c could only end like this…' He coughed again. 'Look after the lads, make sure they get the money, and those in the troop who didn't come. Get their share…'

He took another swig, coughed again. 'Have a drink for me in White's, old boy, a drink, one for the road…'

The sound of gunfire faded, the sky blackened, and the major died.

*

Trent closed the major's eyes, said a short half-forgotten soldier's prayer for the dead, and returned to the other mercenaries.

The men could see from Trent's expression that it was bad news. Corporal Poole crossed himself; Des stiffened his whole body tense with suppressed anger. Nothing else to be said about the major. He concentrated on the immediate problem.

'Still need to get grenades into that building.'

The firing had ceased again and Trent took another look across the yard. 'Corporal, could you get one of those vehicles out front started. Maybe if I drove one into the building, I could get close enough.'

'I could,' the corporal replied. 'Easy, but it would be a suicide mission.'

'Perhaps that's what it needs to break the deadlock.'

They all turned to Illya who started to shout, clearly agitated: 'Major, drook, drook—my friend, my friend. I'll go.'

Before anyone could stop him, he grabbed a hand grenade pouch. His Cossack blood up, yelling strange whoops, he zig-zagged across the grass and the yard dodging a fusillade of bullets. Crack, crack, crack. He pulled a grenade out, pulled the pin, the bullets hit him in a bloody swish, and he collapsed, dropping the grenade. An explosion shook the yard. The Dukh, the Ghost, was gone. Gone to join other ghosts.

They were all momentarily shocked at the speed of Illya's rash action and his demise. A heavy swirl of damp wind blew smoke away towards the east. Illya returning to his homeland? No one spoke for a few minutes, a silent requiem for the Russian.

'I think he knew more a bit more English than he let on. He really bonded with us up in the woods, wanted to join us, the battle seemed to galvanise him. Such a shame.' The sergeant's words broke the silence, he looked sad for a second, then snapped out of it. 'So what are we going to do?'

Again both sides had ceased firing and Trent surveyed the building in the rain. Dawn was breaking in the east, a red sky through the drizzle, a "shepherd's warning". 'We must break this impasse,' Trent said more to himself using a Camille-type word. Corporal Poole looked blank. 'This stalemate, I mean.'

Then an idea hit him. Looking at the thatched roof of the barn, he turned to Corporal Poole.

'Corporal, could you shoot arrows into that barn roof over there?'

The corporal lying down, his rifle pushed through the grass, looked up at Trent quizzically.

'Well, er, yes, I could. Why?'

'Fire arrows,' Trent was still half speaking to himself. He then looked at Poole and replied: 'Fire arrows; we could set that thatch alight.'

'Yes, but where? How do we get the fire?'

The other two were listening, Parker still silent, but Des, inspired, said: 'There's a garage on the other side. Looked in it earlier; there are petrol cans.'

'Of course,' said Trent. 'Come on, Corporal, bring your quiver, we'll make fire.'

'If there's no petrol in the cans, I could always siphon some from those cars,' said Poole, the man of many talents.

He then followed Trent, who muttered: 'Of course, you could.'

Their heads down, they made their way back to the front of the manor and then to the other side and the garage. Gunfire in the background now intermittent, spasmodic. Both sides bored with the stand-off.

In a corner of the garage, there were petrol cans next to a strongbox full of tools. The petrol cans were full. They discovered cleaning cloths, ripped them up, and tied string round them, then fastened them to the arrows. Then they dipped them in petrol. They did this with eight arrows.

They then returned to their place behind the shelter. 'OK, let's get this firework party started,' Trent said to Poole, and then turned to the others. 'Provide some cover whilst the corporal gets ready.'

The two remaining mercenaries opened fire. Sale behind the stables echoed their shots.

'Fire.' Des encouraged Parker and Sale, shots blasted both sides of the barn, and there was a scream from the out buildings and a misty spray of blood rose into the cold air and floated over the cobbled courtyard.

Poole lined up his bow ready to fire, Trent took out his lighter and lit the rags on the end of the arrow. Poole poked his head over the barricade, took aim, and quickly fired. He then ducked as bullets flew, luckily the rain providing some cover.

The arrow sailed through the air and they watched in anticipation, would it? Won't it? Sweat appeared on Des' forehead. Parker was typically unconcerned despite a wound to his arm. Clang! It fell inches short of the thatch, hitting the side of the roof and falling to the yard below, hissing in the puddles. A soft groan from the watching soldiers; a curse from Trent.

'OK, let's go again.' Poole and Trent repeated the procedure with covering fire. Again, the burning arrow flew and again it missed by inches.

Poole, obviously frustrated, took a deep breath. 'Third time's lucky; let's get my rhythm.'

Trent and Poole then got into the swing; further six fire arrows were shot and landed in the middle of the thatch. Twang, twang, twang, they went. Twang, twang, twang.

At first, the fire fizzled and spluttered in the wet, but then suddenly, it took hold and in minutes, the whole roof was aflame and moving into the wooden building below and the stables next door.

The firing from the Zombies now ceased as the gravity of the situation dawned. Then their store of ammunition started to explode in the barn. The flames now really gripped the building, black smoke billowing in the sky; a real bonfire for Guy Fawkes.

Suddenly, there was movement from the stables and five remaining Zombies came out, unarmed, with a white sheet of surrender, one badly wounded. 'We must have killed more than we thought,' Trent said to Des.

But Sergeant Des Williams wasn't listening. He stood up, his 6ft 4in frame shaking with rage. His anger palpable, his machine gun blazed, and he mowed the survivors down.

'That's for the major and the others, you racist bastards…'

Chapter Fifty-One

Trent looked at the sergeant; no longer the gentle giant. He couldn't really criticise but he was getting very fed up now with all this bloodshed. He wiped his forehead and stared out at the mess and the bodies, the fire in the burnt-out buildings slowly coming under control in the teeming rain. Black smoke hanging heavy.

A flock of birds flew across the early dawn landscape. Flying south for winter? Wish he could join them.

His thought again was to pack it all in, get away with Camille, but one more fight…duty, Queen and country. To Swindon, to Mueller, the Z, to his destiny, to save Her Majesty.

He totted up the "butcher's bill" on their side—Major Bob, the Russian, and a wounded Private Parker, who was now receiving attention to his left arm by Corporal Poole. 'Bit of shrapnel got him, will be right as rain,' he cheerfully commented.

On the other side must be roughly thirty dead and sixteen prisoners in the wine cellar. A good outcome for the victors in war but Trent still felt dispirited, even in the victory.

Des' eyes were glazed and he was looking at his machine gun in disbelief. He threw it to the floor in disgust.

'Sorry,' he said to Trent. 'Shouldn't have done that, not professional, not cricket. They'd surrendered!'

'Don't worry, Des, they deserved it. I, er…shot Jones in cold blood…revenge. I understand.'

He looked down at himself, soaked to the skin, covered in mud and blood. 'I'm going to check on the prisoners, try and get cleaned up and changed, and then get off to Swindon. Need to borrow your Jeep.'

Des nodded, said OK. 'We'll still have plenty of room in the Matador.'

'Look, you lads need to get out of here before someone comes. Find the money, load up and go,' Trent said, hoping some money was still in the manor.

Corporal Poole smirked. 'When Sale and me took the toffs to the cellar, nosed around. There's a small store room nearby rammed with cash, we'll take it all…ha ha'

Sergeant Des said: 'Now Poole's sorted you out, Parker, go and fetch the truck. You'll be OK one-armed.'

Trent went back into the Manor House. Talk of Parker's injury brought his own throbbing finger back. Camille's glove hanging now in threads.

He went downstairs to the wine cellar, Poole and Sale not far behind, in search of the loot!

Trent banged on the wine cellar door. There was immediate shouting and banging.

'Now, gentlemen, settle down. Some nice policemen will be here soon to rescue you.'

'You can't leave us in here.' It was that chief constable again.

'You're better off in there; all the others are dead.'

That gave him some food for thought; a few seconds' silence.

'Look, we've no food and drink, no facilities.'

'You've the finest collection of wine in the country, enjoy it whilst you can. Think you'll be locked up for a long time, in prison.'

He left him spluttering in indignation and went back up towards the stairs. Poole and Sale were loading bundles into some boxes they'd found—plastic containers of bank notes; National Westminster, Barclays, Trustee Savings Bank, etc. stamped on the packets.

'Aye oop,' said Poole. 'A right Aladdin's cave; must be over a million in there.' And the rest, thought Trent.

'Have some money as well, Mr Trent.' Poole threw a couple of packets to Trent. 'You've earned it.' He threw another couple which Trent just about caught and stuffed in his pocket. Must be £20,000 there.

'Thanks, Corporal, see you in a bit.' He went up the stairs. He might need that cash for Camille and himself—escape money. Yes, things may get rough from here on in. He then ran up to the first floor, ignored Sir Richard's room and Jones' dead body and looked in the next bedroom.

He found some men's clothes in the wardrobe, which just about fitted. Threw the bloodied Army and Navy clothes on the floor, had a perfunctory cleanup in a sink in the corner of the room, then found a pair of gloves and put one over this bad hand, dropping Camille's ragged gloves into a bin. Finally, he took an overcoat from the wardrobe and felt some way to being respectable.

Outside the house was the army truck which had been driven from Poachers Wood by Private Parker. Poole and Sale were stacking the back with the sealed bank notes. Parker was wheeling, one-handed, a wheelbarrow full of gold and silver artefacts from the house—more treasures, more spoils of the war.

Sergeant Des was supervising. 'A nice little earner this has been. Shame about the major; oh, yes, and Illya.'

Trent approached him. 'What are you going to do next, Des?'

'Well, Corp...and I must say you're looking a bit better. I'm going to take command, promote myself to captain; not major, respect! The loot we'll share with the others who didn't come. Then we've got a mission overseas in about a month; will be a picnic compared to this.'

'You need to get away. What about your weapons?'

'We'll leave them; going to take the major and Dukh with us, bury them somewhere discreet.'

'What about fingerprints?'

'None of us have records, not even the unique Corporal Poole.'

Poole grinned. 'Never caught me!'

'What's the time? Lost my watch at sea.' Trent realised that it was now light and getting on. There was no let-up in the rain either.

'It's 6.13am. Here, have mine.' Des undid his watch and handed it over.

'Think I can afford it. Also, here's the Jeep's ignition keys.'

'Right, I'm going. Can you er...lend me a few coins, quid in change; need to make some calls.'

Trent placed the key and watch into his coat pocket with the bags of money— his "reward".

'Here you are, least we can do.' Des gave him some coins and notes.

'Thanks, will you be out of here in say an hour? I need to phone the authorities.'

'Yes, we'll be gone.'

'OK, best of luck then.' He shook hands with Des, gave a half-hearted wave to the others, and went round to the side of the Manor House.

He stopped at the garage; he remembered the safety deposit box in there next to the petrol. He threw the tools out, found a spade, and then left and walked up the hill at the back of the house towards Poachers Wood carrying the box and spade.

He went past the observation post, the recording equipment still lying scattered about and back down the familiar path into the woods. The rain once again dripped from the bald trees above, mud and slushy leaves everywhere.

Halfway down the path, he stopped by an old dead wych elm tree. This reminded him of the story of *Who put Bella in the Wych Elm* from his youth. This where children in 1943 had found the skeleton remains of a woman inside a wych elm. This being about thirteen miles west of Smethwick in a woods near Hagley on Wychbury Hill. Ever since then, graffiti about Bella appeared on Wychbury Obelisk, on top of the hill, on a regular basis.

The tree made an excellent reference point. He pushed on behind it. Beneath denuded ash trees, through golden brown bracken and brambles. The sky through the branches was still an early-morning angry red through the persistent downpour.

After about 20 yards, he found a small gap and started to dig. He placed the sealed bank notes in the metal box and then buried them. Should he get out of all this alive, enough money there for a new life with Camille. (He hoped.) Covering the freshly dug soil with brambles and leaves, he then walked back to the clearing and through the muddy mass to the Jeep. He turned the ignition and was off, leaving the wreckage of the Battle of the Manor House behind him.

*

Following back roads north, he came upon the B4192 and drove on towards Swindon, the windscreen wipers working overtime. Not far from the outskirts, he stopped at a caravan in a layby selling all-day teas and breakfasts. He ordered a sausage sandwich and a mug of tea and stood under an awning and devoured them hungrily. He realised that he'd lost his cigarettes long ago in the battle. With a sigh, he suppressed the nicotine craving and stared morosely out into the storm.

A little closer to Swindon, he pulled up at a telephone kiosk. Using Des' coins, he tried calling Kev—no reply—he must still be at Number 10, lost in the wheels of red tape. Then tried Camille—again no reply—probably still fast asleep!

He checked the watch Des gave him—a few minutes past 7—and he phoned the prof on the emergency number to his house.

It took Trent a few minutes to convince the sleepy-sounding Prof that it was indeed him, Trent. He then told a disbelieving Prof the whole rigmarole of his sojourn in Wales, the treachery of Sir Richard and Colonel Stewart. Their plans against the country and the planned death of the Queen. How he'd engineered their deaths. He then had to reverse the charges halfway through.

After half an hour, the prof was still the doubting Thomas, so Trent angrily finished off: 'Prof, check with number 10. They have the taped evidence. Hurry them along if you can. Remind them about the assassination plan. Also warn them about the militia in the old RAF base, Bovingdon in Hertfordshire; don't know how many. I'm off now to try and find Mueller to stop him.' With that and with an angry curse, he slammed the phone down.

Chapter Fifty-Two
5 November, Swindon

Nearly 7.30am. He arrived in Swindon, the rain still falling. Lovely weather for the Queen's visit. It was not a town Trent knew, he had copied out the itinerary from the *Swindon Advertiser* in the Marlborough Hotel, and he now needed a map.

He stopped at a newsagent's, bought a packet of Players No 6 and matches, and also an A to Z Swindon street map. He'd probably have to wait for a chemist to open before he could get some painkillers for his finger.

He'd told the prof of the plot and Kev was hopefully at Number 10. He couldn't afford to wait for the wheels of bureaucracy to turn however, he needed to find Mueller and to bring a halt to all this madness for once and all.

Trent sat in the Jeep and smoked a contemplative cigarette. He spread out the map and itinerary and studied them, ignoring the unrelenting deluge battering the windscreen and roof, some of it dripping into the vehicle. He then checked his two guns were in order and felt the comfort of the ammo belt under his coat.

It would seem the Queen and Prince Philip were to arrive at Swindon station on the Royal Train and then make their way to the centre to open the town's new Civic Centre, which included the Wyvern Theatre (at a cost of £7.5 million!).

Times were a bit vague, but it looked as if the opening would be around 10am. The Queen was then to visit the nearby Brunel shopping centre and then Gorge Hill Museum, which was a few miles from the centre. Followed by a civic lunch at Lydiard House at Lydiard Park on the outskirts.

Jones had said Woolworths in Regent Street was the place of attack.

Regent street ran from the Brunel shopping centre to the Civic Centre by way of Regent Square. The Queen's official car would drive down the street to the Civic Centre and also back to the shopping centre. Trent surmised that the

Zombie's strike would be first thing on the way to the centre, at 10.00. He looked at his watch; maybe a couple of hours.

He left the Jeep in a side road and made his way down to Regent Street.

His plan was to make a reconnoitre of her route and the places she was to visit. First, he tried phoning Camille and Kev Bloomer again; there was no reply.

Crowds were already beginning to line up in Regent Street, waiting to cheer their Queen. Police wandered good-naturedly around. No sign of any panic or extra security. Had Kev managed to get the message through to the PM? He stopped at Woolworths, 23/24 Regent Street. A three-floor building of dull brown brick, a white sign at the front: "Woolworths" emblazoned in red. Making sure no police were watching, he slipped down a ginnel at the side. Yes, there at the back was a fire escape. That's the way Mueller would go to prepare for his assault. He'd go up there shortly, but first things first.

The dismal wet day did Swindon no favours, a mist slowly descending over the town. However, the crowds in the street were now growing all ready to have a good time. Surely if the authorities were aware of the plot, then they'd call it all off.

Trent reached the Brunel shopping centre, the second port of call on her itinerary. There was a sign outside proclaiming that this was the only covered shopping centre in Swindon. Well, it was open; small mercies, at least he'd get some temporary respite from the rain.

Trent noted a placard about Isembard Kingdom Brunel. The centre was named after him and his Swindon railway works. Swindon historically was a steam railway town. He gave a small smile, he'd always liked steam trains. The Brunel centre was also filling up with the Queen's loyal subjects, alongside the boys in blue, and St John's Ambulance people.

He found what he was searching for, a branch of Boots, and he purchased more painkillers for his finger; so much for resting it! Joke! He also bought some Lucozade (urgh!) and washed down the tablets.

Back outside Woolworths, he surreptitiously looked about. No one was watching, so he went down the alley and went carefully up the fire escape.

Another rooftop! He'd spent the last week or so up on roofs and here he was again! He scanned the flat rooftop, all wet and slippy. There was no sign of Mueller, or anyone! There was a cluster of chimneys and a water tank where Mueller could have stationed himself. Trent could only think he'd been and checked everything out and would return. Somewhere far off an early firework exploded.

He lay down beneath the water tank, which gave him shelter and also a perfect view of both the street below and also where Mueller should appear at the top of the fire escape. He looked at his watch, 8.22am, hour and half-ish to go. Kev and his tapes must now have been heard by the PM and those that mattered. Where was the cavalry? Was it all down to him?

Smoking yet another cigarette, he surveyed the street and the rooftops opposite. Not that easy to see in the mist. He knew the Palace were very light touch on security and relied on few bodyguards, even with the growing threat of the IRA and other terrorist groups. Even the so-called "Zombie" plot of recent times had not changed their traditional position.

Security was all over the President of the United States, and many other world leaders, as he had seen himself in the past. If this was the president, there would have have been armed guards everywhere and men in dark suits with walkie-talkies all over the rooftops. He saw a few British bobbies and some Boy Scouts. He settled down for a wait, guns at hand.

It was a party atmosphere below—little children waving Union Jacks, the adults sheltering beneath umbrellas. Whatever Mueller had planned, he had no concern for any collateral damage or innocent citizens killed. He'd have to be stopped before any killing started.

Now he must stay awake waiting for his nemesis. He lit another cigarette, chain-smoking to keep himself awake. He hadn't really had that much sleep over the past week.

-   Time ticked on…
-   His, rather Des' watch, then said 8.45am
-   The rain, heavier, was echoing through the water tank
-   Another cigarette
-   Tick-tock. Tick-tock. Tick-tock.
-   A distant church clock then chimed 9am.
-   Rain drummed on the tank roof.
-   Water, splattering, leaking in. Where was Mueller?
-   He should be preparing, the professional. More cigs.
-   God for a drink. Lucozade?
-   Finger ache—another tablet—crunched in teeth

- Ground below filling out
- Expectations/ spirits high
- More fags/ must stop. In a fight, who'd win?
- Mueller v. Trent?
- Mueller is massive but older
- Trent is younger, fitter
- 'Am I?' He said. Broken finger, too many fags. Reinforcements, where are you?
- Kev? Why didn't Camille answer?
- These thoughts swirled through his head
- Tick-tock, tick-tock, tick-tock
- The church bell rang. 9.30am
- Just like High Noon…
- Sweat pouring off him…

Trent was getting worried now. Where was Mueller? The stage was set, the crowds waiting the star of the show, HM due to appear, and where was the pantomime villain, the Zombie?

Knowing Mueller, even if he knew of the massacre at the Manor House, he'd still go through with his plan. Trent looked at his watch again, 9.41. This was not right. Where was he? There was a distant roar of the crowd, the Queen, probably in a Bentley, was nearby. This echoed by a ripple of excitement below. Trent looked out, catching sight of a bank on the other side a few doors down.

Think! Think! Think! Sir Richard and Sir Adrian had mentioned bank several times—their little joke, of course! That bastard Jones had stitched him up even facing death. Woolworths indeed! Talk about Machiavellian! (A Camille word). Trent managed to climb up the slimy wet water tank and he stood on the top. He had a better view of the rooftops and there, though the murk, was Mueller, the Zombie, lying down, a large harpoon gun by his side. He was on the roof of a nearby bank—28 Regent Street, Barclays.

Chapter Fifty-Three

A brass band struck up somewhere: *God save our gracious Queen.*

'Indeed,' muttered Trent, 'or if not, hopefully me.' Twelve or so minutes left, the Queen and Prince Philip slowly coming in an official Bentley with darkened windows. The plan was to drive so far then go on a walkabout. Zombie's attack was to be on the royal vehicle.

Having located Mueller, Trent dashed down the fire escape to the street below. He pushed through the throng, knocking over several spectators in his haste. 'Sorry, sorry, sorry!' He dodged a startled policeman and arrived outside Barclays, inevitably closed. There was no way round the sides to the back, they were bricked up. How did Mueller get up there?

The mist was clearing, but luckily, some wisps still shrouded the rooftops, so it was unlikely Trent would be seen. Anyway, Mueller would be concentrating on the Queen's approach.

The policeman was now taking an interest in him, however with a sudden excited surge in the crowd, he was distracted, and Trent moved away.

There were offices next to Barclays. He found a narrow gap on the other side, at the back in a weed-covered yard was another fire escape which he mounted.

At the top, he went over to the Barclays' side. Yes, that's how he did it. A strong plank went from the one side over to the Barclays' roof.

Down below the national anthem started again, the cheering got louder. Her Majesty must be nearly here. Puffing slightly (cursing nicotine again!), he crossed over.

The Barclays' roof was flat and very wet, mossy and sludgy, a few spent rockets lay about, remnants of an early fireworks party. There was a small battlement-type wall on the roof edge and just about through the dank gloom, Trent could see Mueller hidden behind the wall, his harpoon contraption pointing out. The wall provided the cover needed and would have been the reason the bank was chosen.

In the middle was a small outbuilding with a door on, the way down to the bank. In the corner was what looked like a shed, used for storage no doubt.

There was an old chimney and various aerials.

No time for subtlety, he rushed over the roof; too much noise to be heard. A peek over—the Queen was in line with the bank. 'Hip, hip, hooray! For she's a jolly good fellow!' (Memories of Sir Richard's conference!)

With no finesse, Trent pounced. He kicked with all his force at Mueller's head. Like kicking a blacksmith's anvil! Stunned, the Zombie lost his grip on the giant weapon. Trent also kicked out at the harpoon and it skidded over the wet roof. Trent leapt to the harpoon and pulled out the missile, with some type of explosive on the end. He threw it into a large puddle.

God! What damage to the Queen and bystanders would this have caused?

He then went for his Smith and Wesson beneath the overcoat. Zombie recovered and leapt up with a roar, a man mountain that made Sergeant Des look small.

There was evil in Mueller's face, not from his many scars, but from years of death and hate. All deeply embedded in his features, in his soul.

Before Trent could shoot the beast he lost his footing in the wet, and Mueller was on top of him, the gun skidding away. He had never encountered such strength in a man, even though he was obviously sluggish from Trent's kick.

He hit the Zombie with his good hand, and tried a karate chop—nothing—like hitting heavy metal. The monster then lifted Trent up, squeezing the air out of him, and flung him to the floor. He stood over him: 'Here you die, Mr Trent,' and he produced a gun from his jacket.

Trent noticed he still looked a little woozy from the head blow. He took his chance. He kicked out with both legs with all his strength, straight into Mueller's legs, who stumbled and fell in the wet. It was surprising no one heard him below as he landed with an explosive clatter.

Trent was on his feet and he whipped his second gun, the Beretta, out.

He stood over the giant, gun in hand. 'My turn.' Revenge would be sweet.

'I think not, Mr Trent.' Mueller's German accent was very strong at this point. Suddenly, there was a gun in Trent's back and another pointed at his head.

'Drop your weapon,' another German voice said. He dropped the gun.

'Allow me to introduce my assistants, Hans and Walter. You met them from a distance in Berlin, I think. Helped me with your policeman friend and wife.'

Mueller stood up and weighed the gun in his hand.

Trent turned and looked at the two men, two guns aimed at him. He remembered the three figures in the Berlin yellow gloom. That must have been them, with Mueller in the middle. The two were both very Germanic. They wouldn't have looked out of place in those old war films, the Gestapo or SS.

The Zombie's face gave an evil smile. 'They were sheltering in the storage shed over there, and must have heard our fight, even above this din from the street.'

He gestured to the street below and the noise of a street party. At least the Queen had moved onto safety, Trent reflected. He returned the smile.

'Your bosses, their whole team, are wiped out. You're on your own.'

'Ah, so that's why we can't get in contact with them. Never mind; I've been paid. Not my bosses, couldn't care less about their revolution.'

Trent stood up straight and stared him in the eyes. Yellow/white mist drifting, the English rain enveloping the rooftop. 'You've failed, the Queen still lives.' The band and cheering now becoming distant as the crowd followed their Queen. Far-off fireworks could be heard.

'I think not,' Mueller laughed. 'We'll kill you, then catch up with our target at the Wyvern Centre or the shopping centre, whichever's easier, then kill her. Security is useless. Non-existent!'

Rain dripping down his face, Trent said: 'I've told Number 10 of the plot. Help will be here soon.'

'You bluff, I think. You're a dead agent, a dead hero, ha ha. No one's here to rescue you.'

Bang! With that, he shot Trent in the right knee. A shattering of a bloody knee and Trent fell back to the floor, with a grunt of pain. He passed out in the green filth and puddles.

He came to quickly, the pain excruciating, beyond even that he'd already suffered in his finger.

'Welcome back to us,' he laughed mirthlessly. 'I'm going to kill you. Shoot you slowly. No one will hear with this all noise and fireworks.'

Trent tried to sit up, his blood washing across the roof in the persistent downpour.

'Now the other knee.' The giant raised his gun again.

Bang. Crack! Bang. Three shots went through the ghostly mist. The Zombie fell with a hole in his head. The other two also dead, shot in the back.

Trent gritted his teeth. Who was this? The army, police, Intelligence, the prof?

A shadow, an apparition, appeared in the yellow/white swirling cloud.

Out of the murk, Camille stepped out, smoking pistol in her hand. 'Rescued you again...'

Chapter Fifty-Four

It was a black and white B movie of a day. The cold, damp, misty Barclays' roof.

Camille, wet hair plastered, dripping on her face, was still Hollywood Technicolor, and Trent, despite the pain, felt his heart stir.

She shoved her pistol into her white mac, also sodden, and knelt down, sorrow on her face. She stroked his head. 'I'm sorry I wasn't quicker.'

She took in his wounded knee, blood still oozing, and pulled off her mac.

'Let's see…' She took off her sweater and stood briefly in the rain, only her bra underneath. Faint stirring from the wounded soldier! She then swiftly moved and made the sweater into a makeshift tourniquet to stop the bleeding.

'How come you're here?' Same words as Wallog beach. Déjà vu again! That's the trouble with déjà vu, keeps repeating itself. What was he thinking or hallucinating?

'Ssh, let's sort you out first.' She pulled on her mac and ran to the far corner of the roof. Taking her pistol out, she fired into the air. Most of the crowd below had gone but she attracted the attention of a middle-aged gent walking by, who stared goggle-eyed at the roof.

'There's been a shooting up here. Someone's hurt, please phone police and ambulance.' He stared briefly, nodded his head, and walked quickly to a phone box. A few others stood open-mouthed, looking upwards.

Camille fired her gun again, twice. Trent pulled himself up to the roof wall. He could make out figures through the smog on Woolworths' roof, further down the other side. One of them was the prof with a larger group of uniformed men.

'Prof, Mr Clarke!' (his real name) Camille shouted. 'Over here. Philip Trent is over here, wounded.' A muffled shout responded.

She came back. 'I saw the prof earlier with some uniforms, met him once with the colonel. Saw them go into Woolworths.'

'Yes, I told him earlier that's where Jones said the assassins would be…the liar…' His voice trailed off. 'Now tell me…you should be in London.'

'Must be quick, they'll be here soon when they can find the way.'

He shifted uncomfortably and groaned; he was shivering. She took the mac off again and shoved the gun into her trouser belt. The wet, saturated bra startling him. She covered him with the mac. 'Don't worry about me, I'm a tough Russian. I didn't go to London with Kev.' She shook her head to get the raindrops from her eyes. 'Stayed at the hotel; could hear the distant bangs, knew it was you. Wilf said it was those posh swines having a party at the manor.

'When the rain stopped, I went up there. Saw Des; he told me you'd gone to Swindon. So I went after you.' She paused. 'So so sorry about the major and Illya.'

She continued, rain cascading over her. 'I knew the Queen's route, so came here to Regent Street, saw the prof ferreting about, and then you running across to here. Took me some time to find how you got up here, with all the crowds about.'

'Well, I'm glad you did.' Trent winced with pain. 'When we're out of all this, we'll run away. I'm afraid I still love you. How…How did you learn to shoot like that?' He added.

She frowned. 'At a KGB training base, just over the border from Turkey, in Bulgaria.'

She noted his perplexed expression and before he could reply, she jumped in: 'No easy way to say this, Philip. The deal with the Russians. A hard bargain. For Illya and the equipment, I agreed to go abroad for a mission for them…'

In that second, she'd never looked so attractive, and gently sad. Still matchless, bedraggled and soaked. An image burnt in his mind.

There were noises from the Barclays' rear entrance.

'They're here now. Got to go over that plank. I'm so sorry. Ya lyublyu tebla…'

She kissed him and was gone into the mist, another ghost.

The wet, the puddles blood red, the lingering white mist, the pain…

Trent could make out the unmistakeable figure of the prof and some uniformed men, approaching. An ambulance wailed in the distance.

For the second time in a week, since he was a boy in fact, his eyes watered and tears fell.

Yes, that's love; should have left out the sentiment. With that thought, Trent thankfully passed out.

ENDBIT

(i)

He was dreaming again. Welsh haunted mines, mysterious islands, stormy seas. Circles, going round. Camille waving, vanished in the mist. Ghosts everywhere.

A hand shook him awake. 'Mr Trent, you have some visitors.' The nurse all in blue, stiff, formal, and efficient.

He'd been in this nursing home several weeks and lost track of time. He was somewhere between Haslemere and Hindhead in Surrey. A top-class private establishment, but who normally for? The room was luxury, first class. But looking through the blinds over the immaculate gardens, he couldn't help but notice the barbed wire and guards. A top-class prison?

He knew nothing of his "rescue" from the Swindon rooftops and the days that followed. He'd been drugged to the eyeballs.

The nurses said very little to him, nor the doctors. They said where he was but nothing else. Since arriving, he'd had reconstructive surgery on his knee and proper repair of his finger. The doctors did say that the knee surgery was pioneering and a top surgeon from the States performed it. 'Pioneering? Does that mean experimenting?' He'd asked.

He was now undergoing physiotherapy and exercise three times a day and hopefully, soon could throw away his crutches.

As far as he could see, he was the only patient here at present and he passed his time reading books from a well-stocked library. (Camille would have approved.) He wasn't allowed TV or newspapers, but saw a film show put on twice a week; the last one being Norman Wisdom! He was reading *Flashman* by George MacDonald Fraser, both amusing and an insight into the British army in India last century (and how to lose a war!).

One good thing, he supposed, was he hadn't had a drink or cigarette for weeks, and despite everything, felt remarkably healthy.

Some intelligence men had come to quiz him in the early days.

'Who was in the battle with you at the manor?'

'Who was the woman who shot Mueller?'

'Was it Camille Morris?'

'Where is she?'

'What happened on the Welsh island?' On and on and on…

Trent claimed amnesia; "the drugs, you know" and rang the bedside bell. The nurse shooed the "gentlemen" away.

They came again with a copy of the report he'd done with Camille for Number 10. He was feeling better and bored, so he filled in some edited blanks of what happened after the report was written. This mainly around what the colonel told him on that island. He left out anything related to Camille or the mercenary band.

Now he had some more "visitors". He looked at the window. Snow had fallen and the whole white ground glared brightly in the winter sunshine.

The door was knocked…

(ii)

The door opened tentatively. 'Hallo, hallo,' a voice boomed. 'Brought you some grapes.' It was Kev Bloomer. He came in. 'Well, actually smuggled in this.' He held up a flask.

'Medicinal brandy for the invalid.' He looked at Trent. 'How are you, old boy?' He seemed a lot tidier than normal, Trent noted.

'I'm fine, fine, bored that's all; not allowed any news, nothing. They say I'll be able to walk properly in a few weeks. Thank God. Oh, how's the Albion doing?'

'Absolutely dreadful, old boy. Lost to Stoke the day after, well you know, the fifth. Then continued to lose. Lost 3-2 to Spurs last game and Wolves up next!'

'Every cloud then, shut in here.' Trent looked searchingly at his old friend. 'Now what happened that day at Number 10?'

'Chaos, old boy. We were made to wait for hours—me and the editor—whilst they listened to the tapes. Couldn't seem to make up their minds what to do.'

Kev stared out the window; it had started snowing again.

'Problem was they couldn't get hold of the PM; in a hush-hush meeting somewhere. Also these bods argued whether it was real or not. Some said Sir Richard was a hero and this Trent character was dead.

'Eventually, your prof bloke turned up and persuaded them to get the PM. Things then swung into action. Couldn't afford to delay, the plot might actually exist. My friend, Roger, was also instrumental in getting things moving. They then sent Prof and men off to Swindon and troops to that RAF base in

241

Hertfordshire. That's all I know really. We were served with a D notice and sworn to secrecy.'

Kev gave a big sigh. 'What I do know is that, as predicted, there's been an almighty cover-up and not one word of the plot has leaked to the public. The narrative officially is that Sir Richard Abbott apparently died a hero at the hands of the enemy and the communist plot fizzled out after he and Colonel Stewart thwarted the conspirators. That's the story in the papers anyway, which I'm told you've been banned from seeing. Load of balls!' Kev's anger and frustration boiled over.

'Most of those you imprisoned at the Manor House were quietly pensioned off and had to sign the Official Secret Act. A few leaders of the militia arrested in Hertfordshire were imprisoned, as scapegoats, but that's all. My friend, Roger, can tell you more.'

'Roger?'

'Roger D'arcy. Works with the PM. As I say, helped convince them the conspiracy was real.' Kev paused. He seemed embarrassed, at a loss for words.

Most unlike Kev!

He continued: 'You see…er…um…Roger, my friend, a little more than that now. We've moved in together.'

Trent's eyebrows went up. 'What? You've settled down? Good Lord! What's he like, this madman who's taken you on?' (*And tidied you up*, Trent thought.)

'You can meet him in a minute. He's outside.'

Trent could see a shadowy figure moving about through the porthole of a window in the door.

'He can tell you a bit more about events,' Kev continued. 'By the way, what happened to Camille?'

'I'll save that for another day if you don't mind.'

Kev pulled an envelope out of his pocket. 'For you, old boy. Roger doesn't know. Came to the newspaper office. Have a look when we've gone.'

'OK, let's see this bloke of yours.'

Trent recognised the handwriting but kept his face impassive as Kev swept in Roger D'arcy.

Roger D'arcy was forty-ish, blond hair greying at the temples, and steady, warm blue eyes. He was immaculately dressed, civil service grey pin-striped suit, and a Royal Horseguards tie. Smart, not camp, the total opposite to Kev. He shook hands and sat on a chair next to Trent; a whiff of expensive aftershave was in the air.

'How do you do? Pleased to meet you.' They shook hands.

'Leave you to it,' Kev said, and left.

His right leg crossed over his left, trousers knife-sharp creased. 'A few things to chat about, Trent.' He looked right into his eyes, no blinking; his posh accent from birth, not cultivated like Kev's.

'How do...you're brave taking on our Kev,' Trent said, deliberately pure Black Country. D'arcy gave a brief wintry smile, no reply. 'OK, Mr D'arcy, why are you here?'

'Roger please. This is informal. Thought I'd give you an overview of how HM Government sees this er...interesting...situation.'

He looked out the window, snow falling heavily. 'Hope we'll get back to London.' It was winter afternoon—dark, lights now on in the gardens, casting shadows over the snow.

'Righto,' Roger continued. 'First, may I congratulate you on everything you did for the Queen and commiserate you on your present predicament...'

'But...I sense a but...'

'Well, in certain government circles, you're a bit of an embarrassment. A loose cannon so to speak.' He brushed a minute speck off his trousers. 'They don't know what to do with you. Now where shall we start?'

'Before we start, tell me, what is this place?'

'A government-owned medical centre to keep patients away from prying eyes. They've had PMs with serious illnesses, ministers with nervous breakdowns, and agents returned from abroad who've been through the mill. Even defectors we are hiding.' D'arcy was obviously privy to many state secrets which went beyond the remit of a normal Downing Street civil servant.

He continued: 'First, Kev never said anything about Camille or the mercenaries who helped you. He's been totally loyal to you, and I've never pushed.' Roger's brow furrowed. 'Amazing they never appeared in that report of yours or your later additions; amazing, but never mind...

'Secondly, I must apologise for our delay on the fifth. We couldn't locate the PM. He was in a top-secret meeting with the Treasury about the EEC, his pet project. Took hours to find him. When we did, there was much discussion. Some didn't believe it, said you were dead, Sir Richard, their man, and it must be a communist plot to further destabilise and take our eyes off parliament.

'Finally, myself and Professor James Clarke, your prof, persuaded the PM. We couldn't afford to ignore it. He's a real professor by the way, and now a Sir, runs his own Intelligence Department. Someone had to take the credit for stopping the communist plot, so-called!'

Trent couldn't believe the luck of some people. Well, actually he could! He kept his counsel.

Roger helped himself to some water from a beaker. 'We did two things: Jim Clarke went to Swindon and an army group went to the old base in Hertfordshire. They quickly surrendered.

'In Swindon, we quickly arranged stand-ins, lookalikes from a distance, for the Queen and Prince Philip. They were to drive down Regent Street and would be replaced later by the real ones. The dark windows helped disguise them. The professor and his men searched for this Mueller but couldn't find him.'

For the first time, Trent interrupted. 'My fault. I was misdirected to the wrong roof.' He paused. 'All a bit dangerous for the crowds if Mueller had fired at the car.'

'Not my decision.' Looking at his blue eyes, suddenly as cold as the snow outside. 'I bet,' he thought.

'Anyway, you killed Mueller, and we were then left to tidy up matters.'

'A cover-up?'

'If you like. Well, let's look at your own particular brand of mayhem and what's been done.' Ice was now forming on the windows blocking out the snowy view outside. 'Everywhere you've left a trail of destruction…

'Deaths in Birmingham and Paris, Welsh islands and manor houses blown up. Battles in the shires. Sir Richard, Colonel Stewart, Sir Adrian, so-called pillars of society, dead. A shooting on Barclays' roof. And I'm also told there's a police report in Wales about some bikers being shot. And you, the perpetrator of all this, someone supposedly dead.'

So the bikers did go to the police then, Trent reflected, *wimps*!

'Now I know you were a pawn in this heinous plot, but some may say you've broken every law in the land. Also, we have missing mercenaries and Camille. Your partners in crime, shall we say. So any cover-up also includes you.'

He hesitated, took another drink of water, and carried on. 'We have covered everything else up, yes. Imagine the scandal if this got out! The only arrests were a few leaders of the militia in Hertfordshire. They didn't really know much about anything, so can't say much.'

Here, Roger had the decency to grimace. 'The ones imprisoned in the wine cellar, all drunk when they were released. All now quietly pensioned off I'm afraid, with threats of prison if they talk. Same for other officials involved. Signed non-disclosures, Official Secrets Act…they won't say anything.

'This Welsh Island, the story there is you and Colonel Stewart destroyed the communist plotters on the island and then you vanished, believed killed. We said the original story was incorrect. And that information provided by you led to the ultimate downfall of the plot.

'Finally.' A further face as if he'd swallowed something unpleasant. 'We covered up the Barclays' roof shenanigans with a story of a bank raid gone wrong. Think we've got away with it all, just. Fingers crossed.'

'How did you explain the deaths of Sir Richard and Sir Adrian?' Trent asked, keeping his anger in check, not good for his blood pressure.

'Martyrs—Sir Richard killed stopping the plot, Sir Adrian in revenge. Somehow it all seems to hang together. So far. However, we need you to keep silent about it all. One of the reasons you've been kept here, with no newspapers or TV.'

D'arcy then handed him a copy of the *Times* (of course, it would be the *Times*!) 'Here have a look at this, from last week…'

Trent picked the newspaper up and started to read.

Newspaper article, *The Times*

"An Incredible Coup Thwarted"
Anyone over the recent months who has followed the news cannot have failed to notice the increased terrorist attacks, strikes, and criminal activity.

Thanks to the Department of Sir Richard Abbot and his number two, Alec Stewart, they uncovered a concerted plot to undermine the stability of our nation. The ultimate aim: revolution. It is believed that this attempted coup originated in the Eastern Bloc. Something that Moscow and their allies deny.

Much of what was undertaken by Sir Richard and his men will remain a state secret, and probably won't be revealed for at least thirty years. This is when cabinet papers can be normally released. Our view is it will be even longer in view of the many international sensitive issues involved.

In addition, Sir Adrian Joyce was also assassinated by persons unknown and again full details have been withheld for security reasons.

It is well-known, however, that Sir Adrian had long warned about a Communist plot and had set up the GB National Party as a bulwark against such a threat.

(See obituary page for epitaphs for all of the three above—heroes of our age.)

What we do know of events and what we can reveal is that Colonel Stewart and his employee, Philip Trent, helped uncover the plot. The colonel is now dead and Trent missing...

Trent, in anger, couldn't read any more of the codswallop. He threw the paper across the room, it landed in a waste bin.

'Well shot, Trent; I can't say I disagree with you,' said D'arcy, the probable architect of the cover-up.

Trent's knee was playing up, unaccustomed to sitting in one position for long. He tried to stretch it. Grimacing, he said: 'What if I don't? Keep silent I mean.'

'HM Government would prefer you to remain "dead" for the time being. In fact, we want you out of the country when you've recovered.'

'And if I refuse?' Trent's anger was now surfacing.

'Well, we're not above blackmail. Your friend, Camille Morris, has been dropped in it by the CIA. Seems she upset them somehow, working with you. She's been revealed as a double agent and she's going to struggle to return here without being arrested.

'By the way, the CIA have denied any involvement in the plot, although we do know there have been a few resignations over the issue. The Soviets also deny being part of this—true enough but who'll believe them—anyway diplomacy is interesting at this time.'

He again looked at Trent, now with force and his eyes even icier. 'Now here's the deal. We want you out of the country for six months, on full pay. Things should have calmed down by then and we can decide what story to tell about your return. In return, we'll forget Camille and her activities, and she can return.' D'arcy finished and finally sat back and waited.

Trent knew they had him there, had him over a barrel. He didn't say anything for a minute and then nodded. D'arcy didn't say anything either but called Kev back in.

There were hugs and handshakes and Kev asked him if he needed anything.

'A selection of newspapers in future, please.' To this, Roger D'arcy nodded. To Kev, he said: 'And make sure Tess, the dog y'know, is looked after, and that Mrs McDougal is alright.'

A wave of guilt then hit him. 'I must have missed Steve and Jackie's funeral.'

'Don't worry I attended in your absentia. They all think you're dead. And no blame attached…'

'Thanks, Kev…should have been…' His words failed him, he remembered telling Camille he wouldn't be going to the funeral. What a hypocrite.

Kev and D'arcy then went out into the snow-driven afternoon, a blizzard getting up. He sat looking out of the frozen window, icicles forming around the top. Memories of the 1963 Deep Freeze when he'd been back on leave. After several minutes, he said: 'OK, here goes,' and he opened the letter Kev had given him. In Camille's handwriting with an Istanbul postmark.

Inside, there was a picture postcard: *Venice in the sunshine.*

Written on the back was, *Venice 1972, C xxxx.*

This brought a smile to his battle-scarred face. The more he thought, the more he smiled, and he broke into laughter, and took a swig of the "medicinal" brandy.

For the first time in weeks/months, he laughed at the absurdity of it all and he thought there may be some future after all. He continued laughing, the drink after weeks of abstinence going to his head.

This brought the nurse in, tutting and fussing. Trent didn't care, his mind was on Camille and Venice…

THE END

Printed in Great Britain
by Amazon

48332227R00137